VENDICARE
ANGEL FACES

VENDICARE ANGEL FACES

Carys Jones-Williams
The welsh girl I met at the top of
a mountain while "playing cricket"
Best wishes for your future

TP AKA

Scott Vincent

Matador
9 Priory Business Park,
Wistow Road, Kibworth Beauchamp,
Leicestershire. LE8 0RX
Tel: 0116 279 2299
Email: books@troubador.co.uk
Web: www.troubador.co.uk/matador
Twitter: @matadorbooks

ISBN 978 1788036 795

British Library Cataloguing in Publication Data.
A catalogue record for this book is available from the British Library.

Printed by TJ International, Padstow, Cornwall
Typeset in 11pt Minion Pro by Troubador Publishing Ltd, Leicester, UK

Matador is an imprint of Troubador Publishing Ltd

Author Note

Ten years ago I attempted my first ever writing project; after just six months, it was left to languish in a drawer.

Ywo years ago while sitting in my car waiting to board the Eurotunnel, I listened to a Radio 5 news bulletin on the cruel abduction of 200 girls in Chibok, Nigeria.

With nothing more than imagination and a profound frustration of how global politics tends to balance in favour of getting involved in only those issues that win popularity contensts, I decided to start over and write a story in which the scales get levelled.

I would like to especially thank my three sons, one of whom read every chapter and encouraged me daily to carry on writing. You know who you are! The young Ellie, who first cast her red pen over the manuscript, wielding it like a sword, breaking up the ridiculously long chapters... her first words being, "OMG, this will take a lifetime!" Six months later, together we had finished the first draft. *Isla, Eva and Lila, they are the future...*

Finally, Jo, for always believing in me and supporting me throughout.

Se in un primo momento non si riuscirà, reprovare.

Scott Vincent

CHAPTER 1

VENGEANCE

The only light available to the Somali fishing boat anchored some sixty nautical miles North West of the Seychelles was the bright moonlight, which seemed to illuminate the still ocean. Alhusain Moses and eighteen other countrymen were huddled together against the cool night air, cooking from little gas stoves eating rice and fish, seemingly just like a real Somali fishing crew.

The only difference was that this particular crew were responsible for some of the most ruthless hijackings in and around the Indian Ocean and the killing of at least thirteen innocent hostages. The sea route they now followed had provided rich pickings for Alhusain and his crew in the past, with their ransoms and bounties totalling millions of dollars.

As they devoured their freshly caught fish and wiped their plates with muufo bread, they were completely unaware of the three seabob scooters some fifty metres down in the murky darkness of the Indian Ocean. The Military grade DPD (Driver Propulsion Device) with revolutionary digital sonar could operate in any conditions of visibility. With an electronic limpet compass once programmed the two-man underwater vehicle would remain locked onto to its target.

These pirates were also unaware that they had been monitored for the last four days by Vendicare, in conjunction with the British and Seychelles Navy.

Driving one of these virtually undetectable scooters was Vincent Natalie, who had spent over a year looking for Alhusain. He was now desperately hoping that all the aerial photographs and surveillance material that they had gathered would prove to be correct. He wasn't simply looking for another shoot-out; he had something very special planned for Alhusain.

Vincent was leading the Blue Team convoy with Billie Kjellin. To his starboard side, the Yellow Team was made up of the Devine twins, Scott and Lee. Leading this covert convoy of stealth diving scooters was the Red Team, led by Nikki Hunter and supported by Oliver Natalie, Vincent's son.

Nikki was comforted by reminding herself of the command control back in the Seychelles, who were monitoring their progress using UAVs (Unmanned Aerial Vehicles), which provided thermal and infrared night-time images of every single development in the fishing crew's movements. These were being quickly and constantly relayed to the team below the sea.

"Red Leader to all teams, three miles before target is visible. Over." Nikki muttered through the comms system as she tightened her grip on the steering. She glanced down at her TFT (Thin-Film-Transistor) screen monitoring the team's bios and saw that Vincent's heart rate and breathing had become erratic.

"Red Leader to Blue Team. Vincent, are you okay? Your heart rate's all over the place. Over."

A few seconds passed before Vincent responded. "Blue Team to Red Leader. Everything is okay, I took a little too much nitrox. Over."

Nikki snorted in derision. She was too smart to buy his

bullshit. However, when she checked again, she saw that his breathing was now back under control and his heart rate stabilising. Nikki decided to allow him to focus on what lay ahead of them, increasing her speed again to just less than five miles per hour.

As the water slowly rippled in the darkness all around to accommodate them, Nikki found herself thinking again that Vincent should not be on this mission. Not only was he not trained in the Special Forces, but he also had his own agenda, which she knew would cause a problem at some stage of this operation. However, he was an excellent diver, possibly even the best among them, having achieved the status of Padi Master. He had also passed his marksman course, so his ability to shoot had never been in question. Nikki would never have been able to prevent him from coming, but even so, she hoped everything would come together and he could prove himself an asset rather than a liability.

Back at command control, on board a P32 gunboat everyone was monitoring everything extremely closely, just as they had practiced. Nikki knew that no one would be doing so more than Becci Moore, whom she had left in charge. If Becci had the choice she would have been on this mission in a heartbeat, but Nikki had been adamant that she needed a strong team member controlling this operation. Nikki was well aware of the close bond between Vincent and Becci, which constituted the main reason she had put Becci in overall control. If Becci had been allowed on this mission, she would have had one eye on Vincent and only one on the job in hand. Nikki needed complete focus from her team on the ground.

"Control to Red Leader, we are happy that Blue Team is a positive to go. Over," came Becci's voice over the comms.

"Red Team Leader to Control, that's affirmative, Blue Team is definitely positive to go, I repeat, definitely positive to go.

Over." Nikki replied with confidence, desperately making sure that she had convinced Becci that Vincent was okay. All hell will break loose if she doesn't, she thought inwardly.

"Control, roger that. Red Team Leader, you are one mile to target visuals. Pirates are visible and you have green for go. Over." Becci replied with a hint of anxiety in her voice. Nikki heard the frustration that she could do nothing other than give them visual updates and redeploy the drones if necessary. These drones were flying a grid pattern, giving her total uninterrupted thermal visuals on the pirates. As well as providing the live images, both drones were carrying two hellfires and one pave way laser-guided bomb. She didn't plan on using more than one hellfire.

The team were now less than half a mile away from their target destination, which would take about six to seven minutes to reach, with five minutes needed to position themselves for boarding.

"Red Team Leader to Control and all teams, five minutes to radio silence. Over." Nikki said.

"Blue Team, copy. Over," came Vincent's response.

"Yellow Team, copy. Over.," from Scott.

"Control, copy, will give you any relevant updates until you go silent. Over."

The team were carrying an array of underwater weaponry which included the HK P11 underwater pistol which could fire five rounds with a fifteen metre underwater trajectory, but if used on the surface would provide a kill after thirty metres. As well as the underwater pistol, every team member had a modified Heckler and Koch 416.

A rapid attack had not been planned. They were going in quiet under cover of darkness, so they would be able to take multiple strategic positions. There was no need for flash bangs, which would draw attention to them. The six-man team were responsible for three or four kills each, although Alhusain had to, without question, be taken alive. Scott and Lee, making up the Yellow Team, were carrying C4 detonators, as Nikki had something planned she hoped would satisfy Vincent's vendetta.

"Red Team Leader to all teams and Control, target in sight. Complete silence until attack commences, or abort instructions are given. Over."

"Blue Team copy. Over."

"Yellow Team copy. Over."

"Control copy. Over."

The team now took up their positions. Blue Team took the bow, with Vincent on the starboard side and Billie on the port side. According to the drone images there were five targets for them; three on Billie's side and two on Vincent's. Scott and Lee had the stern, with Scott facing Vincent and Lee looking straight down at Billie. There were seven targets for them; four on Lee's side and three on Scott's. Nikki and Oliver had amidships, with Oliver covering the port side and Billie watching his back, while Nikki covered starboard and kept a close eye on Vincent. She would also be responsible for taking Alhusain alive. The trigger for the attack would be delivered to the team by the Petrel technical dive computers strapped to their wrists; an off-the-shelf computer adapted by Vincent's tech team with a traffic-like colour bar system. Red meant hold, green meant go, and orange would be abort, though they had never seen that colour used before. The dive computers were synced together, with all data monitored by Becci so that she was aware of all their positions and could push the trigger for go when the moment arose.

Vincent and Billie had already surfaced. The twins followed shortly after. Nikki and Oliver were the last to remove their full face masks and fins, clipping them on their belts. The water ran smoothly from their waterproof suits and the only part of Nikki's body that could feel the cool night air was her cheeks. Each team member had a specially designed, quick-release Lanyard clip with a torque spring which would propel them upwards in one smooth motion. All they now needed to do was to screw a mountaineer's clip gently into the side of the wooden hull, attach and wait for the green light. Nikki looked slowly around her, keeping her breathing steady and controlled. The twins were in position, with HK416 in hand, night vision goggles on and ready to go. She thought briefly to herself, please don't let any of these dickheads take a piss now. Everything will go to rat shit.

They now had to wait forty-five seconds to give them the prescribed time they had planned. It would now only change if something major went wrong.

Nikki looked back to her computer, where the red standby was lit. Not long now. She checked her safety was off and the red sight was on. Everyone's finger was on the torque release. Waiting. Waiting. They stared at their computers, waiting for the red light to turn green.

Becci began a countdown in her head. Ten,... five, four, three, two, one. Slamming the green button, Becci broke radio silence, shouting, "ALL TEAMS GREEN FOR GO, I REPEAT GREEN FOR GO."

The last thing the pirates will have heard was the soft sound of the quick release Lanyards which propelled the team into action. Each 7.62 round made no more than a slight phutt noise before they found their targets and buried themselves in either head or chest. Nikki had two clear head shots before putting two in the legs of Alhusain, preventing him from getting to the AK47 he had been reaching for.

Lee and Scott had taken their seven quickly and effectively, with Lee using his six-inch Navy Seal knife to finish off one particularly drunken pirate. Oliver had four head shots, then double tapped them for good measure once he had clambered onto the deck.

Nikki climbed aboard the boat and strode towards the writhing figure of Alhusain. "Red Team Leader to all teams, are we good? Over," she said as she knelt behind Alhusain and tied his hands, almost cutting off his circulation. He was breathing heavily and moaning in agony; the bullet wounds in his legs steadily emitted a crimson flow.

"Good on port side, four sleepers on my side. Over." Oliver said.

"Yellow Team, four my side and three on Scott's. Over."

"Blue Team, Vincent took two and I have three. Over." Billie said.

With the two I've dropped, that's eighteen, Nikki counted, plus Alhusain makes nineteen. From the release of the Lanyard to the last shot being fired, it had been forty-seven seconds. That even included Lee showing off with his knife. That's better by three seconds than our practice runs on the island, she thought with satisfaction.

"Control to all teams, well done guys. I've scanned the thermal imagery, there are no pirates left alive. P42s are on their way to extract you. ETA twenty-five minutes. Hope that's enough time for your little surprises." Becci's voice sounded thoroughly relieved.

Nikki became aware that Vincent had not spoken. She kicked Alhusain hard in the face, warning him viciously not to make a move as she made her way over to Vincent, who was sat with his back to the wooden hull. The twins were already laying the C4 explosives on the floor and getting ready to booby trap the bodies before they created the special surprise party planned for Alhusain.

"Vincent, are you okay?" Nikki asked gently, placing a hand

on his shoulder while he sat facing the two pirates he had shot. Now that she was closer, she could see the blood trickling from the head of one of the pirates as he lay motionless. The shot had gone straight through his cheek bones, smashing his face into a series of pieces. Not exactly a clean shot, Nikki thought, but a kill nevertheless.

"Vincent, it's Nikki, you okay?" she asked again. Then she shook him, hard.

"I'm sorry, Nikki," he said as he turned around and looked up at her, seemingly brought back to life. "It's just not what I thought it would feel like when we eventually got him after so long... I thought I would be ecstatic. But it's such a terrible feeling... like it's bringing everything back." He looked morose.

"Well, pull yourself together. We haven't finished yet," Nikki said brusquely, not understanding Vincent's lack of triumph as she put one more round in each of his kills.

"Control to Red Team Leader, is Vincent okay? Bios are all over the place. Over." Becci said with concern, having used the direct link to Nikki so that the rest of the team could not hear.

"Becci, Vincent is A-Okay, just doing some housekeeping. Over." The last thing she needed was Becci panicking.

"Copy that, Red Team Leader. Twenty minutes to extraction. Over"

Oliver was finished securing the retention wire on the boat for the seabobs while the twins completed their booby traps. Vincent had got up and was walking slowly towards Alhusain when Oliver asked Nikki quietly what exactly she had in mind for him. She glanced over at Vincent. She could see the strong hatred in his eyes. But she could also see a world of morality and emotion which seemed to be replacing his anger and desperation for revenge, which had been the exact reason for this mission in the first place.

"Oli, give Billie a hand hoisting this piece of shit to

the main sail and then tie him up there for everyone to see," Nikki instructed, wishing Vincent had not come along on this operation after all.

"Upside down, arms out, as usual?" Oliver asked.

"Yeah that's great. Gag him too. We don't want him giving the game away if his friends come to rescue him, do we?" she replied with a smile.

With that, Oliver grabbed some thick black Gaffer tape from the twins and stuffed a piece of bloodied rag which he had cut from Alhusain's trousers into his mouth, before fiercely wrapping several layers of tape around Alhusain's terrified face.

"Okay, we've finished," said the twins. "Be careful where you step, or else there'll be fireworks."

Vincent looked on, expressionlessly deep in thought as they heaved Alhusain high up the mast and secured all the bindings. Nikki wondered momentarily what he could be thinking.

"Whatever you're thinking Vincent, drop it. This is what we discussed. It won't be closure, but it sure counts for something. Go and give the signal for the extraction," Nikki said in a commanding voice, physically pushing him in the direction he needed to go. Reluctantly, he headed to the bow, while the twins climbed the mast and set a spring release C4 block on the back of Alhusain so that if anyone attempted to move him, he would explode.

"Is my Dad okay?" came Oliver's nervous voice from just behind Nikki.

"He'll be fine when we get off this fly-ridden heap of shit," Nikki said, gripping Oliver by the shoulder to show him some support. Oliver had always dealt with the reason for this revenge differently from his father. Perhaps it was the Special Forces training he had received. He seemed able to file it away in a safe place in his mind and control it, maybe even forget about it.

Nikki told Scott to set up some cameras to cover Alhusain's face as he hung upside down. The other two would give a stern and bow view in case anyone was approaching. Vincent was now on the communications, telling the team they had two minutes before their lift arrived.

"Everybody good to go?" Nikki said to her team.

"Roger that, boss."

The team disembarked the wooden hull of the mothership, leaving Alhusain hanging perilously close to death from the mast. They headed for the P42s which were now moored alongside while Nikki stood on the deck, checking that the team had left nothing behind. She walked slowly and deliberately towards Alhusain, eventually coming to stand right before him, removing her soaking wet hood to reveal she was female, knowing full well the contempt that this sorry excuse for a human being held for women. She wanted the last face that Alhusain saw on this earth before she sent him to meet his maker to be hers. She saw his eyes widen with fear as she leaned in close and whispered in his ear, "Say hello to Allah for me, you fucker. Let him know he's going to be seeing a lot more of his followers by this time tomorrow." She then viciously spat in his face, knowing that this was the greatest insult he could ever receive.

"We done here, boss?" she heard Lee saying from behind her. "Or do you want a pic of me with this scumbag so we can use it on Fuckbuddy and Twatter?"

"Yeah sure, take a selfie. We'll upload it when his friends have been." Turning back to Alhusain, "I think we're done," she said, feeling as though rage were going to take her over and make her do something that might spoil the taste of the afters. She followed Lee and stepped onto the P42 for the journey back to the Seychelles. The team sat in the corner of the aluminium-skinned boat which would get them back to the port of Victoria in the early hours of the morning. As Lee and Scott cleaned down their weapons, Billie asked them breezily if they were up for a late night casino session when they got back. The team had been booked into suites at the Plantation Club, which, as well as top-of-the-range facilities including gym, sauna, spa and nightclub, had a casino on site.

"Why not, the pit boss from the casino is from Stoke," Lee responded.

"Where the fuck is Stoke?" Billie asked.

The twins looked at each other and laughed at Billie, having forgotten that she was from Sweden and of course wouldn't have a clue where Stoke was. Billie continued asking who else was up for letting their hair down. Nikki sat chatting to Vincent, attempting to coax him back into the real world. He stared into the bleak, dark ocean, seemingly unseeing, but Nikki knew his mind was racing.

Becci was talking to Oliver over the satellite phone, passionately and anxiously questioning him while Oliver said for the third time that his dad was absolutely fine, that they would be back shortly. He signed off with a brief smirk at Nikki followed by a whispered "Fucking hell, she is hard work."

Nikki grinned back, then focused her attention back on Vincent. "We'll be back soon, boss. The job's finished now."

He looked up at her, his face wrought with emotion, and said, "Do you know what, Nikki? I think it's just the beginning."

CHAPTER 2

WELCOME, MIKE

TWO YEARS LATER

As the British Airways 737 BA 2644 flight touched down on the tiny Mediterranean island of Malta, Mike Russell Delaney was entirely unsure of what he was to expect when he disembarked the plane.

Mike had been born in the United States but raised in Surrey. He held a dual citizenship and worked for MI6, with solid connections at the CIA. As he waited in the queue for passport control, he wondered for the hundredth time why his boss had sent him on secondment to an organisation named Vendicare which he had never even heard of, nor could he find any information on whatsoever, based in the middle of nowhere.

As his mind pondered this question yet again, he heard a voice shouting his name from behind. As he turned, he saw a twenty-something girl striding towards him, five foot ten or eleven, with thick blonde hair and Prada sunglasses shading her eyes, dressed in cream shorts and brown flip-flops with a security lanyard hanging around her neck. To Mike, she looked like some sort of holiday representative, or one of those girls who hands out drinks vouchers for bars.

He realised he was staring at her and opened his mouth to say something when she said, "Sorry, my name's Emily, I didn't mean to startle you. I was supposed to meet you airside straight from the plane, but we had an issue landing the helicopter. Some bloody local in difficulty with a hang glider." She smiled and stuck out a welcoming hand. "Welcome to Malta!"

Before Mike could even respond, never mind formulate a question, she had turned quickly and said, "Follow me, you don't need to clear immigration here, we have an... understanding." A cute little smile was playing around her lips and she had an accent that Mike couldn't quite place. It was definitely European, but possibly concealed a hint of the Middle East, he thought.

She swiped the pass on the lanyard and led him through a security door, which opened onto some tarmac where there were several helicopters situated.

Mike immediately recognised one of the helicopters as a Eurocopter AS 365 and another as a Bell Augusta 609. He regularly travelled in helicopters, but never ones as grand as these. His were more... military issue.

"Which one's ours?" he asked Emily.

"They're all ours actually, but we're taking the Dauphin," she responded, gesturing towards the Eurocopter.

As they climbed in, Mike asked, "Where's the pilot?"

"You're looking at her," Emily stated as though it were obvious. "You can ride in the front, if you want."

After completing her pre-flight check, Emily was cleared for take-off by the tower, whom she thanked for the short visit, before the shudder of the rotary blades lifted the Eurocopter off the ground. Mike sat, growing more and more intrigued by this company Vendicare and the way they ran their operations. He decided to quiz Emily about the organisation and attempt to find out exactly why he was there. "I hope you don't mind me asking, but who, and what, are Vendicare?"

His question was followed by silence as Emily headed west towards the island of Gozo. According to the instruments, the journey would take no more than seven or eight minutes.

The radio crackled into life as Emily said, "This is Alpha Oscar Sierra Two requesting clearance to land on Pad One, over."

It was quiet for a few moments, before the radio sounded back again. "Alpha Oscar Sierra Two you are cleared to land, the boss is waiting for you, Emily. Over."

"Mike, if you look down to your left you will see Villa Vincenzo. That's our accommodation block. Don't tell the boss I called it that, as he designed the whole thing and actually got his hands dirty, believe it or not, building it with the Gozitans."

As Mike looked down he could see an amazing villa complex, almost ranch-like in style, with Tuscan features, spread over what looked like several acres and surrounded by perimeter fencing and sunflowers. "Not bad for barracks," Emily said with that trademark grin on her face.

Noting that his question about Vendicare had been delicately avoided, Mike asked, "What's that smaller place over there?"

"Oh, that's Vincent's private place. He entertains there, plus his daughter stops there when she's not at boarding school," Emily replied.

"What's this Vincent like?" Mike asked inquisitively, keen to squeeze any information he could out of Emily. As he was waiting for his answer, Emily swung the helicopter right sharply and descended towards the landing pad, where Mike could see a flight engineer dressed in a high visibility jacket waiting for them alongside a man and a woman.

"That's the boss there, waiting for us," Emily said. She

hovered for a moment before descending, but was slightly too quick in her downward thrust and the Eurocopter thumped heavily onto the helipad.

She cursed. "Fuck, fuck, fuck, I always do that when the boss is about. Oh, he's going to take the piss, I know he is," Emily said to herself as a self-frustrated flush crept across her cheeks. She flicked several switches and the engine noise began to decrease as Mike removed his Peltor headphones and hung them on the clip he had taken them from. As he climbed out of the helicopter, Mike felt the warm Mediterranean air brush his cheeks and the noise from the helicopter slowly receded.

"Welcome, Mike," said the woman, who had striking features and sleek, dark hair. She stretched out a welcoming hand which Mike shook. "I'm Rebecca, but they all call me Nikki. This is Vincent." Vincent shook the hand of their new visitor with a small smile.

Mike noticed that Nikki was dressed immaculately in a similar fashion to Emily, though the Prada sunglasses had become Raybans and her skin complexion was much darker. Vincent also had a slightly Mediterranean look and stood at about the same height as Nikki. He too was dressed down in casual shorts, designer glasses and a short-sleeved shirt. Well this is nothing like MI6, Mike thought to himself.

"We hope you had a good flight, Mike. We would normally have sent the private jet for you, but Oliver and Billie are just on their way back from a job and the spare is being refitted," Vincent explained, apologetically.

Confused that they were apologising about flying him over in business class, Mike replied, "No worries, I had a great flight."

"You have of course already met Emily. I apologise for her landing, she doesn't get the whole 'gentle' bit yet, but we live in hope," Vincent said, smiling at Emily who had now appeared beside Mike.

"Sorry boss, I only ever do it when you're there, honestly," she replied grudgingly.

"Let's go inside and get a coffee. I'm sure you have a few questions for us, Mike," Nikki said.

The group walked along the courtside towards a large, half-round oak door which looked like the entrance to a Tuscan villa. Once inside the refreshing air conditioned building, Mike noticed that, although from the outside everything looked old and grand, inside it was completely modern, almost like a high-tech suite of offices or a medical centre. He also noticed that all the doors and entry points had the latest laser body scanners which seemed a great deal more advanced than the biometric ones they had at MI6. He found himself wondering, not for the first time today, exactly what he was dealing with.

As they waited for the lift, Mike noticed the red laser scan Nikki. She was instantly recognised by the system which stated loudly, "Rebecca Hunter, access granted." As they descended in the lift, Nikki explained to Mike the biometrics of the system. The computer would only identify real people, as well as safeguarding against intruders using force to gain access. If anyone unauthorised was within a ten metre radius of the bio scanner, it would not grant access. "Quite simply, Mike, if you don't exist on the systems and we don't tick the box, then you can't move around this building. Luckily for you, we've ticked your name, so you're safe," she explained.

The lift doors opened and Nikki led everyone out into an airy conference room where they all took a seat. Vincent offered them all coffee or juice from a mini breakfast bar. He made both the girls juice and programmed a latte for Mike and a double espresso for himself.

Once they were all sat comfortably, Vincent turned to Mike. "I appreciate that you have been cleared to the highest level here Mike, but what we are about to tell you, only a select few people in the world know. And most of those people work here." Mike briefly wondered to himself if it were possible that his curiosity could grow any stronger. Vincent then put some of his questions to rest.

"Vendicare is an independent contractor who quite simply deal with jobs that no government or organisation can put their name to. Sometimes for political reasons. Sometimes because they fear reprisals. Sometimes because maybe they don't think that doing it is worth the loss of votes. The world's a dirty place and we are the ones who do the clean-ups. We don't answer to any particular government."

"We only deal with PMs, Kings, Queens, Presidents," Nikki continued. "That way we know what they know. If it's deniable, then we are all in the same boat, so to speak."

Before Mike could properly digest the information he was being fed, Vincent stood abruptly and said, "Mike, I'm going to have to pass you over to Nikki and Emily. I have other visitors arriving shortly. I apologise. I'm sure we will catch up later, and once you've finished your discussions here, Emily will give you some orientation around the place." Vincent gestured at Nikki to take over, and walked stiffly from the conference room.

Nikki apologised again for Vincent leaving, explaining that "AC had arrived." Though Mike was keen to know who 'AC' was, he knew that he wasn't likely to get a response and so kept his mouth shut.

Nikki stated loudly and clearly. "System on." Immediately a large picture on the wall became a transparent, 3D screen. She turned to him. "Mike, do you know anything about Senaullah, the leader of Boko Haram?" she asked.

Mike knew who he was. "Apart from him being a vile terrorist that gets away with kidnapping one hundred innocent children?" he replied, incredibly irritated by the mere mention of this man's name.

"In four days' time, he will be snatched and in the hands of MI6, with all the girls back with their families."

Mike was astounded for a moment. Then he sighed, knowing it was a little bit of wishful thinking. "Providing those poor girls are still alive."

"They're definitely alive. We've seen them." Emily chipped in, eagerly.

Mike turned, feeling utterly bewildered. Nikki quickly explained. "Our colleagues, Oliver and Billie, have been sent out to Nigeria. They are posing as a couple on a honeymoon safari. While they've been there, they have made contact with several assets of ours in the region, who have confirmed that apart from the obvious distress of being kidnapped and some brutal sexual trauma experienced at the hands of the guards, they're all alive and well. They are being held in one place, which is not what's been reported. There have been several media reports on them being held in numerous places." Nikki frowned. "It's all deception to stop us mounting a credible rescue."

Hundreds of thoughts came rushing into Mike's mind. How on earth did they know all this? This was information that even MI6 had no way of knowing. What have I got myself into? was becoming a recurring thought.

Nikki touched the screen on her desk and images appeared of a dense jungle area. Some old breeze block outbuildings interrupted the greenery and Mike could see guards stationed outside every visible door. "That's where they are holding them," Emily explained simply.

"How old are these pictures?" Mike asked, breathless.

Nikki looked at him as though she were having to explain the obvious. "These are real time."

Mike did not respond. He looked from Emily to Nikki and back to Emily again with a blank expression on his face. That's not possible, he thought. How could these people have live images of one of the most wanted terrorists in the world? The superpowers with all their billions of dollars spent on trying to locate them haven't got the faintest idea of what they're doing… let alone where they might be. He knew from his briefings with people at MI6 who were in direct contact with those the CIA and other US security offices that no one had a clue.

He finally responded with, "How the bloody hell do you have satellite and drone images of Boko Haram?"

"That's not really important at the moment, Mike," came Nikki's evasive response. "More importantly, we need to get you up to speed in less than four days. We will be on site and you're on the team." Nikki looked almost apologetic for a split second, but the sympathy vanished as soon as it had appeared. She quickly explained, before he could object, that there was a full operational briefing tomorrow at 10.00hrs and that for the remainder of the day Emily would show him around and introduce him to the rest of the team.

Nikki made a move to leave the conference room, but before she did, she invited him to a get together later that evening at Vincent's villa. "Just drinks and a barbeque around the pool," she said. Mike nodded to say he'd be there. Nikki promptly left, instructing Emily to continue with Mike's induction.

Once she had left, Emily turned to Mike with a smile and said cheekily, "I hope you've got some shorts and flip-flops. We don't stand on ceremony here." Then she turned on her heel and led him out of the conference room to take him on their orientation trip. "Ask any questions you want while I show you around."

Mike inwardly wondered if this time his questions would actually be answered, but thought he might as well give it a go. "How come I got selected for this team? And who am I replacing?" he asked.

Emily stopped suddenly and her cheeky smile disappeared, being replaced with an expression of grief.

"Mike, I apologise if I sound evasive..." Surprise, surprise, he thought. "I don't mean to, but I don't know why you were picked. That's Vincent and Nikki's bag. They do the hiring and the firing, but I guess you must be bloody good, or you wouldn't be here. As far as replacing anyone... we lost one of our team in a shit storm of an operation recently and Vincent won't let us operate one down. Nikki won't let Vincent go in place of them. So, they compromised," Emily said in a strained voice.

Mike didn't say anything, realising that it was an incredibly sensitive topic, and Emily said after a few paces, "Here we are, our accommodation block."

The bio scanner examined them and then they heard, "Welcome Mike Delaney. Please enter." Emily followed Mike into the room and explained that all private residence suites could only be initially accessed by the person the room had been allocated to.

The suite itself was enormous, with a beautiful wet room, dining room and balcony and an infinity pool that looked out across the Mediterranean. Emily explained that from his desk area he could access all comms and IT. The only thing he wouldn't be able to access were the drones, although he would be able to see the images he had been shown in the conference room.

She then took Mike down to the restaurant area to introduce him to Jodie, who was in charge of catering. As Mike walked towards her, he looked around. Who picks the staff here? he thought to himself. Every single girl around this building is to die for. It wasn't anything like what he was used at MI6, that was for sure.

As Emily led Mike down to the restaurant area, she explained to him how Jodie had got the job. Vincent had met her at one of his favourite Italian restaurants in Rome called 'Panaro's' and although Jodie was only twenty-one, she had worked in that family business for over ten years. Vincent had discovered Panaro's some eighteen years previously when a business colleague took him out for dinner.

Since that day, Panaro's had become Vincent's favourite restaurant and he visited whenever he could, with the Panaro family becoming his incredibly close friends; so much so that when Jean's husband Mario was killed in a car accident, she contacted Vincent before anyone else and he immediately flew to Italy and spent a week with her and her daughter. He had first met Jodie when she ran around the restaurant, just three or four years old. As a child, she had looked up to him and even called him 'Zia Vincenzo' – 'Uncle Vincent' in Italian. Whilst on a visit a few years ago, Jen had seemed somewhat troubled. After much probing and threats of staying all night until she told him, Jean revealed that teenage problems were causing her sleepless nights after she had discovered that Jodie had been going off the rails: staying away from home, not studying, being involved in drugs... and although Vincent knew that all would pass with time, he felt obligated to help.

"...so Jodie has now been at Vendicare for two years. Although she's not operational, she's one of the family," Emily said with a smile. "Jodie, this is Mike. He just started today," Emily said, introducing them.

Mike stared at Jodie. He couldn't believe how good looking she was. She was a mixture of Latin, most likely from her dad, and European from her mother. She stood at nearly six feet tall, with long dark hair and piercing aqua blue eyes. She was dressed in figure-hugging black jeans and a pink chef's top which read her name, embroidered next to an Italian flag.

She glanced at him quickly and said, "Hi Mike," giving a quick dismissive wave of the hand before kissing Emily on both cheeks and erupting into a conversation in very fast Italian, as though she were annoyed at something. Emily looked taken aback for a few moments and then held her hands up in the air to stop Jodie from rambling.

"Jodie! It's rude to speak in Italian when I'm introducing you. We can discuss that issue later," Emily said sharply.

"Sorry Em but it pisses me off. I've been asking for six months and still he keeps ignoring me."

"Whatever, but let's talk about it at the barbeque or another time, please," Emily said in the same sharp tone, looking irritated but also faintly embarrassed.

Mike looked on bemusedly, finding Jodie cute when she swore in English with her strong Italian accent.

"Are you doing the barbeque tonight, or is Mel?" Emily continued in her conversation with Jodie, apparently having forgiven her for her misconduct.

"I'm doing all the prep and setup, but you're cooking it yourself. As if you lot don't think I work hard enough," she answered with a laugh, then stuck her tongue out at Emily before retreating back into the cold room.

Mike and Emily stood in silence for a few moments before Mike said simply, "Bloody hell. She looks a handful."

Emily didn't respond, only shook her head in obvious exasperation before continuing with Mike's orientation.

She led him to a building which she introduced as 'the killing house'. Mike recognised it as very similar to ones he had previously seen in Hereford and at Fort Bragg, but this one was different. It was entirely electronic. He looked at Emily in wonder, making it clear that he needed a bit of explanation.

She grinned at him, looking proud and launched right into the story. Vincent had looked at the designs when they had originally built it, wanting to use the same technology as they used in electronic gaming and after having been on a visit to EYA, a games company in Surrey, and having had further meetings with one of their chief designers, together they developed a thin layer base suit which could be worn under combat gear. When using different background mock-ups, such as 'house', 'train' or 'plane', they could use laser technology linked to a computer programme which generated a different simulation each time. The main advantage to this was that there were fewer accidents and no stray ricochets; an arrangement which had been very important to Vincent following a ricochet which had hit him whilst training for Operation Pirate over two years ago..

The difference was notable. Unlike the screen simulations he was used to, this was a real, move-around environment using day-to-day weapons which had been adapted. On top of the standard killing house, they also had different simulations, which even included a ship actually based at sea. It was all scarily impressive.

Emily continued to show Mike the simulation village which had been constructed for the training of Operation 'Angel Faces'. Mike looked up and was about to ask what this mysterious sounding operation was before he remembered that all of his questions so far had been deflected. He let out a quick sigh, shook his head and kept quiet. Instead, he looked at the amazing detail of the simulations. One was absolutely identical to the images he had seen coming in live from Nigeria earlier on.

"We use the same joiners and builders as they use for making the Game of Thrones sets," Emily said matter-of-factly, answering Mike's unasked question. "It's pretty neat really, because they think they're building a film set, which means no one asks any unwanted questions."

***

A few hours later, as Mike's orientation was nearly complete, Emily signed out a new tablet and phone from their stores for him and informed him that personal weapons would be issued tomorrow at the briefing. Mike had noticed these 'personal weapons' being carried around the base. He had seen almost everyone carrying a Heckler and Koch Compact, recognising the carbon fibre hybrid design, which meant that it would be as light as carrying around a water pistol and very easy to conceal about your person. Emily also informed him that these guns contained a whole host of extra features, such as palm print recognition which only responded to members of the teams. Mike was well and truly baffled by the enormously high standard of weaponry that Vendicare possessed, significantly better than MI6. Rather than again questioning how this was possible, he turned his attention to his new phone and asked a different question that had been bugging him since he'd arrived.

"Why doesn't my phone work here? Why do I have to be given a whole new one?"

"Oh, right, yeah, sorry, should have explained when you first got here. There's a 10km black out perimeter here covered by a cloaking device, which creates a communication bubble. None of your MI6 issued equipment will work here. It gives us an extra layer of security. No external communications equipment brought here would work. The blocker system was developed by our communications team and is on twenty-four-seven. The same software and technology cloaks the villas, so no one can get satellite pictures or aerial photographs unless approved by us and the area above is a no-fly zone. We have complete and total privacy here."

She then took him to see the garage, which contained not only operational vehicles for European jobs but also some 'toys' for the boys and girls, Mike noted with interest. He'd always been a bit of a petrolhead. However, Emily explained, there were two vehicles that no one touched; those being Vincent's Aston Martin DB7 and Nikki's limited edition McLaren MP4 12C SPYDER which Vincent had given her for her birthday. "Other than that, anything else goes. Feel free to just take the keys off the board and go for a drive," Emily said.

Mike stared around him once again in wonderment. He had never seen such an array of cars. Before now, all he was used to were the Fords and Vauxhalls kept by MI6 in their underground building in Chelsea. He noticed that apart from Vincent's DB7, there were two original Mercedes G-Wagons, a 2011 SLS AMG Gullwing with a 6.2 litre V8 engine and two Range Rover Sports, which he guessed were more for operational use. There were also several Chevrolet SUVs with bulletproof glass and Kevlar reinforced door panels and an insane amount of Porsches and BMWs. There was everything in the motor pool from motorbikes to sports cars and off-roaders to road cycles. I'll bet no one's bored around here, Mike thought to himself, looking around in ecstasy at the motor fantasy that surrounded him.

Emily's voice broke off his fascination. "Mike, if you're alright here, I'd like to go and get ready for tonight's barbeque."

"Yeah, no problem, sorry," he smiled apologetically. "What time does it start again?"

"I'll knock on for you at seven, if that's alright with you, and we'll walk across together. After all, I wouldn't want you bumping into the twins without already being introduced. You won't stick around until the morning if that happens," she said with her trademark grin. She turned to leave. "Oh, don't forget to dress down. Shorts are good," she added as she left him standing alone in automobile heaven.

CHAPTER 3

THE WEDDING BELLS

Oliver and Billie were on their way back from their 'honeymoon' in Lagos, travelling via London. Vincent had asked them if they could pick up his daughter, who had just finished boarding school for the summer. Oliver had not seen his little sister for over six months and was looking forward to catching up with her. Vincent and the team at Vendicare had grown rather protective over Kerry because of past events; the past events which had, in fact, created Vendicare in the first place. On top of the main reason, which was vengeance, Vincent had felt that things were happening in the world that governments wouldn't readily stand up against most of the time, due to votes and popularity, so someone needed to do the jobs no one else would put their name to.

Oliver remembered that night, two years ago, where his and his father's vengeance was fulfilled. Eight hours after they had hoisted Alhusain up the mast and strapped enough C4 to him to bring down a small building, they had watched the ship explode back on the Seychelles via the hidden surveillance cameras, killing seven other barbarians who had attempted to rescue Alhusain. Since that day, Somali pirates had avoided that area by a 500-mile radius. They definitely got the message, Oliver thought with grim satisfaction.

His deep thoughts were suddenly interrupted when Billie asked in her standard, cheeky voice, "Do you think my new husband will have time to take me shopping in London before we pick up your sis?"

He smiled to himself before responding. "Firstly, let me tell you, Billie, that we are now divorced. Spending seven days with you as your husband has completely traumatised me as far as marriage is concerned. In fact, when I get back to base, I'm gonna book myself some counselling."

"Fuck off, you totally loved it. I saw you checking me out when I was in the shower; you know full well that if it wasn't for your dad's stupid rule you would have made a play for me," Billie retorted, grinning widely at Oliver.

"Thank god for Dad's rules," Oliver muttered under his breath, thinking to himself that it wouldn't be Billie that he'd go for if his dad's rules weren't in place. He didn't pursue the conversation, knowing that she was only attempting to wind him up. Anyway, even if his dad did have a rule about the team not being allowed to be involved with each other, he loved her more like a sister than anything else and would do anything to protect her.

"I'm just going up front to check with the pilot how long until we are on the ground at Heathrow. Why don't you knock yourself out while I am away?" he said, giving her a playful crack around the back of the head as he left his seat.

"Argh, that hurt," she screeched. "I knew you'd bite," she said grinning. "Now ask the pilot if I can go landside and shop, there's a good husband."

Oliver shook his head as he joined the two pilots in the cockpit of the Gulfstream GS550, which was cruising through a mild, cloudy sky at 560 miles per hour. They were about seventy minutes out of London Heathrow. Vendicare operated two Gulfstreams and both had been adapted with a new Airborne

Early Warning System and Enhanced Vision System. The communication and IT on board was so advanced that no other agency in the world had anything even remotely similar. Oliver admired the two systems for a moment before focusing on the two pilots. William and David were both ex-RAF and, although they only worked for Vendicare, both were non-operational personnel and didn't know too much about the ins and outs; exactly as Vincent wanted it to be. The less people knew, the safer the team would be.

"Good afternoon chaps, how long we got to go?" asked Oliver.

"We're on a direct flight path boss, no holding pattern for us today. The tower has cleared us for about sixty-five minutes," William responded.

"That's nice of them," Oliver said. "Any idea how long on the tarmac, Will?"

"Normally thirty minutes tops for refuelling and then we should be on our way."

"Any chance you can patch me through to my sister's security details so I can check where they are?"

William switched the channel from standard airline frequency to the communications system which Antonietta and her tech team at Vendicare had developed. The system used a new MAG-7 Satellite system which bounced a scrambled signal through normal tele-comms networks which was then unscrambled by the recipient with no interference whatsoever, making it completely untraceable.

"This is Alpha Oscar Sierra One calling Kilo Sierra One, please acknowledge," Oliver said into the piece.

"Alpha Oscar Sierra One, this is Kilo Sierra One. Go ahead," came the response a few seconds later.

"Hi guys, it's Oliver. What's your ETA on Heathrow and how's my darling sister?"

"Hey Oliver, it's Steve. Just clearing tarmac security at Gate 5, and your sister is sprawled on the back seat fast asleep, I think."

"Thanks guys, we will be on the tarmac in fifty-five minutes or so. See you then."

Oliver sauntered out of the cockpit and informed Billie that she could have twenty-five minutes or so in T5 shopping, if she really, desperately wanted to. Her excited response confirmed her intentions.

As the plane touched down in London, the co-pilot was already talking to the ground crew arranging refuelling while Oliver and Billie prepared for a quick dash to T5; Oliver to pick up his little sister and Billie to do some shopping.

Oliver's sixteen-year-old sister Kerry was waiting for them in the VIP lounge with Steve looking after her. When she noticed Oliver walking towards her, she gave a little shriek of delight and ran over to him, giving him a huge hug.

"My god sis, look at you! I can't believe it's only six months since I've seen you." He gave her a critical once over. "I hope you've got a change of clothes for when you get there. Dad's going to go mental with you dressed like that."

"Oliver. You're a dick," Kerry responded passionately.

"I can second that," Billie chipped in.

Kerry shrieked another high-pitched welcome when she saw Billie standing there. They had a close relationship which had been built up when Billie used to escort her to the villa during school holidays.

"Do you fancy a quick thirty-minute shop in T5?" Billie asked with a grin.

"Err...YEAH. Let's go!" Kerry replied.

"Billie, find her something to wear that's more appropriate please!" Oliver chirped in, laughing, before they walked off arm in arm.

Kerry turned around and gave him a very long, hard death stare and shouted in exasperation, "Hello! I am here and I can hear you!" before dashing off with Billie to do some quick shopping.

CHAPTER 4

WHO IS AC?

In a private, secure office within Vincent's villa on Gozo, Nikki and Vincent were sat with their visitor, staring at the live images on the screen coming from Chibok, Northern Nigeria.

"So we definitely have your full support for an evacuation if we run into a shit storm?" Nikki asked.

"Nikki, you have all the support you need. Obviously, that goes without saying! I have to be able to deny that it was a British operation, but the SAS will evacuate you if anything goes wrong. I believe they are already on exercise in the area awaiting your contact," AC responded, glancing away from the live images.

Vincent quickly relayed the necessary information to him without going into a full operational briefing. He told him what was happening and the fact that they had put the Red Cross on standby to collect the children immediately. He declined to expand on issues relating to casualties or what would happen to the Islamist Sect. "It's better you didn't know, then you can answer honestly in PM's Questions," Vincent justified grimly.

There was a slight nod of the head from AC, which confirmed to Nikki that everyone was on the same page.

"Vincent, if that's all you need me for I have to get some stuff ready for the briefing tomorrow," Nikki said.

"That's fine. I will catch up with you later at the pool," Vincent replied.

"See you later," Nikki said to their visitor, shaking his hand quickly.

"Absolutely. I can't wait to see the team again. I'm looking forward to seeing Kerry and trying to get her to reveal who Sarah is seeing at school. She has been rather evasive lately," their visitor replied with a smile.

"Good luck with that," Nikki said, snorting, as she turned to leave with a half-smile playing around her lips; she knew full well that Kerry would never give anything away as easily as that.

Vincent watched as Nikki left the room and then turned back to AC. He sat quietly, listening intently while his visitor discussed the Ukrainian crisis and potential governmental fallout if it escalated any further. Since the President of Russia, Sergei Gorelov, had reclaimed the sea port and was heavily arming the separatists, things were just going from bad to worse. He could see not only AC's but also the entirety of Europe's nerves mounting.

"Okay, so let me get this straight. You and Washington D.C. are looking to take out Gorelov? Is that seriously what you're talking about?" Vincent asked, not even trying to force the annoyance out of his voice.

"It's not just us. His own people, particularly the Oligarch's, are worried that the rest of the world is going to turn on them. If we have to start sanctions, London could lose billions!" AC said emphatically.

Vincent sat momentarily, looking at the wall for inspiration.

"Look," he said agitatedly. "We are in no way interested in a military coup to overthrow Gorelov. That's not what we do, especially since the only thing he can actually be accused of is the retaking of Sevastopol from the Ukrainians and jailing the Pussy Riot band, neither of which in my opinion constitute justification for him being overthrown, let alone assassinated."

AC replied quickly, with mirrored irritation. "You managed to sort out our little problem in Libya for us without us having to twist your arm half this much. What's the difference here?!"

Vincent stood up sharply, indicating that this conversation was over as far as he was concerned. "Let's not spoil a good day, shall we? I will chat to Nikki later and let you know what our thoughts are. But, for the record, Gaddafi was a real bastard, up there with Saddam, Bin Laden and that Sociopath in Syria." He gestured for AC to rise and he did so unenthusiastically, a sour expression on his face. "I assume you will need some privacy to contact your office. You know how it all works, any help you might need ask Jen, she's just outside. She'll show you to your suite once you're done and I will see you later at the barbeque," Vincent said, before extending a formal hand and shaking AC's with a firm grip.

As he left the room, he glanced at his watch. Oliver and Billie should be arriving at the base with Kerry in about twenty minutes. They were en route from London and Lee and Scott should be taking the Eurocopter for the short hop to collect them from the airport in Malta.

When Vincent entered the operations room a few moments later, he saw Nikki with the Vendicare technology team, Antonietta and Damien. They were all completely submerged in working out the attack strategy planned for Operation 'Angel Faces.'

"How's it all going, guys?" Vincent asked.

Nikki turned around sharply and visibly relaxed when she saw Vincent standing in the doorway. "Oh hey, Vincent. Yeah it's going well! Just typing up some notes for tomorrow. Oh, by the way, I've moved the briefing forward to 0830hours, as I want the simulation to start by ten, if that's okay with you," she replied.

"Yeah that's great. You know I'll be up anyway, though I can't speak for the rest of our lot. Let's keep them off Jacks tonight then, beer only I think," Vincent said with a smile.

He made his way over to Antonietta and Damien and asked them if they had any eyes or ears on the Ukrainian situation.

"Not really at the moment, Vincent. We are monitoring the general chatter all over the world, of course, but if you want me to look at something specific I'll get right on it," Antonietta replied, ever eager.

"Well, communications between Gorelov and his magic circle and anything between them and the Ukrainian pro-separatists would be great," Vincent replied, thanking them before standing up to leave. He gave Nikki a meaningful look which he knew would translate as "We need to talk about this later." She gave a slight nod, so small she wasn't even sure he had seen it, and turned back towards her desk to continue working on her notes for the briefing tomorrow.

Vincent then made his way over to his villa, hoping to see Jodie there so that he could have a quick chat about the evening's barbeque and special requirements for their new visitor, AC. Although Jodie lived in the main house with the rest of the team, she often spent time in Vincent's villa watching TV shows with Nikki. It wasn't unusual for Nikki and Jodie to pull an all-nighter watching a complete season of what Vincent described as 'ACTV' - American Crap Television. On several occasions he had woken up early in the morning, either to go cycling or to visit the gym, and had found them both fast asleep on the sofa with the television still blaring an episode of this or that. Rebecca Hunter's nickname 'Nikki' had actually come about because of Vincent and Jodie teasing her about watching repeats of Nikita. As the team already had a

Becci, Nikki was an ideal nickname that since had just stuck with everyone.

"I've been looking for you all day," came a familiar voice from the sofa as Vincent entered his luxury villa, breaking up his thoughts.

"Nice to see you too, Jodie. When were you last in touch with your mum?" Vincent responded light-heartedly, keeping his wits about him. He knew full well what he was about to deal with; Emily had tipped him off as to Jodie's annoyance only a few hours ago.

"You promised that if I worked hard you would let me join the team!" Vincent knew Jodie would be trying her best to keep the whiny teenager from her voice, but nevertheless it was there. Well, don't beat around the bush, Jodie, he thought to himself.

"Okay, hold up there missy. Firstly, I didn't promise anything. I said I would consider having a chat with Nikki and maybe... see if we could put a training plan together," Vincent replied in his most reasonable tone. Jodie had been pestering him for the past six months to get involved with the team. Unfortunately for Vincent, he'd made a promise to her mother Jean that he would keep her safe. How on earth would he be able to manage that if she were to go on missions with the team? It was now obvious that every promise he had ever made about keeping his team safe were nullified... since...

He felt like a rock stuck between two hard places. He saw Jodie visibly deflate with disappointment and she started to turn away from him. His heart went out to her and, having always been too soft-hearted for his own good, he tried to comfort her. "Before you get all funny with me, if you could maybe get some cover in the kitchen for the next five days, I will have a word with Nikki and see about setting up some training for you, okay? But for the complete avoidance of doubt or confusion, this is for training ONLY," Vincent said forcefully.

Jodie leapt up and threw her arms around Vincent's neck, almost squeezing the breath out of him, screeching her appreciation. As Vincent attempted to prise her off him, laughing all the while, Nikki arrived back. She took in the scene and then laughed openly at Vincent, knowing full well that Jodie had just got her way yet again.

"Listen Jodie, that's not a priority right now! I need to talk to you about something else. I want to check that you have all the food details for our guests tonight at the barbeque," Vincent said, trying to get off the subject of Jodie's training before speaking to Nikki about it.

"Yes, yes, don't worry, all sorted!" Jodie squeaked excitedly. "I'm going to go ring Mum and tell her the good news!" She shouted as she bounded off the sofa and sprinted out of Vincent's living room, whooping.

Vincent shook his head, dismayed. He would have much preferred to make that phone call first, knowing full well that Jean would be extremely worried, but there was nothing to be done now. Jodie will have already told half of the people she knew in the last thirty seconds alone.

"You know both her and Kerry have you wrapped around their little fingers, don't you?" Nikki said playfully, only half-jokingly. Vincent knew it.

"Well you may as well just add you, Emily, Billie and Oliver onto that list for good measure. Throw in the twins and everybody else I've ever employed," Vincent said with a half-smile on his face.

"This is the first time I've seen you smile for a few days. Are you okay? Are you still thinking about Becci?" Nikki asked, trying to sound empathetic, even though it didn't really suit her.

Vincent really didn't feel in the mood to talk about it. He respected that Nikki was concerned about his feelings and appreciated her trying to help him. Although he knew that everyone understood that people dealt with their grief in different ways, he was really struggling to cope with the first loss of a team member.

"Nikki, over the next few days I want these guys drilled and drilled, okay? I was so close to jacking all this in... but then that would have meant that Becci died for nothing...and... I can't go through this again." Vincent's voice broke with emotion as he said Becci's name.

Nikki's heart went out to him, but she dealt with her grief in a very different way from Vincent. "You know someone sold us out, don't you?" she said with anger.

Vincent sighed in resignation. "Oh absolutely, someone did. But who?"

"I don't know, but when we get back from this job, we sure as hell will know," Nikki replied, positivity seeping from her every word.

Vincent smiled in agreement, but his insides felt dead. Just at that moment, his phone bleeped. He looked at it and saw that it was Jen, his CEO, informing him that she had finished the monthly reports for VirtualTech, the gaming business attached to Vendicare, and asked if he wanted them bringing over tonight or leaving in the office. Vincent replied telling her to leave them at the office.

VirtualTech was one of the largest online gaming businesses in the industry, which had put Vincent in the top twenty richest men in the world before he was thirty. However, he'd always kept himself to himself, with all of his financial and personal information kept away from the prying eyes of the public domain. Vincent's VirtualTech team had developed software which crawled through the entire internet and online media systems deleting any reference made to him personally, or any member of his team at Vendicare. It was as though they didn't exist. Just how Vincent wanted it.

Jen, his CEO, had begun working for Vincent eight years ago as a twenty-two year old, a young post-graduate fresh out of university. She had begun in the finance department and quickly worked her way to joining the board at only twenty-five. Vincent hadn't had any trouble spotting her work ethic nor her enthusiasm – it was clear for everyone to see – but it was her loyalty which drew him to her. Two years ago, he flew her to Panaro's restaurant in Rome and told her everything about his plans to start up the new operation of Vendicare in Gozo. He asked her if she would head VirtualTech so that he could concentrate on Vendicare. He remembered vividly her response. She had just finished a spoonful of pea and mint risotto made by Jean and Jodie. She then looked up from the table and said, "So you mean, like, I'd be Pepper Potts out of Iron Man?" Before Vincent could respond to the absurd question, she just said, "Yeah, sure, sounds good," and took another mouthful of risotto, as though all he'd done was ask her to do a little overtime. When he understood what she'd meant, he had burst out laughing and didn't stop for a very long time that evening.

The rest was history.

Jen ran everything, including finance, marketing expansion strategies, even dealing with human resources issues. Vincent only ever got involved if she needed someone to chat to and to look at the monthly reports. She was also responsible for all offshore funding and payments for Vendicare and the private finances of all the team, which meant Vincent didn't have to worry about any of them. In fact, no one ever even mentioned the money. If they needed something, they just spoke to Nikki or Jen and they got it. Although, Vincent supposed with an inward grin, that wasn't strictly true. He recalled the time that Oliver had asked Jen for a Ferrari and she had simply laughed at him, telling him to use the pool cars rather than ask stupid questions.

Despite being in control of pretty much all the financial aspects of Vendicare, Vincent hoped that she didn't know about one particular thing. Each year, he had placed shares into an offshore account in Jen's name, meaning that by now, she owned about eight percent of the company making her one of the richest women in the world. Or at least, he knew for sure, she was definitely the richest woman in the world her age.

By the time Vincent was making his way to the evening barbeque, he had changed into some casual trousers, flip-flops and a slim fitting Prada T-shirt which Nikki had bought him whilst on her last visit to Italy. When he arrived, he saw Jodie checking on all the fresh meat which had just been brought to the pool area whilst giving instructions to Mel, who was going to be cooking the food. When she saw Vincent she grinned, ran over to him and embraced him in a bear-tight grip for the second time that day and informed him that her mum would be ringing him later. Oh crap, Vincent thought before pushing it out of his mind. Nikki then appeared, looking striking as usual in white shorts with a pink and black sports shirt.

Generally, his team was looking well, Vincent thought to himself. The Mediterranean climate and lifestyle, plus the level of fitness they maintained, was probably the main contributor towards that. This was reassured for Vincent when he felt a slap on his back and turned to see AC, who congratulated him on the surroundings.

Vincent then thought he heard the sound of rotary blades and looked up into the darkening Mediterranean sky. His heart lifted when he saw the Eurocopter arriving back from Malta, knowing that it was carrying his daughter. It had been months since he had been in London and had the chance to see Kerry. Although at times he felt he was overprotective of her, he loved having her at the villa with the team.

The pool area had begun to fill up. Vincent headed over to where Emily and Mike, their new team member, had just arrived. As he was making his way over to them, he saw Kerry arriving ahead of them, flanked by Billie and Oliver. He could see her on the balls of her feet, anxiously looking around. Emily quickly embraced her and attempted to introduce her to Mike, but she was far too distracted to even look at this new person and so Emily laughed off the introduction, saying, "Don't mind her, Mike. Sorry, she's just far too interested in seeing her Dad." She began to introduce Billie and Oliver to Mike instead, as Scott and Lee also arrived from the helipad.

It was at that moment that Kerry's eyes met her father's. She shouted to him then hurtled towards him. He opened his arms just as she threw hers around him, gripping him tightly.

"Wow, have you missed me then?" Vincent asked, making a joke as he attempted to hide his emotions. Although they spoke every day, it had been months since he'd last seen her and the feelings overwhelmed him. When Kerry finally finished embracing her father, she moved onto Nikki, who received a similarly affectionate hello, then whispered something into her ear that Vincent couldn't quite catch.

Kerry disengaged herself from her friend, flushed with joy, and saw AC loitering nearby. "Oh, hi Mr Coombes," she said, rather shyly, "how are you?"

"I'm really well, thank you Kerry. Sarah wanted to be here, but she has gone to see her grandmother with her mother. She's asked if she might be able to have a week here later on in the summer, if your father is okay with that?"

Alistair Coombes' daughter, Sarah, was Kerry's best friend. They went to school together and had grown up enduring similar security bubbles, which meant that they had been able to relate to each other. In fact, it was true that the majority of Coombes' security team were trained at this exact base and so

Vincent could almost rely on Coombes' protection as strongly as his own when he allowed them to look after Kerry.

Just out of earshot, Mike suddenly turned to the twins in shock and whispered loudly, "Holy shit, is that the PM?!"

Lee glanced around at Alistair and turned, laughing. "Yeah, yeah, we get 'em all here, in person and all."

"We had You-Know-Who here once too," Scott put in, chuckling.

"What? The UK PM is actually here? Where's his shadows? His entourage?" Mike questioned, confused at the whole notion of the PM standing a few feet away from him.

"Oh, he doesn't bring them here. It's just the way we operate."

"He's pretty cool actually, I chatted with him for about half an hour once," Lee put in.

Vincent leaned in towards Nikki, as Kerry did her niceties with the PM, and muttered savagely in her ear. "Nikki, when my daughter is finished, will you please find her something in her extensive wardrobe that is more appropriate than what she is wearing now?"

"Dad, seriously?!" He heard Kerry object loudly.

Damn.

"I'm sixteen now! You can't be serious. Actually? Seriously, tell me you're joking?" Nikki slid her arm surreptitiously through Kerry's and began to lead her away. "Oh, seriously?!" Kerry shouted, then shook her head and sighed. "Fine."

As Nikki and Kerry slipped away from the assembled group, everyone's attention was drawn towards the returned 'newlyweds' Billie and Oliver.

"Go on, husband, fill them all in," Billie said, as she held out her hand to show everyone the enormous diamond ring that adorned her wedding finger...

A ring which Vincent had borrowed from one of his

jeweller friends on the island to make their 'honeymoon' legend that bit more believable.

"Do you get to keep that ring?" Jodie asked inquisitively.

"Nope, it's going back tomorrow," Vincent responded for Billie as he stepped into the circle, to audible disappointment and a groan from Billie. He gave her a rueful smile and a quick kiss on both cheeks as a welcome. "How was everything with Oliver? No serious dramas, I hope?"

"It was alright boss, other than the fact that he was pestering me the whole time. Are you sure you told him that the wedding was a scam? I think he thought it was real," she responded with a wicked grin on her face.

Before she could continue with her wind-up, Oliver stepped carefully in front of her. A few seconds and a slight nudge later, Billie had lost her balance. She attempted to grab onto Jodie for support but ended up pulling them both into the pool with an enormous splash. Cheers and laughter followed from the assembled crowd.

Oliver smiled apologetically at his father who was frowning at him. "I'm sorry Dad, but she so deserved it. She's been driving me crazy for the last ten days!" he said, as all the lads around him patted him on the back and jeered at the two girls in the pool.

Jodie was the first to resurface, looking most displeased. Vincent knew she would have spent hours getting ready and her long dark hair now resembled a straggly, dripping mess. Billie fared no better, appearing from the pool with black panda eyes from the make-up she was wearing. She climbed out of the pool and stood at the side staring at Oliver with contempt in her eyes.

"This. Is. War!" she shouted over to him.

Vincent laughed enjoying the banter. I'm so lucky to have this amazing team, he thought. Once the whole pool fiasco died down, Vincent drew his son to one side and asked him if he would make their new visitor Mike Delaney feel like part of the team. It had always been important to him that his team bonded well with each other and he knew Oliver would make it his business.

"Yeah sure Dad, no problem. He seems like an okay guy. I am sure he will fit in perfectly," Oliver responded, though Vincent knew he was distracted, in case Jodie and Billie exacted their revenge upon him.

Once the two girls had dried off, and Nikki had returned with Kerry dressed in clothes that covered her skin more appropriately, Vincent called for everyone's attention.

"No big speech or anything, everyone, but from tomorrow, you have three days to get ready for this mission. Though none of us want to dwell on our last operation, I just need everyone to know that you have to be one hundred percent. I need you all. This operation in particular requires you all at your best." He received a hushed cheer, before he continued. "Oh, and just so everyone is aware, after six months of being pestered, I have now agreed to let our dear Jodie do some training with us. Starting tomorrow. So, up at eight, Jodie. We are starting with a ten kilometre run. If you can keep up with me, you get some time in the killing house," Vincent finished with cheers and a round of applause as everyone turned to congratulate their caterer.

If looks could kill, Jodie's would have had Vincent flat on his back. She glared at Vincent, who grinned back at her. Not quite what she was expecting, hey, Vincent thought to himself, almost unable to stop laughing. Nikki then drew everyone's attention to her, which Vincent was grateful for, as he could see Jodie tackling him to the ground any moment.

"Hello everyone. I just want to introduce you all to our new recruit Mike, who has joined us from MI6," she said, gesturing towards Mike, who smiled almost bashfully. "I also just want to make sure that everyone is aware of the briefing tomorrow at 0830 hours, bright and early, so that we can be ready for simulation at ten. So don't stay up too late and don't drink too much!" Though Nikki's words were met with a collective laugh, Vincent knew they were unnecessary. This team had never had problems with discipline. Hell, he thought, they'll even all be in the gym an hour before briefing.

Vincent took a seat with Alistair Coombes once everyone had begun to chat amongst themselves and watched as Kerry went to eat with Billie and Emily. Nikki joined them and they chatted for a little while about things that didn't concern the mission tomorrow, such as bringing Kerry and his daughter Sarah together at the base at some point so that they could do some kidnap and evasion training, which Alistair agreed with emphatically.

"That's agreed then," Nikki said, "I'll arrange it for when we get back from the current job. Providing nothing happens, of course."

"Speaking of things on the agenda, I was having a bit of a chat with Nikki earlier on, Alistair," Vincent said. "We've agreed that we will... keep an eye on things for you, regarding...what we discussed earlier."

"Thank you," he replied. "That's just what we were expecting and hoping for. It's very much appreciated."

"What's all these gifts wrapped up that I'm seeing everywhere?" Nikki asked the PM, changing the subject.

"Oh, I forgot to mention. They're just a small token of our appreciation for all the work you guys do for me and for the country. It was Geraldine's idea, as you looked after Sarah whilst we had our... little scare," Alistair said.

The rest of the evening passed by uneventfully for Vincent. Alistair Coombes excused himself and went to his room not long after, as he had a breakfast meeting with the Maltese PM. Vincent wandered around the groups with Nikki, taking part in small talk with his team before making his excuses to go to bed too. He knew he would be able to catch up with his daughter sometime soon, but just before he left, he leaned in to ask Oliver to keep a close eye on her. Last time she'd been at base, she'd ended up getting wasted on JD when everyone was under the impression that she was drinking cola. Vincent did not want a repeat of that.

When he arrived back in his room, he made his way over to the bed and picked up the phone, dialling an Italian number.

"Buonasera,"

Vincent smiled when he heard the voice on the other line, "Hi, you."

"Hi stranger! Thought you didn't care about me anymore," came Jean's voice jokingly.

"Don't start that again!" he laughed, throwing himself down onto the pillows. "How many times have I asked you to sell up and come out here to live at the villa?"

"What's this about my daughter joining some Special Forces team, hey?" Jean asked abruptly, making it clear that jokes were now being put to one side. "I couldn't stop her babbling on about it earlier on. I've never heard her so excited."

They chatted for another thirty minutes as Vincent reassured her over and over again that Jodie wasn't joining any special forces, she was just going to be put through some physical training with the team. Having eventually put her worries to rest temporarily, he knew, he put the phone down. His mind flooded with questions about Jean that he just couldn't push away, but after a while, following the eventful day, he drifted off into sleep with the phone lying next to him.

CHAPTER 5

THE TRAINING

Nikki awoke the morning after the pool party feeling fresh from a good night's sleep. She was going through her notes for the hundredth time in preparation for the briefing later that morning, when Emily popped her head around the door.

"Morning Nikki, are you going to the gym?"

"Yeah, give me five. I'll catch you there."

With that, Emily's head disappeared. Nikki continued trying to check over her notes, but eventually shook her head, smiling at herself. She'd been over the notes enough to know them by heart. She threw on her lightweight clothes and began to make her way down to the gym.

When she arrived, she saw everyone there, working hard at each of their strict exercise routines; though she noted the absence of Oliver and the twins, who preferred to mix up their exercise by occasionally going on runs. Billie was already on one of the cross trainers, looking red-faced and covered with sweat. Nikki guessed she'd been there for an hour already that morning. Amanda, another team member, who had joined them just after the Pirates operation of two years ago, was doing weights in the corner looking equally exerted. Even Jen, Vincent's trusty CEO, had joined them this morning, completing a cycle track on one of the 3D simulators which Vincent had recently installed.

As Nikki set herself up on another cycling machine, Mike Delaney appeared at the door of the gym. Emily made her way over to him. "I'm glad you found us Mike. I'm sorry I completely forgot to show you where the gym was yesterday!"

"Oh, no worries. The twins told me last night at the barbeque," Mike replied. Nikki could see him taking in the magnificent exercise arena that surrounded him. She'd almost began to take it for granted, although now she took a moment to look around herself. She could appreciate that it was the kind of gym that wouldn't seem out of place even in a five-star hotel, perhaps being more appropriate for someone training for an Olympic gold medal.

"What's this?" Mike asked no one in particular, pointing towards what looked like a dinghy in front of a 180-degree large screen.

"It's a ribbed dinghy simulator," Nikki responded. "It simulates rapids, or any other programme you input, and responds accordingly. It's great for practicing water extractions. The tension and simulation is so real; it even sprays water on you. Oliver holds the record at the moment for forty-six minutes down Victoria Falls without drowning," she said with a laugh.

"Hey Mike, if bikes are your bag, check out the Ducati simulator. It's the shit," Amanda said, who had only met Mike briefly last night at the barbeque and knew she ought to get to know him more. "Did you not have anything like this at MI6?"

"Not at all! I might not have left if they did," Mike said, clearly impressed.

The team all did a good hour of training before the lads arrived back from their run at about 0715. Oliver announced that he was going for a shower and then something to eat as he was starving. The twins nodded in agreement before heading towards the showers.

Mike began to follow Billie from the room when he asked, confused, "Where the guy's showers?" Nikki grimaced, knowing what was coming next.

Billie turned to him and, without changing her facial expression, said, "Mike, the showers are communal here. No secrets allowed."

Mike stopped dead in his tracks. Nikki couldn't tell if he was pleased, or horrified. Probably a combination of the two, she thought, amused. "Billie, leave him alone and stop teasing! Haven't you learnt your lesson after last night and the pool incident?" Nikki said, laughing.

"Mike, the men's showers are over there. Follow the twins and, from now on, ignore everything Billie tells you," Amanda informed Mike.

"Unless she's behind you on a mission and shouts 'Duck'. I'd listen to her then. She's not the best shot," Emily added, clearly loving making Billie the brunt of their banter.

After their showers, everyone piled into breakfast together. "Stand down, Jodie, we're here!" shouted Billie in warning.

Jodie's assistant Mel responded, having just finished replenishing some fresh fruits and cereals. "No Jodie today, guys," she announced. "She's booked the next few days off."

"Yeah Billie, weren't you listening last night? Or was this when you decided to wash your hair in the pool? Jodie's getting some training in," Lee said.

"God help her," Scott added.

"Don't be tight guys, Vincent's in for a bit of a shock I think. Nikki's been putting Jodie through her paces to make sure she at least passes the physicals," Emily informed them all.

"God, you girls do stick together don't you?" laughed Oliver.

Once they'd all finished their breakfast, they made their way to the operations room. Nikki stood, waiting to get all of their attention, and they eventually quietened down.

"Right then guys. We need to get our game faces on. In less than four days, we will be on site. What do we do until then? Practice, practice and more practice makes..." she looked over everyone for an answer.

Lee put his arm in the air and responded in a childlike voice to collective giggles, "Perfect, miss."

"Very good, Lee. Have a gold star. That's enough of the chatter now, this is serious," Nikki said, regaining their attention before going into full operations mode. As she began to discuss the logistics with the team, Antonietta uploaded their visuals and all the data and tactics to their personal tablets so that they could observe as well as listen. Nikki felt it extremely important that the team knew their target personally, so she presented a detailed and up-to-date profile on their mark.

"Senaullah Yosuf," she said. "Aged between thirty-nine and forty-one. His alias is Darrel Tawheed, or 'toe-rag' as the boss calls him. This is who you're dealing with. He was born in a Nigerian village called Shekau and was number two to the radical Mohammed Yors. If reports are to be believed, Yosuf killed Yors and three of his wives before taking his fourth wife and marrying her when she was only twelve. According to the report, the three other wives had their breasts sliced off and were then cut open from their genitals." Nikki knew the team understood the gruesome reality of the person they were dealing with, but if they didn't, pictures were being shown to them by Antonietta on their tablets. All the girls physically recoiled, looking faintly sick, and Nikki saw that even the lads found the pictures too disgusting to look at. God help Senaullah when this lot get their hands on him, Nikki thought grimly.

The room had an air of deathly silence as Nikki continued.

"Boko Haram, as you all know, translates as 'Western Education is Sin'. Just so you are all aware, these guys actually managed to get kicked out of Al-Qaeda. In fact, rumour has it that Osama Bin Laden wanted to trade them, but unfortunately for him, the Yanks didn't see Boko Haram as a credible threat."

"That's the Yanks for you, boss. They never know their arse from their elbow," Scott chipped in, before flushing once he'd realised that Mike was present, who had American blood and connections. "Ah, sorry, Mike, only joking, of course."

Mike nodded and agreed with Scott good-naturedly. Nikki continued with the briefing, explaining that the live visuals they were seeing on the big screen was the building in which the girls were being held. "Kukawa is based in Northern Nigeria, a part of Adamawa, Mube and Numan. All of these regions are controlled by Boko Haram; we're talking a few thousand raghead followers. If we get this wrong, we will have a shit storm ahead of us like we have never seen before.

"Fortunately for us, there's only about thirty or so of them watching the girls. If you take six protecting the entrance to the building, twelve on the perimeter duty and the remainder, say, smoking weed, drinking rum or playing with themselves, then it's just another night at Gozo's finest nightclub," Nikki said to a grunt of laughter. "The only downside is that there are several women in the building that are not necessarily 'friendlies', but we are struggling to get exact confirmation that they are to be treated as enemies, because the drones' infrared cameras aren't accurate enough at the altitude we are having to fly them to avoid being seen. So, for now, we will have to assume that they are not friendly to our cause and if they are, it's a bonus."

She then went on to explain the entry and exit points for the mission. It had been decided that entering through Lagos would leave too many footprints, even with Vendicare's incredible technology, you would have to rely on bribing officials to scrub everything clean. The team couldn't risk it. Nikki had already contacted some of her 'off-the-grid' friends at the French Foreign Legion and managed to arrange for the team to fly into an ex-military airfield about sixty miles north of the capital N'Djamena. The team would then be based at the most northern point of Lake Chad, only forty to fifty clicks away from where the girls were being held by Boko Haram in Kukawa. This would make for an easy extraction. The team would be going in on a camel train, disguised as nomadic pastoralists, but once the hostages were away in the Chinooks and in the safe hands of the Red Cross, the team would be evacuated via two helicopters, with SAS back-up if needed.

Nikki knew that the most complicated part of the operation, and the one which the team needed the most extensive practice for, was planting the incapacitating agent to take out the guards. While discussing the original risk assessments with Vincent, they had to rule out dropping it from the air, or using a lethal agent, because of the risk to the girls. The idea of an incapacitating agent was not new; they had been used before, even as early as the year 184 BC, when Hannibal's army had used a plant called Belladonna to disorientate their enemy. More recently, the Russians had used Kolokoi 1, a derivative of Fentanyl, killing nearly all of the hostages they were attempting to rescue. Due to the obvious risks, Vincent and Nikki had eventually agreed upon using a non-lethal agent called Hypernol, which had been originally developed to put large animals to sleep, with no side effects whatsoever. This meant that even if the girls were to come in contact with the agent, they would be unaffected, aside from a little drowsiness. They needed to have zero casualties, which was a big ask under the circumstances, but was definitely necessary.

Once the mission was underway, they would have full drone cover on top of being assisted by a US Marine blimp which had first been used in Afghanistan and would stealthily hover over two kilometres in the sky, giving the control room full eyes and ears in the pitch black. Cameras would provide full night vision using the latest green filters, which could switch to thermal if necessary. This blimp wouldn't be used until night had fallen, just in case they were spotted.

Nikki continued to explain their immaculately thought-out plan. "Scott and Lee, you will provide 180-degree sniper cover of the main entrance to the building where the hostages are being kept. This will make it impossible for anyone to enter or leave, relieving the threat from the hostages. You will also need to give cover to Emily and Mike, who will be climbing onto the roof of the building to cover the forward positions and then preparing to drop into the building to take out any internal hostiles.

"I'll be leading the ground team which will consist of Oliver, Amanda and Billie." She gave them all a nod. "We will extract the girls using a human chain system toward the rear of the building, where they have identified a clearing less than 500 metres away, where two Chinook CH-47s will land, one after the other, to extract them in groups of fifty." Each of these Chinooks would be carrying two medics and two Special Forces members who would secure the landing zone and stay on the ground to provide extra cover and assistance, if the team needed it. There would also be two gunners on the ramp armed with 7.62mm machine guns. Nikki was confident that they wouldn't be needed; the fewer the casualties, the better.

"Any questions?" Nikki finally said to her fully informed crew. She watched them as everything she had said was being consumed.

"What's the delivery method for the gassing agent?" Mike asked.

"There are 750mg aerosol cans with digital timers with

a release time set for 2255 hours, which you and Emily will place around the building, taking out the guards in under five minutes," Nikki responded immediately. Mike nodded to show he understood.

"Weapons, Miss?" came the question from Billie, with a smirk across her face.

"As well as your usual kit, Scott and Lee, you will be using HK417, slightly modified sniper rifles, each with five extra twenty round magazines. Same for you Emily, but Mike will have an M200 just in case we might need to take any vehicles out. We all will have silencers effective for up to 200 metres, so no one will know we are there until we are on them."

"What if the gas doesn't work, boss?" Emily asked.

"It will," Nikki said, confidently. "We will all get to try it before we leave."

"Well no one is gassing me, I can tell you that much," Billie said defiantly.

"According to Oliver, Billie, you had to be gassed every night on your 'honeymoon' so that you didn't take advantage of him while he was sleeping, isn't that right Ol?" Amanda challenged, laughing, with everyone else soon joining in when Billie couldn't come back quick enough.

"Who will have eyes on us, other than the operations room back here?" Mike asked curiously, managing to keep focus.

"We will have the PM watching our backs, as well as Timothy Davies Smith from Hereford. President Baker and his Chief of Staff and, for the first time ever, the German PM is starting to take an interest, so someone from GSG9, their special forces, will be keeping an eye on us," Nikki said. She explained that there would be more eyes on them than usual because another project in the pipeline would need German support, so it might be prudent for them to be opened up and aware of just what Vendicare were capable of.

She finished off with some general housekeeping rules, before dismissing them all, telling them that they need to get their training to one hundred percent. "Oh and everyone, can you make sure that all of your jabs are up to date please? Everyone will be checked on the return as well, what with this Ebola outbreak. And don't forget, no alcohol from now until the mission is over!" she finished. Her words were met with a collective groan as everyone began to file out of the room.

"Mike," Nikki shouted. He turned at the sound of his name. "Can you please go and see our on-site doctor? He needs to go through your medical stuff as we have no records here. I'm in no doubt that you're entirely healthy, it's just the way we do things here."

"Yeah, sure thing, Nikki," Mike responded.

"Sniper practice begins today at the compound simulation; ground team need to meet to get our evacuation plan drilled. Everyone must be ready for a full midnight practice run tonight! Remember we only have two more practices after this and we need one hundred percent from everyone!" Nikki shouted at the team's retreating backs as they went to get their kit together and dressed into their simulation suits.

***

Half an hour later and the team were all changed into their training gear and Nikki had them familiarising themselves with the mock-up terrorist site. Emily and Mike had taken up their positions on the fragile rooftop, having to be extremely careful with their footing, and were now setting up their quick release bindings for when they would need to descend through the roof.

"Nikki, how does this roof compare to the real one?" Emily asked through her comms device.

When she got no reply, she went in search of Nikki and eventually found her. She tapped her ear and pointed at her. Nikki flushed and then Emily got the reply, "Sorry Em, that's really not a good start. I forgot to plug in. What did you say?" she said as she plugged in her communications pack.

The group had been split up into their three assigned teams: Alpha, Oscar and Sierra; Alpha being the ground team assault, Oscar being Scott and Lee with their sniper rifles and Emily and Mike making up the Sierra team.

"Alpha 1 to Sierra 1, comms check," Nikki said.

"Sierra 1 to Alpha 1, ten out of ten," Emily responded.

"Let's just hope we get ten out of ten in the outback, okay? And yes, the roof and all of this mock-up is a complete replica that has been reproduced from our recon pictures."

For the next two to three hours, everyone familiarised themselves with their positions, timings and equipment, particularly Scott and Lee, who were firing rounds into simulated bandits.

Emily continued with the roof descent, tightening her bindings every time so that she could see the difference in speed. It would never do to be too slow, but at the same time, she couldn't exactly hit the deck in a heap, especially with the presence of internal hostiles. Mike would have to do the same with his bindings, but for now was working on making fine tune adjustments to the M200 and dropping a few rounds into an old simulated land cruiser.

An hour later, Nikki and her team sat cross-legged on the floor as they all took a break from their physical training.

Satisfied with the progress so far, she concluded the training for the evening.

CHAPTER 6

MASTER GICHIN

Vincent awoke early on the morning of the briefing, just as the sun was starting to break through the blinds. He could feel the light, already warm on his face and, though he had fallen asleep in his shorts and T-shirt he felt like he had had a comfortable rest nonetheless. He never needed more than five or six hours these days. He jumped straight into the shower to wake himself up before setting off for his morning cycle ride.

As he made his way from his bedroom down the marble floored hallway, he noticed Kerry's bedroom door was slightly ajar. He peeked in and saw her fast asleep in the middle of her super king-sized bed, with her big brother Oliver on one side of her and Jodie on the other, both with an arm sprawled over her. He smiled to himself and began to back out of the door quietly when he saw Oliver stir.

Oliver saw his dad standing in the doorway and slid out of bed, creeping quietly across the floor so as not to disturb the girls. Vincent wondered to himself if there had been a drama at the barbeque and looked inquisitively at Oliver. He put a finger to his lips, as though to say, we'll talk about it in a moment.

They walked down the hallway together, making their way

to the kitchen, where Vincent poured them both a glass of fresh orange juice.

"Kerry found out about Becci last night," Oliver said, by way of explanation. "She took it pretty badly. To make matters worse, it was a few hours before we found out that she had been mixing vodka into her coke, or coke into her vodka. I'm sorry Dad... we just didn't really notice." Oliver looked sheepish.

"Don't worry Oli, it's not the end of the world. I guess she will just have a bit of a headache when she wakes up," Vincent replied, eager to take some of the guilt Oliver was feeling away from him. They both smiled awkwardly at each other before Oliver announced abruptly that he was going to go for a run. Vincent followed him and went to the garage to take his bike for some mileage around the island.

When he arrived back almost two hours later, he made his way to the restaurant area, where he found his entire team in fits of laughter. Is it just a coincidence that it's always when I walk into the room that they laugh? Vincent found himself asking, but he shook it off. He sat down next to Jen, who was watching them all having their little joke with an absent-minded smile.

"Jen," Vincent said gently to get her attention. "I was wondering if you had any free time later so that we can talk about making some more charity donations. I've been looking into some organisations which specialise in conflict areas and helping with the effects they have on children in particular. I was wondering if you could set up some meetings for me."

Jen responded eagerly and they chatted for another ten minutes or so before agreeing to discuss it more later on. Just as he was about to turn and leave, having finished his breakfast of a croissant and a black coffee, he handed her a piece of paper which read a number plate and some car details; 'Black BMW3 Series ZMN 969'. He asked her to pass it onto Antonietta to do some vehicle checks for him.

Jen looked up perplexed. "What's this about? Is everything okay?" she asked, concerned.

"Yeah, there's no problem, some local idiot just nearly knocked me off my bike. I wouldn't mind finding out who it is," Vincent said, before leaving the restaurant area. Entering his kitchen he bumped into Jodie, who was groggily pouring herself some juice from the massive double American fridge. She stood, yawning, wearing just some boxers and a baggy shirt. The sun shone on her face and Vincent could still see sleep in her eyes.

"Sorry that I didn't get to the gym this morning, Vincent. I didn't want to leave Kerry like she was and..." failing to suppress a yawn, "you won't change your mind about the training, will you?"

"Don't be silly. A promise is a promise. Anyway, I hear that you don't need to do the run, as it has been rumoured you have passed all the physical tests," Vincent said, smiling to himself. The team is right when they say I don't miss much.

Jodie put her arms around him and kissed his cheek, but paused, holding his shoulders, before saying, "Then can I go back to bed, pretty please?"

Vincent actually had other plans for the girls rather than lazing in bed all day, which he didn't quite approve of. He had arranged, at very short notice, a week's training on Aikido, an ancient form of martial arts. All the team had trained in as part of their programme after joining Vendicare. The martial arts teacher was a descendant of the original master who had developed the technique. Normally, the team's personnel would go to Japan for a month's intensive training, but Vincent had managed to convince Master Gichin to spend a few days at the base training. Obviously a few days would not be long enough for Kerry and Jodie to master Aikido, but it would be enough to give them some basic self-defence skills. At the same time, it would be an opportunity to evaluate Jodie to see if she had what it took to join Vendicare's team. He couldn't help but worry about what he would say to Jean if she did pass all of the necessary criteria. It will be a few years away yet, Vincent tried to convince himself. As a treat for the girls, Vincent had also asked Gichin if he would do a day on Iaijusu; the art of mental presence and immediate reaction, which would give them the opportunity to use both samurai swords and an array of knives.

"I'm going to try and coax Kerry out of bed. I need you both at the studio for 1100 hours to meet Master Gichin. Please work hard for him, he's doing this as a special favour for me," Vincent said with eyebrows raised.

He made his way along the corridor and saw that Kerry's bathroom light was on, meaning she must be awake. However, as he got closer, he thought he could hear the sound of retching. He grimaced, hoping she was alright, knowing the last thing she needed right now was to know her dad was witnessing this. He continued walking, deciding that he could leave Jodie to fil her in about Gichin's visit. They could have their own little conversation later on, when she would be feeling better.

Vincent got changed out of his cycling clothes and went to meet Gichin at the helipad. He had arrived in Malta yesterday; Vincent knew that in addition to training, he was here to gamble, so he had set him up in his most exclusive casino The Club. As part of his online business and for private entertainment, Vincent had acquired three casinos on the island, but The Club was by far his most special, where Gichin would be able to gamble and relax without being noticed. He had thought many times before about offering The Club to Jean, so that she would leave Rome, but he had never got around to asking her, mainly for fear of her saying no. Jodie had helped him there several times and had introduced them to authentic and rustic Roman food before spending the night playing roulette with Vincent and Nikki. Most of the team had been there at some stage; Vincent would often close it for private functions so that the team could dress down and have an evening of light-hearted gambling.

By the look on Gichin's face, Vincent could gather that he had enjoyed a good night at The Club, as Vincent had hoped he would. However, he was keen to start work and felt it an honour that Vincent had chosen him personally to work with his daughter, saying that it was a high honour in Japanese culture.

"How do you feel about dinner tonight? I have flown in a chef named Hiroyuki from London especially for you," Vincent said, smiling. He enjoyed Gichin's vivacious personality.

"Thank you kindly, Vincent! Though it is true that I would be happy with anything that your Jodie prepared. She is my favourite chef and if I would not offend such a good friend as yourself, I would steal her away and take her to Japan to cook all my food, my friend!"

"She's far too much hassle, Gichin, you'd have your work cut out. I wouldn't wish that upon anyone," Vincent said, laughing. He told him that the girls would be ready to meet him at 1100 hours in the studio just off the gym and made his excuses to return to the villa to hurry the girls up.

"She's still upstairs," Jodie said quickly as Vincent arrived back into the villa. "Though she isn't as bad as I thought she might have been. Must be that she's used to drinking." She received a death stare from him and very quickly added "Joking! Sorry!!"

"Can you keep an eye on her while you're training with Gichin please? Don't either of you offend him. Oh, just so you know, he loves your cooking so much that he wants to take you back to Japan with him," Vincent said in a lighter tone, the smile back on his face.

"You're kidding me right? He must be a hundred years old, at least!" Jodie said, though he knew she was pleased by the compliment.

"I'm not joking. But play nice, he's the best in the world and you've got the opportunity to learn a lot from him."

Kerry then walked into the kitchen, looking... well, better than Vincent had anticipated. She had a slight colour to her face and was probably starting to recover after being sick. She looked at him anxiously, clearly expecting a reprisal, but didn't receive one.

"I'm off for a shower, Kerry," Jodie said. "Then we need to get going. Make sure you have the Judo kit I brought for you on. This old dude is full of tradition and crap. I'd really like us to try our best not to piss him off."

Kerry watched her go without responding, then turned back to her father with tears in her eyes.

"Dad, why didn't you tell me about Becci?" Her voice, full of sadness, made Vincent's heart ache.

"Kerry..."

"Dad."

"To be honest sweetie... I didn't know how to. I haven't really began to understand what happened yet. I still believe she might walk through the door any minute. I haven't felt like this since... since..." Vincent found himself unable to finish his sentence and teetered off into silence. He felt his eyes growing red, fighting to hold back tears, not wanting to break down in front of his teenage daughter.

Wordlessly, Kerry crossed the distance between them, held him in her arms and whispered, "We will work this out together, Daddy."

"Kerry come on, we really need to get... oh." Jodie had walked into the room and seemed to be taking in the scene, drying her hair as she walked into the kitchen. "Sorry, am I interrupting?" Vincent turned away, anxious not to show his weak or vulnerable side to anyone.

"Jodie, have you never heard of knocking?" Kerry said, clearly irritated.

"Actually I have, missy, and if I hadn't, I certainly would know now after having watched you knocking all that vodka back last night," she pointed an accusing finger at Kerry, who flushed, obviously thinking that they had managed to avoid the conversation of her alcohol consumption the night before.

"Dad, send her back to Rome!" Kerry begged, though Vincent knew she was joking. She adored Jodie; that much was obvious from their love-hate relationship. She turned back to Jodie and defiantly stuck out her tongue.

Vincent stared at her with his mouth hanging open. What on earth had he just seen...? "Kerry!" he said, taking a step towards her. "What the hell have you got in your mouth?"

"Ha, whoops," Jodie laughed.

Kerry went bright red and looked as if she wanted the floor to swallow her up. She shifted her weight from side to side and stared at Vincent's feet. "Dad chill, it's only a piercing. It's not like I got a tattoo or anything. I promise."

"Yeah Vin, I've got six tattoos altogether now. Check out my latest," Jodie said, pulling down the side of her underwear to reveal a slot machine style cherry.

"Don't call me Vin, Jodie, and stop being such a bad influence on my daughter!" Vincent said testily.

"Vin.... Vincent, I'm only teasing!" Jodie said, laughing, as she finished drying her hair.

"Look, you two," Vincent said, eager to change the subject, never having been much of a disciplinarian. Marie had always been the one who could scold their children. "Do either of you fancy going to your Aunt Julie's in Morzine?" Vincent said.

"Dad, Morzine is great, but not in summer. It rains every day, it's only really good for skiing in winter and Aunt Julie is a nightmare! She always moans at me for staying in bed..."

"Rightly so..."

"...and last time she actually said I was lazy! She actually said that! And that bloke she lives with, George, is it? Is always going on about bloody cheese and wine! He's so BORING."

"Or maybe, if you feel up to it, Kerry, we could go and tidy up the villa in the Seychelles," Vincent asked, testing the water carefully, knowing neither of them had been there since the tragedy.

"Oh yes, Kerry, let's go to the Seychelles, I love it there!" Jodie said excitedly.

"That sounds like a deal to me. After this next operation, we'll go for a week."

Kerry groaned. "Won't you be bored Dad, with just me and Jodie for company?"

"Well," Vincent said, trying to sound indifferent, "I was thinking of asking Jodie's mum to come with us... if you're both alright with that." Even to his own ears he sounded sheepish.

Kerry bounced up into the air. "Told you, TOLD YOU!" she shouted at Jodie, delighted. "Dad, you know you don't need to say 'Jodie's Mum'. We both know you like her. Just ask her! Jean thinks a lot of you, I know she does, but she isn't a bloody mind reader. Just go for it!"

Vincent paused, trying to take it all in. I guess subtlety has never been a strong point of Kerry's, he said to himself. He didn't want to delve into this with his sixteen-year-old daughter. It was perfectly obvious that both of their assumptions had been correct.

"Go and see Gichin, right now. I don't want to hear any more about it," Vincent said, attempting to regain control of the situation. "I'll see you both later for dinner." They both disappeared out of the door, whooping and giggling, as Vincent shook his head.

An hour or so later, Vincent was in the operations room when Jen arrived. "There you are!" she said in an exasperated tone that suggested she'd been looking for him for a while and that he had been hiding from her.

"Jen, I was hoping to see you. Listen, I'm a little worried... I feel like Russia is going to be a leper colony soon; anything connected to it will be infected. Do we have any interests, financially or otherwise? If we do, get rid. Something bad is going to happen, I can feel it. Antonietta has informed me that there has been some chatter from pro-Russian separatists in the Ukraine. It's pretty scary stuff. Also, and this is for your ears only, I am going on a visit to the UK tomorrow, as the PM is at the top of our agenda. It seems like we may end up getting drawn into this Russian crap-fest after all." He sighed. "How does dinner fit in with you for later this evening? We can discuss that charity stuff in a bit more detail. I'd quite like Kerry to start taking an active interest in the business, now's as good a time as any to start."

"I'd love to," Jen said, having taken notes down on everything Vincent wanted her to look into. "What time?"

"Let's say about 7.30, for 8."

"Great, I'll see you later," Jen said as she packed up and left the room.

Vincent decided to put a call into the head of the Special Forces, Major General Timothy Davies Smith, whom he would be meeting with tomorrow in the UK. As the PM was travelling back to the UK that night, Vincent felt it would be a deal easier if he could hop over there.

Antonietta started up the live link to Hereford and, after a few seconds, they heard "Good morning, Vincent," calling over the screen. Major General Timothy Davies Smith, the youngest ever commander of the regiment, could be heard but not seen.

"Give me two seconds, boss... hold on... aha! Live feed," Antonietta said as the Major appeared on the screen.

"Morning Tim! How's the family? Well, I hope!" Vincent enquired cheerily.

"They're great, thanks Vincent. How's Oli and Kerry doing?" Tim asked.

"Oliver is training at the moment; well, they both are in truth. Gichin is here at the moment giving Kerry some personal tuition," Vincent said.

"Oh great, pass on my regards, I love that guy."

Once the pleasantries were over, they got down to business. The call was really just to arrange a time and flight path for Vincent, as he would be landing at RAF Brize Norton. Tim had made all the necessary arrangements and told him that he would be sending two of his team to meet him. One was an American girl, named Saxby, who was a lieutenant in the US military. The other was Sergeant Steve Daniels, whom Vincent had known for many years and who had, on occasion, joined Vendicare on their operations.

"What are you doing with a lieutenant from the US army?" Vincent asked, curiously.

He saw Tim grin. "I thought that might throw you. I'll explain tomorrow, if that's okay with you."

"No problems, just curious," Vincent said, then added, "By the way, I will have company tomorrow. I will need clearance for Antonietta Martina. I know what you guys are like with the PM and all his security details." Vincent could see Antonietta ogling him from out of the corner of his eye, but he avoided looking at her.

"It won't be a problem, Vincent. Coombes wouldn't let it be," Tim said.

They finalised their arrangements for lunch, as Mr Coombes was insistent they have something to eat after their chat. The flight time was about two hours and twenty minutes, so Vincent agreed to leave at 0900 hours so that he wouldn't need to change his morning schedule much, plus he would have the chance to have a heads up with Nikki before he left.

"Great. Looking forward to seeing you tomorrow, Vincent. Over and out." The screen went black before Vincent had the chance to reply. It was only now that he turned to look at Antonietta, who was staring at him, shocked. She had no idea that he had been thinking of taking her, especially to something as high profile as this.

"It's about time you got more involved, Antonietta. You're always twenty-four-seven with this company; you never get a chance to leave these screens," Vincent said by way of explanation.

"Oh. My. God," she squeaked. "I won't be sleeping tonight!" She then looked embarrassed at her outburst and regained control over her grin.

Vincent laughed, before getting up to leave, to head over to the gym. His new favourite toy preoccupied him greatly at the moment, which he preferred even to going out on his morning cycle. It was a road bike 3D simulator, which allowed you to programme hundreds of preset routes. It was an identical simulation of actual cycling stages, including potholes.

He set the programme with the intention of tackling a part of the Tour de France which had previously caused him some issues: The Joux Plane Pass. It was fifty-two kilometres long, with a 1,250 metre climb over 1,700 metres above sea level, and was without a doubt one of the most difficult alpine climbs in the world. Vincent had tried this particular pass twice already on the simulator. He had given up both times. On this occasion, he felt that maybe he had channelled enough energy and thought to get him all the way to the top, believing that cycling ability was seventy percent down to training but also thirty percent responsive to mental strength. He had psyched himself up for this challenge, especially since finding out about his daughter's piercing. He pushed that thought out of his mind, before he exploded. Some thirty kilometres into the cycle, just before he began to climb from Samoens, he realised he was smiling to himself.

***

Antonietta and Damien were hard at work in the communications room, investigating Vincent's request.

"Toni, are you getting that?"

"Yeah," Antonietta responded, with the same amount of anxiety in her voice as Damien. They had been picking up a lot of chatter and unusual search requests on Vendicare over the past twenty-four hours; far more than they usually did.

"Whoever is orchestrating these searches is using variable DNS servers and also multiple IP addresses..." Damien explained.

"What do you reckon?"

"Well... it could be a terrorist? Hackers? Or a government agency? All I know is that it's definitely not an accident," he responded.

"Are you certain it's nothing to do with the upcoming mission?"

"Well, from what I can see, I'm fairly sure it's another agency. Give me another day and I'll find out, but I'm pretty sure... I will see if we can trace the signal using a Vectra search!" he said excitedly. Damien always enjoyed a challenge.

"Okay, great. I'll fill Vincent in tomorrow during our flight; I'll send out a daily intranet report to all the senior staff, just so they're aware too," Antonietta said decisively.

***

"Well, don't you look pleased with yourself," Nikki said with a grin as she passed Vincent crossing the courtyard. He was dripping with perspiration and felt as though he was in serious need of a shower, but had a grin that stretched from one ear to the other.

"I just managed to get all the way up the Joux Plane Pass. It was my third attempt," he said, still grinning, sounding like a child at Christmas time. "It was the thought of Kerry's tongue piercing that really got me through those last kilometres. How is everything going with training?"

"Everything is going perfectly to plan. I've given the team a couple of hours rest before we have a go at our first proper run tonight."

"I won't be able to come and see it, even though I'd like to. I'm entertaining the kids plus Jen and Gichin, but could I have a quick twenty-minute chat with you before I leave tomorrow?" Vincent asked.

"Yeah sure. How about 8am? I'm going to let the team have a bit of a lie in tomorrow," Nikki responded.

"Perfect," Vincent replied. "See you tomorrow."

Back in the villa, about to get showered and changed, Vincent heard the sound of the girls giggling, who must have just finished their training with Gichin. He tapped on the door and entered when Kerry shouted, "Come in!" They were picking out some clothes for dinner and chatting about their training.

"Well? Did you enjoy it?" Vincent enquired.

"Oh my god! Dad, are you insane? It was the coolest thing ever! The next boy that messes with me won't know what happened to him," Kerry said with a wink, putting her fists up in the air.

Before Vincent could interject and say that wasn't exactly what he had in mind, Jodie interrupted calmly, as if to settle the air between them. "The training was incredibly useful. We have both learned an awful lot and we're looking forward to tomorrow. Oh, what's the dress code for tonight, while you're here?"

"Casual. Whatever you feel comfortable in," Vincent said, before looking at Kerry. "But not anything like what you were wearing when you first arrived, please, if that could ever be described as comfortable." She looked to stick her tongue out at him, but evidently thought better of it, so instead grinned at him. "I'll leave you to get ready. I'm so glad you enjoyed your training with Gichin. I'll see you on the terrace in an hour for drinks."

Their guest chef from London had arrived earlier that day and had been in the kitchens all day preparing Japanese cuisine for them. Though Vincent and Jodie had had a look at the menu, they had both decided that they were not specialists in Japanese food and thus left the choice up to the chef.

Chef Hiroyuki Tanaka had learned his trade in the Roppongi district in Japan and, after meeting with Vincent and Gichin a few years ago when they had dined in his restaurant, had kept in touch. When Tanaka decided he wanted to come to England to set up a restaurant, they had both agreed to help him along the way; a decision which neither of them regretted in the slightest. The restaurant in Soho had already received a Michelin star. Tanaka had also set up a sushi academy, teaching European chefs how to prepare sushi correctly, rather than the poor fast-food version which he had seen too much of.

Vincent had tried to convince Jodie to go and learn to cook Japanese food, but she had laughed and told Vincent that the day that Tanaka mastered Italian food, and only that day, would be the day that she would learn to prepare sushi. Vincent had dropped it soon after, knowing that he couldn't push her towards a decision without shoving her into the opposite direction.

Once Vincent was showered and changed into casual shorts, he made his way to the terrace just at the side of their pool, overlooking the Mediterranean. Though the dress code was only casual, Tanaka had set the table with a beautiful, simple elegance and Vincent found himself looking forward to the meal greatly.

Gichin arrived soon afterwards, wearing a typically-styled Japanese kimono. Vincent, well aware of Japanese customs having spent some time with Gichin in his home, clasped his hands together and made a short bow. "Watashi no yoki yujin konbanwa," he said in his best Japanese accent.

Gichin replied with the same, "Good evening to you too, my friend." They then continued their conversation in English; Vincent's Japanese was entirely limited to greetings and chit-chat. Vincent enquired as to how the girls had got on during his teaching today and Gichin complemented the girls passionately. He insisted that they were both capable of graduating in Aikido, but specifically thought that Jodie had a single-mindedness that drove her. Gichin said that he could see in her eyes the ability and desire and suggested to Vincent that if he truly thought she could become a team member, perhaps he should consider sending her to his training school in Japan. Vincent considered this for a few moments, thinking that perhaps that would be a brilliant idea, and was about to respond when the two girls arrived onto the terrace.

Both looked stunning. Jodie's olive complexion glowed in the evening light, her long dark hair blowing softly in the wind as she walked arm in arm with Kerry, who stood only a few inches shorter but looked just as beautiful, dressed appropriately for once, in white shorts and a striking turquoise top which she had purchased from Terminal 5 in Heathrow.

Gichin turned and drew in a deep, exaggerated breath and bowed deeply to the girls. "Mottano utsukushi on'nanoki ni konbanwa," he said. Vincent translated the sentence quickly in his head. 'Good evening to the two most beautiful girls.'

"Konbanwa," the girls responded, smiling, thanking him for the compliment.

Kerry gave her dad a quick hug and thanked him sincerely for the training. She then placed her arm in Gichin's before cheekily saying, "Now you've trained me hard all day, the least you can do is buy me a drink!" She led Gichin, who laughed, towards the waiter stationed behind the bar, with a quick backwards wink at her dad.

"Wine please, Kerry. And no more than one glass!" Vincent cautioned her, more loudly than he may usually have done. He knew he was becoming an overprotective parent, but felt he had no choice. He did not want Kerry to become the rebellious teenager that Jean had said Jodie had once been. She was too precious. He and Jodie followed Kerry and Gichin to the bar. Gichin ordered himself a Dirty Martini, before ordering a glass of Soave Classico for Kerry. Vincent and Jodie both ordered a glass of Monfortino, an iconic and classical Barolo known as 'the King of Reds'. Vincent had a passion for wine, but not to the extent he liked to think he had become pretentious about it. His wine cellar in the villa and at the casino contained some of the world's most famous and expensive reserves, including a renowned and sought-for champagne collection. Jodie and Vincent had made several visits to local Italian vineyards to buy particular vintages and had built up a great relationship with the brothers, Dario and Andrea Tierpon, who had a fabulous vineyard near Mount Etna in the Pompeii region. The area, because of the volcanic rock, gave the wine a certain acidity, making it fruitier and giving a more delightful flavour. Jodie would go over once a year to do a tasting. If she was satisfied, which she usually was, she would buy a whole pallet every time she went.

"Is there one for me?" Jen said from behind them in a chirpy voice, making them all turn so that they could greet her.

"Of course, Jen. What would you like?" Vincent asked.

"I'll take a glass of white for now, if that's alright. I might try the red with dinner."

The group mingled and chatted lightheartedly before Tanaka came rushing out to usher them all into their seats.

Chef Tanaka had decided upon a starter of Tuan Tataki, which was slices of seared tuna served in a ponzu sauce, accompanied with aubergine Dengaku – grilled aubergines with a red Miso paste.

As everyone tucked in to the Japanese cuisine, Vincent began a conversation with Kerry about the charity work that VituralTech were involved in. He wanted to know if she had seen anything that she might like to be included in. Though she was young, and Vincent didn't want her to have any true exposure to their operations just yet, he did want her to show an interest in what VituralTech did and the positive effects that it had.

Jen interjected, explaining that as an international business, VituralTech made donations of over three million pounds per annum to Save the Children, The Soldier's Charity and one that Vincent was particularly interested in, The Railway Children, which looked after vulnerable victims who were in danger of getting caught up in child trafficking gangs. Whenever Vincent heard about this particular charity, his expression hardened. Soon, after their upcoming operation was complete, half the team would be on standby to take out a Romanian trafficking gang; Vincent could not wait.

"Well, Kerry? Is there something you're involved in at school, or that you've spoken to your friends about that you've taken an interest in?" Jen asked.

"Now that you mention it, Daisy Marne, a girl in my class, lost her sister recently... She was only nine, it was some obscure cancer... We were all thinking that maybe we could do a bike ride to raise some money for the charity that helped them. I think it's called Days of Sunshine..." Kerry trailed off and looked down at her food.

"I have an idea," he said. "What if Jen sets up a bank account, separate to your trust and school funds, and we charge it with some money so that you could do some event planning and use the money to raise more?"

Kerry looked up eagerly. "Honestly, Dad?! That would be awesome! I could get Sarah and all my friends involved, they'd love it!" It warmed his heart to see his daughter so excited to help other people.

"Well, if you're going to get Sarah involved, how about I talk with Alistair Coombes and see if we can do something together. Maybe a bike ride, or a charity tennis match or something? I'm sure he'd be up for that," Vincent said. And even if he isn't, I'm sure I can twist his arm.

"Dad... that's fantastic, thank you," Kerry said. Vincent could see that he had really cheered her up.

"Kerry, you can email me when you are all set up, I don't mind doing something to help too," Gichin said. "Just let me know."

Tanaka and his staff then returned and served the main course: a grilled black cod marinated in Saikyo miso – Vincent and Jodie's favourite. Once the mains had been eaten and cleared, Tanaka then served the dessert, a pumpkin crème caramel, which no one had ever tried before but everyone agreed was absolutely delicious.

"It gives your Banutella brioche pudding a run for its money," Vincent teased Jodie.

Jodie looked defensive. "What are you saying, Vincent?" She sounded insulted. "Do you not like my pudding?"

Vincent looked at her, confused. Worried that he had upset her, he he looked at Jen desperately. "Help me out here!"

"I'm only kidding, boss, you know I don't upset that easily," Jodie said, knowing she had caught Vincent hook, line and sinker. She nudged Kerry, laughing at how easy it was to wind her dad up.

Vincent ignored their jibes and indicated for everyone to

help themselves to coffee or any drinks from the bar. Jodie and Kerry continued to chat with Gichin and Tanaka, complimenting the chef on his delicious food. Vincent discussed Kerry's charity functions with Jen and subtly confirmed that he didn't want Kerry's name attached to it at all. "It's not that I don't trust her, of course. I just don't want her to get any publicity. The media is dangerous," he explained. Jen simply nodded. She didn't need telling; she knew the drill. It was the same for all the team, not just Kerry.

After thanking Tanaka for a glorious meal, Vincent made his apologies, saying that he must get to bed as he had an early start in the morning. Gichin bowed and said he would also look forward to that. Kerry gave her dad a goodnight kiss and, before he could even mention to her to take care with her drinking, Jodie put a finger to her lips behind Kerry and mouthed, 'I'll handle it'. He looked at her gratefully and retired to his bedroom.

He knew he had already sorted his personal documents out for tomorrow, but thought that now might be a good opportunity to catch up on the world news and maybe put in another call to Jean before going to sleep. He switched on the television and decided to do exactly that.

"Hey Jean, it's me, Vincent. How are you?" he said while lying on his bed. He had the TV on mute, but watched as the pictures and news articles concerning the Ebola outbreak in Nigeria flashed up on the screen.

"I know it's you. It comes up as 'my man from Gozo' on my phone," Jean said, he could hear the smile in her voice.

"Oh, I'm 'your man' now, am I?" Vincent said with a hint of flirtation in his voice.

"Vincent, you will always be my man. You know that already, I hope."

Vincent's heart stopped for a beat, but he decided that now might be a good time to ask her about the Seychelles trip. Jean would need to know in advance so that she could get someone to look after the restaurant.

Before Vincent had even finished the first sentence of his proposal, Jean had said yes.

"But you don't know what I'm asking you," he objected.

"Oh honestly, Vincent. The Seychelles? You? Me? And the girls? Did you genuinely think Jodie was going to keep that to herself? You don't know the girls one bit, do you?" she added with a laugh.

"Obviously not! I'm glad you find that so amusing," Vincent said, feeling rather played by them all.

"Sorry, Vincent. Jodie felt she needed to warn me because you might not get round to asking, that's all."

They chatted for a few more minutes before Vincent decided it was time he went to bed and said a quick goodbye. He insisted that he would ring her from the plane on his way back home tomorrow before hanging up the phone.

CHAPTER 7

THE SIMULATION

The team were gathered around in the restaurant area having a late meal before the simulation that evening. They were all having to structure their diets and eating times, so as to coincide with what they would have to be doing on the mission ahead. All the foods eaten by the team were prepared on site, made by Jodie and Mel. On the days before missions, the two always had to work especially hard, putting together their ration packs with specific requirements geared to adapting their bodies to the temperature, climate and time of day, to give the team an even greater edge. Vincent and Jodie were forever discussing the fact that not only did the team need to be physically fit, but they also needed to have diets that complimented their tough, intense environment. The team were lucky; Jodie was not only a trained chef since her early teens, she had also been to Rome University, completing a two year honours degree in Food Technology and Biological Processing which Vincent had requested. The team had made a joke of the fact that their ration packs looked more like first class airline food to be served to the rich and famous. This particular mission being only a hop, skip and a jump meant that they would only require protein food and drink for the forty kilometre camel hike, then the team would not eat once in position. They would have been given everything they needed for twenty or so hours and, if everything went well, they would be treated to nourishment packs when they were on the plane home to fill their calorie and protein requirements before they returned back to the base to begin training for the next mission.

After they had finished their meal, Nikki gathered them all into the briefing room. She opened up a Peli case which contained the new toys that she couldn't wait to show them all. The team were very fortunate in the fact that they had people who never delayed in finding them the next cutting-edge technology.

Gargo was a new watch which Nikki brought out of the case to show them. It used part Garmin hardware and part Google software and was only reliant on one satellite for a fixed point. It even had two-way communications, using similar technology to the one the team had developed for their own comms. It also had a sensor pad on the reverse which could monitor heart rates and other biological metrics. But first and foremost it was a watch, which when synced with the others became one unit, all on the exact same time.

Nikki handed a selection of these out to the team and told them to become familiar with them over the next few hours for tonight's exercise. She also showed them a new base suit to go under their uniforms which was primarily made from carbon fibre, but was also spun with Nomex and coated in a Kevlar polymer, meaning that it weighed next to nothing.

The team didn't quite react as excitedly as they had to the watch.

"Well what's new about this, boss?" Amanda asked pointedly. "They look the same as the old ones."

Nikki explained that these new suits had extra Kevlar, which covered all vital organs, but more specifically the heart and stomach. Though it wouldn't stop a bullet, she explained, it would give them an extra layer of protection. The other new factor to these suits was that they had a thermal cooling system. This meant that when the suit was attached to an external battery on their tactical belts,t could operate as low as sixteen degrees Celsius, keeping its wearer cool in the humid conditions they would be facing. These particular base suits had been designed by NASA for astronaut use, before Vincent's tech team had managed to get their hands on them and made some modifications. Nikki noticed that the team had perked up about the new gear once she had explained these modifications.

"Now then, does anyone have any questions before our penultimate simulation run?" Nikki asked. "Just so you are aware, Vincent will be around for the final one tomorrow. Let's get it perfect tonight; he needs to see us at our best tomorrow." Nikki said.

"Boss, are we sticking with our old night vision gear, or using the new?" Amanda asked.

Nikki quickly explained that for now they would be sticking with their tried and tested equipment.

"Make sure that after tomorrow's exercise, all of your operational equipment is packed away and ready to go; you never know if we are going to need to move things forward a few hours," Nikki instructed them. "Oh, just so you are aware, a shit storm is going down in the Ukraine at the moment. We aren't really sure what's going on, but you may as well know that we may have to go straight from one mission to the next," she warned.

"Missions here are like London buses," Oliver joked. "Nothing for two hours, then five come at once." Everyone laughed. "Who's doing the recon on the next mission, Nikki?"

"Your dad's got it sorted, but will brief you all about it when he gets back from his trip tomorrow," she said. "I need you all to be aware also that tomorrow night's simulation will involve some new people. We will have Jodie and Kerry playing our enemies, but they don't know it yet; Vincent wants to surprise them."

Two hours later, the team were in place, ready for the simulation to begin. Nikki gave the green light to go and they all launched into action. Within six minutes of this signal, the team would be in a position to start moving the hostage children. For the purpose of the simulation, they had assumed that there were four female enemies within; Emily and Mike would have to take two each, though of course if this wasn't the case it would make the job much easier and quicker by several seconds. The team flew through the simulation and were done in record time.

Afterwards, control switched the floodlights on so that the team could have a debrief. It was great, Nikki thought, to be able to discuss the operation while they were all still breathless and filled with the energy from it.

"Well done everyone. As long as they don't shoot back we should be home in time for one of our Jodie's special lunches," Nikki congratulated them.

"Boss, can we sort out my bindings? I felt like they might have been sticking on the way down," Emily said.

"How about yours, Mike?" Nikki enquired.

"Mine felt fine," he said. "I guess I'm a few pounds heavier than Emily."

"A few?" Billie laughed.

"Okay everyone. You're free to go, except you Emily. Tomorrow you can all have a lie in. Briefing at 0930 hours." Nikki dismissed them and they all left, cheering. With that, Emily and Nikki made their way to the roof to test the bindings. Nikki did the descent several times and, by the end, was confident that they wouldn't stick.

A good evening's work, she said to herself, feeling satisfied as she shut down the simulation and left the building.

CHAPTER 8

THE GORELOV AGENDA

Vincent was up early the morning of his trip to England. He spent some time in the gym before grabbing a quick juice and receiving an update from Nikki. They had discussed Antonietta's concerns already this morning over the increased chatter, but had all agreed that it was not relevant to the current operation and that it could wait until it was done. Vincent had however suggested that they raise their security level to Orange.

After their brief chat, Vincent changed from his gym clothes into a lightweight Armani suit over a thin blue shirt and, having said goodbye to his daughter, he headed over to meet Antonietta at the helipad. She was already waiting for him, looking stunning in an extremely smart charcoal grey suit and carrying a Bridge briefcase. He wondered how long she had been standing there waiting for him and hoped it hadn't been too long.

"Morning Antonietta! You look business-like. You're going to turn all the heads at Hereford," he said smiling.

She blushed slightly and muttered, "Thanks, Vincent."

Vincent had decided to fly the helicopter himself on this particular journey, as he needed to keep up his hours. The next few minutes consisted of a series of checks, flicking all the necessary switches before getting clearance for Malta International Airport.

The flight was only seven or eight minutes long and Antonietta wasn't too talkative. He had guessed a while ago that she didn't much enjoy flying. On several occasions he had noticed her journeying to the mainland by driving and taking a ferry, rather than simply hopping in the helicopter for a far shorter journey. He tried to make the experience as minimally traumatising as possible and eventually made the smooth descent to their own secure area at the far side of the airport.

"Good morning, Vincent," their pilot, William, said cheerily as he greeted them both at the small retractable aeroplane steps.

"Morning, William. You've met Antonietta before," he said with a gesture towards her.

"Morning Toni, nice to see you again," William said with a smile.

While William was doing the passenger greeting, David, the co-pilot, was just completing the final checks so that by the time Vincent and Antonietta had strapped into the plush leather chairs, the engines were already at their optimum for taxiing.

"This is Alpha Oscar Sierra One, requesting permission to take off," William said over his comms to the control tower.

"Alpha Oscar Sierra One, you are clear on runway one. Please head North, North-West before taking up your non-specified flight path," came the response from the tower.

"Thanks. Over and out," William replied.

And with that, the GS550 roared to maximum thrust down runway one. It was a familiar feeling for Vincent, but one that he enjoyed every time he travelled by air. The plane gently eased up off the runway and began its ascent into the cloudless morning sky, taking the North-West route off the island. He was aware that the tower would be curious, as they rarely logged a flight plan, unless it was to pick up Kerry from London or perhaps the odd pleasure trip to Rome. However, today was on a need-to-know basis; the tower did not need to know about this specific trip to Brize Norton.

Once they were safely cruising, Vincent jumped up out of his seat and offered Antonietta some fresh coffee, letting her know that the flight would probably be just over two hours. "We should be on the ground by ten GMT."

Antonietta drew her gaze away from the window for the first time since they'd taken off. Vincent couldn't tell if she were mesmerised or terrified, but from the fact that her face had paled considerably and that she was gripping the armrests of her chair, he guessed it was the latter. She coughed. "Before you go boss, Jen asked me to find those details for you on the black BMW? Here's the file I found," she said, handing him a brown flip-file.

Vincent took it, quickly scanning through before analysing the picture inside. It showed the driver, who was perhaps around twenty. He could only be a body builder judging from the size of him. He stared for a minute, wondering if the guy was on steroids or something, before committing the picture to memory and handing the file back to Antonietta. "Thanks,."

She took the coffee he offered her a few minutes later. For the next hour or so they talked about Vendicare and the Gorelov chatter coming from the President of Russia that was concerning them both. Damian had most certainly uncovered some fairly serious talk that they had clearly identified as Gorelov and the pro-Russian separatists. Antonietta explained to Vincent that a Special Forces unit called Gorvorkov, whom no one had ever heard of before, were supplying arms and, worse, surface-to-air missiles to the separatists. She then dropped a bombshell on Vincent by telling him that they had also intercepted similar communication to Islamic State. "I'm sorry I didn't mention it before we came, but Damian has only just picked it up. He's still working on it now."

"How certain are we?" Vincent asked.

"I'd stake my reputation on it," Antonietta said bluntly.

Vincent drew a deep breath. "Okay. Well now I know it's serious. My god, there's a lot going down at the moment."

Before Antonietta had time to answer, the phone built into the seat bleeped; it was their captain, William, letting Vincent know that they had been cleared to land in the next ten minutes. Vincent thanked him, stretching his legs before disposing of the coffee cups and strapping himself in for their descent.

A few minutes later, there was a slight thud and the screech of wheels hitting the tarmac as the GS550 landed at Brize Norton. The G-forces made Vincent's head spin slightly, which he always enjoyed, and then they slowly pulled to a stop.

Vincent and Antonietta stood waiting to disembark the plane and saw a Range Rover with blacked out windows, displaying diplomatic plates, waiting for them. Beside the car stood two people; a young woman wearing a smart black suit, whom Vincent assumed was Saxby and the sergeant, who Vincent knew well, wearing his standard military uniform. William was the first to leave the plane after extending the steps to the ground. He was followed by Vincent and Antonietta.

"William, are you going to be alright waiting here? We probably won't be back until about three o'clock," Vincent said to the pilot, wondering what he might get up to while they were gone.

"Yeah, don't worry, we have got lots of old friends to catch up with," William replied.

"Alright then. See you later," Vincent said with a wave. Antonietta gave a small smile to say thank you and followed Vincent in the direction of the two waiting escorts. As they approached, Sergeant Steve Daniels stood to attention, giving them a salute. Before Saxby could stand to attention also, Vincent had waved his hand away.

"Steve, how long have we known each other?" Vincent asked him.

Steve thought for a few moments before he responded, "A good long while now."

"And, apart from the army, what do I hate the most?"

"Saluting, boss. Gotcha," Steve said, laughing. He extended a hand, which Vincent shook with a grin.

Vincent turned to the woman standing next to him. "You must be Saxby." He extended a hand.

"Yes, sir."

Vincent turned to Steve, with the smile still on his face. "What's the second thing I hate the most, Steve?"

"Being called sir would be an appropriate guess, I think," Saxby responded before Steve could.

Vincent grinned. He introduced Antonietta to both of them before jumping into the plush leather interior of the Range Rover. "Does anyone object to me travelling in the front?" Vincent asked. "I hate feeling like I'm being chauffeured."

No one objected. Saxby sat in the back of the car with Antonietta.

"What's our ETA?" Vincent asked Steve.

"Just under an hour, I think. It depends on traffic. I mean, we could have brought outriders and sirens and been there in under forty, but I didn't think you'd want the pomp and procession for the sake of twenty minutes," Steve replied. Vincent was always happy to take his time. He hated fuss when it wasn't necessary.

He turned again. "Comfy?" he asked Antonietta, who looked a little stiff. He could tell she was nervous.

She gave him a little smile. "Fine thanks, boss."

He turned to Saxby. "So, tell me a little bit more about

yourself? What are you doing over here in the UK?" He was curious to know why Tim would send Saxby here to meet him. There must be an ulterior motive; there always was with the military.

"Well, I joined the military from university. I did a Biotechnology degree at Cal Tech. I'd always wanted to join the Navy Seals, or some other kind of Special Forces unit, but I guess the powers that be only ever paid me lip service. It's only more recently that the Special Operations Forces Report started looking into women in the Special Forces. I did get the chance to take the entrance exam to the Navy Seals and the Counter Assault Team which I passed pretty well, but they wouldn't attach me to any units. I did a year or so with the CIA as an undercover agent, which was fun, but I'm not sure if it's really for me."

She looked a little nervous, as though she may have said too much, but Vincent smiled and gestured for her to carry on. She did.

"When I was at Virginia Beach, which is where the Seal Team is, I was working on a Biotech project for the Navy and saw this memo going around asking for female officers to take selection at Hereford as part of a new unit. It sounded perfect, so I pulled a favour out of everyone I knew to get here; now I'm just waiting for the results."

"Well, Steve? Did she pass?" Vincent asked the Sergeant.

Saxby turned her head sharply. She obviously was not expecting this.

"The smart money is on flying colours, boss," Steve replied.

"Well done Saxby. Did you know you are one of only five girls to have passed the selection?" Vincent congratulated her.

Saxby looked confused. "They told me I was the first girl ever to have taken the test."

"That's another story for another day. But if I am a betting man, which I am on occasion, I would say that you will be joining us on our return flight," Vincent said. Saxby looked bewildered and Vincent nodded at Antonietta, having finally understood why this girl had been sent to meet him from the plane.

The blacked out window lowered as the car pulled to a stop; Steve showed his credentials to the two armed security guards at the gates to Hereford. Once they had been cleared, they drove towards a barracks-type building with several offices adjacent to it. Vincent was pretty familiar with the layout of the base, having been here many times before with Nikki.

Major General Timothy Davies Smith was waiting for them as the Range Rover pulled up outside the office block. Antonietta opened the door and he extended a polite hand to help her get out as Vincent climbed out of the front seat.

"You must be Antonietta. It's a pleasure to meet you," Tim greeted her with a smile.

"Thank you, yes," Antonietta responded.

"Call me Tim," he said as he greeted Vincent with a firm handshake.

Sergeant Daniels and Saxby stayed with the vehicle while the rest of the group headed into the closest building. The PM Alistair Coombes was waiting for them, drinking from his seemingly obligatory Royal Doulton tea set.

"Vincent!" Alistair said, standing up and proffering a hand when Vincent walked in. "Seems like only yesterday, hey?"

"Hi Alistair. This is Antonietta, I'm sure you've met before," he replied.

"Only briefly. But thank you for all the work you have done on our surveillance over Gorelov. You've been a great asset to our research." Antonietta blushed slightly at the compliment and muttered a thank you.

Everyone took their seats. As Tim poured the tea, Vincent

got straight down to business and began to explain the seriousness of the information that Antonietta had delivered to him on the flight over. Tim and Alistair were evidently shocked at what they were hearing. It was clear that neither MI5 nor MI6 had picked up on any of what Damian and Antonietta had found and, if their friends across the pond had, they had not felt obliged to share their findings yet.

"So wait. Let me get this straight. Are we saying that Sergei Gorelov is not only sponsoring pro-Russian separatists, but that he is also behind Islamic State?" Coombes asked incredulously.

Tim opened his mouth to speak, but before he could, Vincent raised his hand. "We know for a fact that Gorelov has been in contact with pro-separatists. We can prove that with a paper trail. But Islamic State is a work in progress; I'm sure that as we look into this in more detail we will be able to unravel it."

There was a long, unnerving pause, which was eventually broken by Tim.

"Well. That's a bit of a hand grenade. We weren't expecting that this morning! Who's in the loop so far?"

"Because we only found out early this morning; the only people who are aware at the moment are Nikki and Damian back in Gozo and the people in this room. If I can make a suggestion, why don't you and Alistair speak to your relevant offices while Antonietta sorts out a live link, then we can pick up this issue later on?" Vincent suggested.

"Do we have a secure line?" The PM asked, looking at Tim.

"My office. I'll show you."

Tim and Alistair stood. Tim leading him towards an adjacent office while Vincent indicated to Antonietta to start things rolling with the live link. Sergeant Daniels then entered the room, saw Antonietta getting out all of her equipment and asked her if she required any help with plugging into their IT. Though Vincent knew she was perfectly capable of doing it alone, she graciously accepted, evidently thinking that might go down better than a refusal. Vincent then caught Tim trying to catch his eye from the adjacent office. He glanced over questioningly and saw him gesturing to come and join them. "Give me two minutes," Vincent said, taking his leave of Toni and Sergeant Daniels who, both engrossed in their work, barely looked up.

Tim closed the door behind him and began to speak with Vincent quietly as the PM briefed his home secretary on the secure line.

"Listen Vincent. The Americans have a planned operation going down imminently, with the intention of rescuing some hostages and taking down the inner circle of the Islamic State," he said in a rushed whisper.

Vincent tried to take it in. "How long have you known this?"

"About twenty-four hours. Even Coombes didn't know until this morning."

Just then, the PM put the phone down and turned to see the two of them whispering. "Well, that's screwed up his day," he said with a sigh.

Tim continued his explanation to Vincent. "The Americans had a full-scale operation in place, planned to go ahead in forty-eight hours, involving all of their Special Forces Units backed by the CIA."

"Well that's not perfect with us already set up to go," Vincent said.

There was a knock at the door which interrupted their thought processes. Tim shouted at them to come in. Sergeant Steve Daniels entered, apologising for the interruption, but requesting everyone's presence in the other room, as they'd managed to get the live link up. They filed into the room and were immediately shocked by what they were presented with on the screen. The large monitors showed a picture of a seven-year-old boy holding the decapitated head of, based on the hat, an Iraqi soldier, which had been posted on a Twitter feed with the comment, 'That's my boy!'

Vincent tore his eyes away from the horrific image and looked around the room. Saxby was staring at the image with dead eyes and everyone else was avoiding each other's gaze.

"That's Islamic State for you, I suppose. Violent and cruel," Tim said.

"Well," Vincent tried to draw their attention away from the horrifying image on the screen. "For the moment everyone, let's park up Gorelov and Russia and crack on with our rescue of the children tomorrow. Then we will see how our American friends are getting on."

"Vincent, I've just had a message from Nikki. She's in the control room with Damian and Emily. They're ready to join us with a conference call. The rest of the team is preoccupied;" Antonietta said.

"Yeah great, get them onto conference call," Vincent said.

"Going live in twenty seconds," Toni confirmed.

Vincent turned and saw Alistair looking toward Saxby and Steve. "Coombes, if it's alright with you, I'd quite like Saxby and Steve to sit in on this; it might be beneficial later," he said.

"Are they cleared?" Alistair asked, looking at Tim.

"Yes, sir. They're cleared to the highest degree."

Just as Coombes nodded his consent, the screen blinked into action and Nikki appeared on the split screen with Emily and Damian stood behind her. Vincent introduced everyone and Nikki confirmed everyone present in the communications room.

Nikki immediately took control of the meeting, showing the live feeds of the breeze block building hidden within the dense undergrowth. She explained that they had to go in forty-eight hours, as they had discovered that Senaullah, the leader of Boko Haram, was due to be back at that time also. Apart from the obvious positive that it would be an opportunity for his extraction, they also did not want him to have the opportunity to move the hostages. She also explained that they had constant tags on his whereabouts, so that if he decided to leave the south of the country sooner than they thought, they would move everything up. The spare GS550 was fuelled and on a one-hour standby on the runway at Malta, ready to go immediately if needed.

"Well, it seems like you've got all points covered," Tim said, obviously impressed by what he had heard.

Vincent added onto what Nikki had said by saying that the team were ready to go. "If we didn't want Senaullah so badly, we could have already been in and out before the Americans have the opportunity to start kicking up a shit storm in Syria. Nikki, if they are planning a hit on Islamic State around the same time as us, are there issues with any satellites, drones, comms, anything?"

"Absolutely not boss, all independent, other than the blimp; we have their word that it's in position and ready to be deployed."

"Nikki, do you want me to check with the man himself, just the be sure that it's in place?" Alistair asked.

"It would definitely be good to safeguard, for sure," she replied.

"I will make that call as soon as he has woken up," Alistair said, leaning back in his chair, evidently pleased that he could offer some form of assistance.

Nikki then brought the assembled people up to speed with Islamic State. "We now have a footprint that leads us all the way back to Gorelov, but one of the messages we translated is extremely disturbing. We believe that they have provided both the Russian separatists and Islamic State with surface-to-air missiles. I'm not talking SA7 hand-held, we're talking big boy stuff, like an SA11 GADFLY with an altitude of 80,000 feet, twice the distance the commercial carriers are flying."

"Surely the separatists and Islamic State can't have anyone actually capable of firing these things, can they?" the PM asked with incredulity.

"Well, there's no mention of operational staff that we've heard, only equipment and rendezvous points," Nikki said.

"Couldn't we just take them out before they arrive at their destination?" Tim asked.

"Unfortunately they were delivered approximately three days ago, before we could even look specifically into the chatter," Nikki said dismally.

"For now," Vincent put in, "neither of these two factions have used them. So, they are either waiting for the opportunity, or they haven't found any available operators."

"Either way, it's a ticking time bomb," Tim said.

"Nikki, if the Americans manage to take out Islamic States' inner circle, how long after finishing our next mission could we be ready to take out the separatists and any serious hardware?" Vincent asked.

"We can be mission ready in as little as three or four days, boss, but that's not the issue. We don't know who or what we are taking on, let alone where they are," she said. "Unlike our hostages, which are all in one place and can be contained by a small team, the Ukraine problem is made far more difficult because of the size of the country and the extent of the separatist outbreaks. The Ukraine is the largest land mass in Europe and has a population of almost forty-four million people. How are we going to find who is responsible? Honestly, I think we would need to put an undercover team in Poland and pull on all the resources from both the United States and the UK for a week, at least, and then I would be able to give you a much clearer picture."

"Tim, Alistair, I have an idea. I'll try and pull it altogether on the flight back to Gozo and will let you know when I finalise the details, but for now, we need to go. Saxby, Steve, I need you to come with me. If you are available and willing," Vincent said, pulling himself up out of his chair.

Both Saxby and Steve looked to Tim, who nodded. "We're ready, sir," they replied together and, with that, Vincent beckoned to Antonietta to wind up her gear and get ready to leave.

"Tim, I'll ring you from the plane once I've formulated the plan. Saxby, Steve, I'd go and pack some basics." They both left the room hurriedly.

As Antonietta packed away her kit, Vincent quickly concluded with the PM that the Gorelov factor had now become serious enough to take action, although Vincent did add that this was less of a surgical strike, which Vendicare specialised in, and more of a politically driven war. "I am sure we will be able to resolve this, but keep me up to speed. We will be a little preoccupied over the next few days, but do keep me informed." Vincent extended his hand.

"Yes. Good luck on your operation. I'm sorry we didn't get the chance for lunch. Safe journey home," Alistair Coombes said, taking Vincent's outstretched hand and shaking it.

This time, the Range Rover was accompanied by outriders and flashing, wailing sirens as they sped towards Brize Norton, back to the waiting aeroplane. William had completed the pre-flight procedures and welcomed Vincent, Antonietta and their new passengers on board. Vincent allowed everyone else to board and take their seats. "Boss, the PM had some snacks loaded on; he said you didn't get time for lunch." Vincent smiled and acknowledged what he'd said as the plane doors slammed shut. William retreated to the cockpit as everyone got comfortable and within a few seconds Vincent could hear the engines winding up. He strapped himself into a large leather chair facing Steve and Saxby. William announced over the speakers that they would be taking off in one minute, then thanked Brize Norton for their hospitality over the radio. He wheeled the plane around and began to accelerate quickly down the old, military runway. Vincent watched out of the window as RAF Brize Norton, the largest station in the Royal Air Force with over 6,000 service personnel, got smaller and smaller as the plane gained altitude. It had been built in 1935 to provide aircraft support during war time operations, the most famous of which being during the Second World War, when all the glider operations had been based there for the D-Day landings, which had been made famous in the film 'A Bridge Too Far'.

The GS550 made a sharp eastward turn before taking a south-easterly route which would take them through French airspace directly over Paris, then Turin and the Tyrrhenian Sea before descending on Malta's international airport. The journey was a comparatively short 1,300 miles, but with a head wind against them, William told them that he had calculated an approximate two hour and thirty-minute journey.

Vincent passed around coffees to everyone while Antonietta searched through data on her laptop which she had connected to the larger screens built into the fixtures on the plane.

"Anything new?" Vincent asked her.

"Not really, I'm just looking at the footprint data that Damian just sent me to confirm it," she replied, distractedly.

"Excuse me for interrupting, but are Steve and I going to be involved in this hostage rescue that you were talking about? Is that why we are on this flight?" Saxby asked, evidently wondering how she had ended up on a flight to Malta.

"I'm sorry, both of you, I know this must all be a little bit of a shock." He was aware that if Vendicare had to be mission ready for another operation prior to the first being completed, they would need some serious intelligence. They didn't have the same resources as the Special Forces, who always had eight to ten teams on standby, though the eventual long term goal of Vincent's was to have two operational teams on standby with a smaller team which could do advanced recon on upcoming missions and also provide emergency cover should anyone be injured. Unfortunately, they weren't quite there yet.

What Vincent had planned for Saxby and Steve, which he now explained to them, was a quick induction in Gozo, watch the team in action tonight and then, once the hostage mission was complete, the two would head to Poland to set up a forward operating base ahead of the team's arrival for the next mission. Steve had worked with the team before on at least two joint ventures and felt comfortable with the whole thing, knowing that Nikki's operational planning was exceptional. Saxby was evidently less confident. She was surrounded by utter strangers, but found herself oddly comfortable in everyone's presence.

Once Vincent had briefly explained his plan to them, they began chatting to Antonietta about technical specifications on the communications, which gave Vincent the opportunity to put a call into Jean to explain that they may need to put the holiday back by a few days, as everything had started to get rather hectic. She was fine with his proposal; he quickly rang off to talk to Kerry, who didn't answer her phone. He left her a brief voicemail asking her to change their reservation for the meal tonight from four people to six, knowing it wouldn't be a problem; the family who owned the restaurant were his friends.

Once he'd made his phone calls, he turned his attention back to Saxby and Steve. "So, are you two okay with Italian tonight? I had planned an early meal, then we can all watch the team in action."

"Well, you know me Vincent," Steve said, smiling. "I'll eat anything."

"My favourite," Saxby agreed.

Vincent could see through the aeroplane windows that they were now only a few minutes away from Malta; he could see the distinctive outline of the island just south of Sicily.

William's voice shouted, "We're on our final approach guys, we are six minutes to landing."

Antonietta unplugged her laptop and packed everything away before strapping herself into her seat. Saxby and Steve did the same, staring out of the window at their new home.

"The journey from Malta to Gozo is only a few minutes by helicopter, so we will arrive at our base by just after five local time, which will give you a couple of hours to explore before dinner at seven," Vincent briefed their new team members. They both nodded wordlessly and returned to staring out of the window, their faces reflecting the bright yellow, afternoon sun. Vincent turned to Antonietta. "Can you upload their bios to the security system for me please, Antonietta?"

She smiled knowingly at him. "One step ahead of you. Got them off Tim at Hereford and sent them straight to Damian. I bet they'll all be uploaded by now."

Vincent grinned at her blatant pleasure at knowing what to do before being asked. It was exactly this quality that had made him decide to have her on the team in the first place. Antonietta quickly explained to Saxby and Steve the security system in place at the base, how it used biometrics and informed them that any personal devices they had with them wouldn't work within the base, but that Damian would give them some temporary mobile phones and tablets.

After making a quick descent, the GS550 hit the runway

with a slight bump and within a minute was making its way to their side of the airport, where the helicopter they had used this morning was sat waiting for them. They disembarked and Vincent thanked William quickly for the flights, showing them all to the Eurocopter. As he walked towards it, Gianni, one of the team's flight engineers, was stepping away. "I've already done all the pre-flight checks for you Vincent, you're good to go."

"Great, thank you," Vincent said appreciatively, knowing that would save them some time. He climbed into the pilot's seat, putting his Peltors on before starting the rotary blades. "This is Alpha Oscar Sierra Two requesting permission to take off. Over," Vincent said to the tower.

"Alpha Oscar Sierra Two, you are cleared to take off to Gozo. Over and out," came the reply.

And with that, Vincent ascended a few hundred feet before swinging the Eurocopter to the west and then heading north over Mellieha, following the ferry route, before hugging the west coast tightly and coming in over Dwejra Bay, where their base sat glistening in the sun. Saxby was sat next to him with her mouth slightly open, leaning forwards to take in the breathtaking views of Gozo and Comino.

"Well, what do you think of the island?" Vincent asked.

"I was brought up on Virginia Beach, but I've never seen anything like these islands before," she said, awestruck.

Their conversation was interrupted by Nikki's voice coming through the radio, giving them clearance to land on helipad two.

"Control, thanks, this is Alpha Oscar Sierra Two approaching to land," Vincent said as he banked right to head over to his villa. He pointed out his daughter and Jodie sunbathing by the pool to Saxby, saying, "That's my daughter over there!"

As Vincent pulled up and began to descend gently onto the

helipad, Nikki and a flight engineer appeared. Once Vincent had safely landed and turned off all the controls, the team disembarked and headed over to where Nikki was waiting for them.

"Okay, Nikki, Steve, you've met before, and this is the newest member of our team, Saxby. Saxby, this is Nikki." They all shook hands politely. "Nikki, can we show Saxby and Steve to their accommodation? Antonietta, thank you for everything you've done today, it's been a pleasure having you with me." Antonietta grinned and thanked Vincent for even considering to take her to such an important meeting. She turned on her heel and headed off to the communications room, no doubt to catch up with Damian on the day's occurrences.

"Shall we?" Vincent asked the group, gesturing in the direction of the base. He led them over to their new private quarters. Although Steve had worked with the team before he'd never actually been to the island or seen their base and made it very clear that he was impressed by the accommodation. Saxby was equally in awe and stood at her balcony for several minutes.

"You know, on a good clear day, you can see the coast of Tunisia from this balcony," Nikki said to her. Saxby looked at her and just gave a small smile, as though she didn't quite believe what was happening.

As promised, Damian had left phones and tablets on the table, which all looked very top-of-the-range, already set up so that Saxby and Steve could use them. Nikki suggested to them that they could either chill out for an hour or so before dinner, or maybe they might like to explore. "I would avoid the simulation areas until you've had a chance to be properly introduced to our team. They're a handful at the best of times."

"Oh, before you go, what is our dress code for dinner?" Saxby asked Nikki.

"It's very casual, just shorts, t-shirts etcetera," Vincent

answered. “We’ll leave you to get settled in, I’ll pick you up at 1845 hours for dinner.” They both turned to leave as Steve made his way out of Saxby’s room to stare at his own beautiful balcony view. “Nikki,” Vincent said as they left the private accommodation. “I think I’m going to head over to the gym to shake of the five hours of plane travel. I’ll see you later at the simulation?”

“Yeah boss, see you later. Hope you had a good day?” She was obviously wondering how on earth they now had two new team members.

“I’ll fill you in later,” Vincent said, giving her a knowing look before heading off in the direction of the gym. What a crazy day, he thought to himself. And it’s not even over yet.

CHAPTER 9

SISTERS

Kerry and Jodie were lying by the side of the Villa's pool, attempting to catch the last rays of sunshine before the end of the day.

They had awoken that morning to the sound of Vincent's helicopter taking off. Knowing that they had another full day of training with Gichin ahead of them, they had decided to take a swim. Jodie had been excited about the day, really looking forward to training, but Kerry had inwardly thought to herself, Goddddd, I just want to lie around the pool all day and get some of these rays. I'm so pale after a year in London. But she had gone to training anyway, knowing that it was what her dad wanted her to do, supposing it was good for her after all.

They had found a note on the fridge asking them if they would like to book a table tonight at the Italian on the sea front, or would Jodie like to cook Italian at home.

"Well, that's a no brainer," had been Jodie's response, as she picked up the phone to ring Beppe and book a table.

Soon afterwards, they had made their way to training with Gichin, who had installed several new training aides for the girls: a heavy duty punching bag and two Shaolin wooden dummies. It was hard to deny that they enjoyed themselves, though by the end of it they were both aching and hurting in several places from the strenuous attack-and-defence workout.

After their lunch break, Gichin had announced that he was going to show them some close-quarter combat and how to disable an armed assailant using a gun or a knife. After several hours of working at this, Gichin announced, "Well girls, seeing as you've progressed so quickly, I think we may call it a day as a reward. After all I do have business on the mainland that I must attend..."

The girls had wandered over towards the water machine to rehydrate before Jodie had whispered to Kerry, "'Business on the mainland', my arse. He's off to your dad's casino."

They had both broken into fits of giggling before Kerry said, "Who cares, I need to get some sun on me anyway. Let's go back."

And so they had found themselves at four-thirty laying at the poolside, talking about their upcoming holiday to the Seychelles.

"Do you reckon your Dad will let you come to some beach parties? I know how protective he is over you," Jodie asked Kerry.

"Well, I wouldn't worry. You know you and I can both work on him; he'll soon come round to the idea," Kerry said with a laugh, knowing that she was not the only one who could have her dad wrapped around her little finger. She tapped a finger on her nose at Jodie and they both giggled again.

"Your dad's funny, isn't he," Jodie said, placing her sunglasses back over her eyes and leaning back onto her sun lounger.

Kerry leaned forwards and stared at her. "What do you mean?"

"You know. He's just... funny."

"No, I don't know. Tell me what you mean," Kerry said agitatedly.

"Calm down, Kerry, it was just a stupid comment."

"Fine." She lay back down. A few minutes later, she asked, "What are you going to wear tonight?"

"Well, it's a difficult decision. But I'm probably going to go with what your dad bought me for my birthday, those red Valentino shorts and this leopard print shirt my mum says must have cost over a thousand Euros," Jodie said, pulling her copy of Grazia off the table next to her and aimlessly flipping the pages.

Kerry felt her frustration stirring again. "Jodie, how the hell does my dad know what to buy you?"

"Kez, your dad's cool. He knows what's what, have you ever seen him not looking immaculate? No, didn't think so," she replied with a similar amount of annoyance.

"So what, do you fancy him or something now?"

"I would... but I couldn't put up with his baggage. I don't know if you've met his daughter, but she's a self-opinionated spoilt brat; I couldn't put up with her as a step daughter," Jodie replied with an air of nonchalance.

Kerry sat up sharply and threw the ice bucket that had been cooling their drinks all over Jodie.

"You bitch!" Jodie shouted as the ice hit her.

They both screeched names at each other and grabbed hold of each other, each attempting to throw the other into the pool. After a little while, they both collapsed breathlessly into a heap, giggling uncontrollably.

"Seriously though, Jodie, you don't fancy my dad, do you?" Kerry asked, trying to regain her breath.

"Oh Kerry. Seriously, I love your dad as much as you do. Get over it," she said, slapping Kerry around the head with her copy of Grazia.

A familiar buzzing sound was coming from the east and they both looked to see a helicopter flying towards the villa.

“Speak of the devil,” Jodie said. “I guess your dad’s back from that trip to England.”

Kerry grabbed her phone to check the time. “We’d best start getting ready for that meal. Oh, I’ve got a voicemail, hang on.” She called, receiving the message her dad had left her asking her to change the booking for their evening meal.

“You go do that,” Jodie said, commandingly. “I’m going to go get in the hot tub before we get ready. It’s starting to go a bit cold.”

“I’ll meet you in there,” Kerry said, gathering up her things and retreating inside to call Beppe. She was glad to know that Jodie did not actually fancy her dad and she had begun to realise that she loved him in the same way that Kerry did; as a father. She smiled, thinking that it might not be too long before they were actually sisters, by the way her dad seemed to feel towards Jean. Don’t get your hopes up, she said, grinning, as she picked up the receiver and dialled.

CHAPTER 10

REAR MIRRORS

Vincent was at the control panel in the gym, taking a set of Bluetooth Bose headphones from the rack before programming a playlist of music. 'The Best of Queen' seemed good to get him into the right frame of mind for his forty-five minute workout. Nikki and Antonietta had put this personal music system in place after every member of the team had complained about Vincent's choice of music, which was either all from the seventies or very current boy/girl band stuff. It also used to drive Vincent mad when all he could listen to was Will.I.am, or Eminem, which the rest of the team seemed to be in to.

He found himself on the rowing machine for a change, keeping a studious eye on the big screens which surrounded the gym's interior. They showed a variety of channels, including BBC News 24, Sky News and CNN, all of which seemed to be showing the same images of a Russian truck heading towards an obscure border point.

Vincent frowned. It was only two weeks ago that these screens had all been showing nothing but Senaullah and the hundred young girls he had taken as hostages, the sole reason for the mission which was to be undertaken in twenty-four hours. Now, it wasn't even mentioned as back story. This was worrying for two reasons. Firstly, that the media's, and the world's, attention, could be diverted from a serious issue so quickly; secondly, because Senaullah was no longer receiving the media attention that he had been, which meant he may do something drastic to rekindle that interest and may ruin the team's plans and chances of success.

Just as he came to the realisation that he was overthinking everything as usual, his vision was suddenly disrupted by a towel which had been thrown at him. He pulled it quickly away from his face to see Emily standing before him. He pulled the headphones off his head. "Time's up, boss," she said, pointing at the screen, which showed that he had been going well over his forty-five minute programmed time. "Not bad. You must have been giving it some. It says you've burned 700 calories."

"Hello Emily. Thanks for that," Vincent said, though he was happy to see her.

"We've just been finalising tactics and going over routes in and out before tonight's major simulation. Nikki sent me over to check you definitely want Jodie and Kerry and our two visitors acting the parts of terrorists?" Vincent nodded in response. "Okay, well, they need to be in position by ten pm at the latest."

"That's fine, I'll have them back here for nine-thirty. Can you ask Nikki for me if she is happy to get everyone together for a final briefing straight after simulation tonight? I think I might be considering moving things forward."

"Yeah, no problem, I'm sure that will be fine," she replied, then left to deliver Vincent's message.

About twenty minutes later, Vincent was in the car, driving Saxby, Steve, Jodie and Kerry down to Marsalform in one of the Mercedes G-Wagons, parking directly in front of Beppes, which faced the sea front. Antonietta had been intending to join them, but had decided that she needed to go over some of the more recent Gorelov data with Damian and had asked Vincent to bring her back a takeaway so she didn't miss out on the food. Joseph, the owner, and his son Beppe, both of whom Vincent knew very well, met them as they took a seat at an outside table. The formal greetings and introductions took several minutes before the group could get around to ordering.

"Now everyone, if you're happy, we could just trust Jodie to take care of the ordering. You will not be disappointed," Vincent suggested. Everyone responded enthusiastically, so Jodie picked up the menu and began discussing the order with Beppe in her native Italian, only stopping every now and then to make sure that the table liked certain things.

"Grazia, grazia. Okay everyone, we are going to have an Italian tapas-style meal, so there's going to be lots of little things for everyone to taste," Jodie said once she'd finished her discussions with Beppe, "I hope that's okay with everyone!"

"What about drinks?" Vincent asked.

"Joseph said he's got a nice wine for you to taste which will suit the meal. I thought Kerry and I ought to have soft drinks really, seeing as it's a school night." She gave a sideways look at Kerry, knowing full well that she would get wound up by that comment. The result did not disappoint.

"No, you can both have a glass of wine if you want. Saxby, Steve? Would you like wine?"

"I'll just have a beer, please," Steve said to Beppe.

"A glass of wine would be lovely," Saxby said.

Beppe nodded and disappeared with a full order sheet. The group settled into easy conversation. It was a mild evening, the sea giving a calming soundtrack, lapping gently against the beach. Vincent was interested to know how Kerry and Jodie had fared with their training with Gichin during the day. Kerry was clearly impressed with herself, bragging to the table about how she had disarmed Gichin while he threatened her with a knife and that he was on the floor before he knew what had happened. Saxby was clearly impressed and congratulated Kerry.

"So, are you two happy with your accommodation?" Vincent directed the question at Saxby and Steve, knowing that they would be, but wanting to engage them in conversation.

"Mine's fantastic... I just cannot get over that view!" Saxby said with a sigh.

"Almost as good as the regiment, boss," Steve said, which received a laugh from the group. Vincent laughed in response, having always enjoyed Steve's company, when something caught his eye. He looked out towards where the cars were parked and saw a parked black BMW, with a huge guy climbing into it accompanied by a girl. He watched them for a few more moments, before excusing himself from the table.

"Excuse me, I just need to go and... say hello to someone. I'll only be a moment." No one made an objection, all carrying on with their casual chatter, all apart from Jodie, who stared at Vincent as he pushed his chair back from the table and made his way over to the car park. He calmly walked the fifteen or so metres towards the car, stopping at the driver's side. The guy who had caught his eye was already sat in the driver's seat, fumbling with his keys while his passenger, of about twenty or so, got in the other side.

Knowing that he hadn't been noticed yet, Vincent gently tapped on the window. The guy looked up and saw him, pressing the switch to bring the tinted glass down.

"What?" he asked bluntly, looking bored.

Vincent pointed towards the central mirror. "Ever use that?"

"Piss off, old man," the guy said, before making a move to shut the window.

In one quick, sudden movement, Vincent had him around the collar. "I really would appreciate it if you used that mirror," he said calmly. "You very nearly knocked me off my bike the other day. I don't appreciate that one little bit." He released him and turned away, but not before the guy had climbed out of the car. Vincent turned around and could see him squaring up to him.

"I don't care who you are, but I'm going to beat the shit out of you for talking to me like that." The young guy spat on the ground between them.

Vincent found himself firming his stance, a small smile on his face. Let him think he's got me. "This doesn't seem like a fair fight. You're so much bigger than me."

"Look, do you have a death wish? I'll snap your puny body in half, then beat you bloody for even touching me." When Vincent didn't reply, the guy pulled his arm back and aimed a swing at Vincent. Quick as a snake, Vincent dodged the huge, clenched fist and, in the same action, took the guy's arm and twisted it one way, then quickly the other, then up and behind his back. Before he knew what had happened, the BMW owner found his face pressed against the bonnet of his own car. Vincent then held his arm straight and upright, allowing the guy absolutely no movement.

"What were you saying?" Vincent said, smirking.

"You're breaking my arm. LET GO!" he bellowed.

"You didn't call me old man this time." Vincent said, enjoying the power he felt overcoming an opponent.

Someone in the corner of Vincent's vision made him jerk his head; he saw the girl from the passenger seat climbing out of the car with a baseball bat in her right hand, making her way towards him.

"Let him go!" she screeched, swinging the baseball bat viciously. He looked towards the girl swinging the baseball bat to the man he had contained beneath his grip, wondering how to react to this one. But he didn't need to.

"Are you going somewhere?" came Jodie's voice from behind Vincent, startling him. She stepped forwards to meet the girl. "Be careful. If you don't put that bat down, there's a chance someone may get seriously hurt." The girl looked as confused as Vincent felt as he watched on with interest, holding the guy firmly. The girl appeared to gain some confidence from the bat she clutched in both hands as she shouted at Jodie, "You scrawny posh bitch, let's see what you look like when I'm done with you!"

Safe to say that's her last mistake of the evening, Vincent thought to himself. Jodie proved him absolutely right. As quick as a flash, she had kicked the bat out of the girl's hand and had dumped her on the ground face first, before planting a foot firmly below her neck to stop her from moving an inch.

She looked towards Vincent for some form of explanation. "Scrawny is a first. I don't think I'm scrawny. Am I scrawny?"

"I'm pleased to see you've been listening to Gichin, nice work! And no, you're not scrawny," Vincent burst into laughter. "Okay you two," he said to the two trapped beneath his and Jodie's grip, with a patronising edge to his voice. "What I want you to do is to stay very calm. We're both going to let you go. I want you to walk away without another word. Sound like something you can do?"

The guy being held by Vincent began to squirm and said something inaudible, muffled by the fact that his face was pressed against the car. Vincent pressed him more firmly in to the car and repeated the question. When he received no reply, he let go of him, with Jodie doing the same, and shoved him away from himself. The guy shrugged himself free and flexed his fists. Vincent continued. "I'm going to keep a hold of these keys. I want you to go for a walk; don't come back for a couple of hours. I want to enjoy my meal in peace, if that's alright. Thank you, you may now go." They both stared at him with daggers, before wordlessly turning away and walking towards the sea front. Jodie looked at Vincent who gave him a grin.

They walked back to the table arm in arm, as Jodie whispered in his ear, "Remind me not to cut you up on your bike."

"Remind me not to call you scrawny," he whispered back.

They came back to the table and sat, apologising for their absence. Kerry looked between the two of them, knowing something was amiss, but kept quiet. A few seconds later, Beppe arrived with a host of dishes, which Jodie jumped into action to explain. "Here we have aubergine cooked in egg, garlic, basil and breadcrumbs... ooh, ooh! Ecco il petto di pollo croccante con salsa di pizza e..."

"Jodie!! English, please!" Vincent interrupted, laughing, knowing she had gotten carried away.

"Ah, mi scusi, mi scusi!" she said, looking slightly flustered. "Er, it's crispy chicken breast with a pizza style sauce."

"KFC – Italian style," Kerry said, laughing.

"In Italy, we don't eat KFC and we most certainly don't copy it," Jodie said, frowning at Kerry.

"Sorry, Jozza, just getting you back!" Kerry said.

Jodie made her way through the rest of the dishes which, among other things, included grilled prawns with squid chilli and lemon mayonnaise and thinly sliced beef with parsley and olive dressing. One of Vincent's favourite things about Italian food was that they kept it nice and simple.

Everyone was thoroughly enjoying the food. Saxby chatted to Kerry about going to school in England and what she might have planned for university; Steve spoke to Jodie about life in the regiment, while she hung onto his every word.

Vincent took the opportunity to glance at some emails which Toni had sent him. One which had been marked 'For your eyes only', read: 'Julian Assange to leave Ecuadorean

Embassy followed by a confirmation that the increased chatter and internet requests for information on Vendicare and any other secret special service force units appeared to be linked to 'Wikileaks' servers based in Russia'. Vincent knew that if it was Russian servers, they would be hard done by to trace the footprints, unless they were communicating outside of Moscow. The email went on to explain that they had connections within the Ecuadorean Embassy, Wikileaks and also in Moscow but, more importantly, to Gorvorkov, the unknown Russian unit.

Looking up to check that the others were still deep in conversation, he quickly replied to Antonietta to thank her for the information and that he had ordered her a salmon and penne pasta to take away.

She replied within seconds, with only two words. 'Garlic bread?' Vincent smiled and grabbed Beppe to add this request, before replying with the affirmative.

Jodie broke up everyone's individual conversations, drawing Vincent's attention away from his phone, to ask everyone if they would like a sweet. Everyone agreed that they would like one and Vincent asked, "Oh, Jodie, what's the name of my favourite? It has Limoncello in it, doesn't it?"

She immediately said, "Yes! Crema di limoni e Limoncello! It's a lemon and Limoncello mousse. I used to make it in Panaro's and showed Beppe how to make it. It's now Vincent's favourite dessert."

"Every meal you make is my favourite, Jodie!" Vincent replied with a smile.

When the dessert came, everyone tucked in, 'umming' in appreciation.

"That. Is. Heaven." Saxby said.

After a quick coffee, the team headed back to base using the coastal road. Vincent felt happy that he hadn't seen the

BMW driver since he'd asked him to leave and gave the keys to Beppe, apologising if any of his guests had witnessed the scene.

As the team arrived back, Vincent pulled up and asked Jodie to drop off Antonietta's food in the communications room. "Meet us in the simulation room in half an hour, thanks!"

"Aye aye, sir!" she yelled back, saluting.

Vincent felt everyone else's eyes on him in the car to see how he would respond to his two pet hates being delivered in one smooth blow in a blatant attempt to wind him up. He just looked at her for a moment and turned away with a shake of his head. Saxby and Steve laughed at Jodie, asking Vincent if she was always like this.

"Yes. Believe me. She is," Vincent said, sighing, but with a wide smile on his face. "Are you ready to meet the team?" He asked, pulling up outside the simulation block, ready to see the final practice before their big mission: Operation Angel Faces.

CHAPTER 11

PRACTICE MAKES PERFECT

In the simulation room, the team were going over their final drills. This would be their third go at this. Nikki knew for a fact that they could have gone after their first, but it was always practice makes perfect at Vendicare, so they were doing it one last time. Everyone milled around in their full gear, ready to get going, as Vincent pulled up in the G-Wagon.

Nikki greeted them at the car. "Did you have a nice meal?"

"It was amazing, thank you. Jodie sure does know her Italian food," Saxby replied.

"Great! Listen, you two, Saxby and Steve, I need you to act as our enemy. Basically, I want you to think how they would, do what they would, react to what happens as they would, make this as realistic as possible," she quickly explained. Saxby and Steve nodded, very serious now that they were needed. They had both participated in similar operations before. Steve was used to this type of thing at Hereford, as they used several of the normal military regiments to act as enemies for simulations and Saxby had also participated in several CIA and FBI training operations of a similar nature. "Other than the fact that this is your base, and that you are protecting about a hundred hostages, you aren't going to know anything about what we are going to be doing so that you can be as unaware as, hopefully, our enemy will be."

"Got it," Steve said.

Nikki looked over to Kerry and Jodie, who had just walked through the door of the simulation. They were both stood, motionless, staring at the team. It was true that they had never seen them all in their full kit before, she supposed. They both looked stunned, not knowing really why they were there.

"You two!" Nikki shouted at them. They both jumped slightly. "I need you to do what Steve and Saxby are doing. You're going to hide amongst the cardboard cutouts of the hostages that we have. They're spread out inside the breeze block building. Then, just wait. Here are some veils to cover your faces, they're called Niqabs." She handed them over and watched as they attempted to put them on. Saxby had to help the two girls, but eventually they were all dressed in them, with only their eyes to be seen. "And here are your replica Kalashnikovs. They're simulation guns, so they aren't going to actually fire bullets, but they will send laser shots; if anyone is hit by them, it will register on the computer system and we will know what we might need to change about our team's whereabouts. Good luck," Nikki finished, dismissing them, walking over to the team.

Steve led them all into the dark, dingy breeze block building. It was eerie inside. The cutouts looked lifelike in the badly-lit mock-up. Steve sent Jodie and Kerry to separate corners on opposite sides of the back building to watch for the ground team to breach as he anticipated that was what they might do. He took off their safeties and told them that if they saw anything, any movement at all, to shoot. He then expected a second team to enter, either through the front door, or by abseiling through the roof. Saxby placed herself near the front door with her Kalashnikov to cover the entrance. Steve then took a position across from Saxby but covered the skylights, thinking that they may enter from there. They all then sat, waiting, still and quiet.

Vincent wished Nikki good luck and headed over to the control centre to watch on the big screens with Antonietta and Damian. Antonietta thanked Vincent for the pasta, which she had only just finished, and passed him a tablet with all the updated information before turning to the big screen to watch a live feed of the BBC 24 hour news as the team got into position. A solemn-looking Frank Gardener, the BBC Security journalist, appeared on the screen, being interviewed by Kate Silverton. In the background, Vincent could see pictures of the American journalist James Marshal, who had just been executed by Islamic militants. Vincent stared at the monitor, wordlessly. If Vendicare had received the necessary intelligence from the CIA and MI6 three months ago, they would have rescued James Marshal and the five other hostages that Islamic State held and Becci would probably still be alive. The team had gone into Syria with less-than-accurate intelligence and in fact, it had turned out to be compromised; the Jihadist guarding the hostages on behalf of Islamic State was waiting for them. Vincent from that point on had refused to take on any mission which didn't involve their own intelligence. He had lost trust for anything he couldn't be in control of.

Antonietta saw him watching the screen. She said quietly, "If you want to see it, boss, we have the footage of the hostage being executed."

Vincent merely shook his head. "Was it Islamic State?"

"Yes, but a specific faction, called 'the Beatles'. This guy was called John... he's British. Neither MI5 nor MI6 had him on the radar. In fact, believe it or not, I had a call off them earlier on asking if we had any information."

"Brilliant. We are a small independent group with about a dozen employees and these agencies have thousands of staff, satellites and huge buildings, and they're asking us if WE know anything," he shook his head again in dismay.

Damian interrupted them both, which Vincent was grateful for, telling them that it was five minutes until show time. He turned the BBC news story off, replacing it with the live video footage of the simulation which was happening in the room below them. Even though they were using thermal images and infrared cameras, the only thing to see was the still heat signatures from Saxby, Steve, Jodie and Kerry, who were expecting their attackers any second now. They also had sound and biometrics on all the team, which Antonietta assured Vincent were all tip-top. Vincent watched the figures in the building. They were staying incredibly still; he could tell they were all on high alert, not knowing what was going to happen next.

"Okay boss, it's all starting now," Damian said and, as he did, Vincent detected movement at the back of the building. Two red heat signatures had appeared against the back wall, which he knew to be Oliver and Amanda. They would now be inserting Borescopes through the back wall which would allow all the team to have eyes inside the building. Once they had inserted them, the 4G wireless receivers would transmit the pictures back to base for Antonietta and Damian, but also to the individual team members.

"Alpha Two to Alpha One, you should have visuals on the east side. Over," Vincent heard Oliver say over his radio transmitter.

"Alpha Three to Alpha One, same here, visuals going live on west side now. Over," came Amanda's voice.

"Sierra One to Alpha One, in position. Visuals 10/10 identified; two hostiles at door entrance. Over," came Emily's voice.

"Sierra Two to Alpha One, in position. Visuals 10/10

identified; two hostiles east and west of breach wall. Over," Mike said.

Scott and Lee confirmed their positions and provided cover while Oliver and Amanda placed the explosives to breach the wall. Vincent watched each of their signatures moving with his heart beating quickly. Nikki and Billie had already placed the dummy canisters with the incapacitating agent which were now armed and due to dispense the non-lethal spray in two minutes, which gave the team five minutes to go.

Vincent checked the bios of the team and saw with a smile that the cooling system on the new suits were working a treat, keeping their body heat signatures close to invisible.

"Alpha One to all teams, canisters are dispensing. Be careful; use your respiratory masks. Over." The team acknowledged Nikki's instruction and got ready for the countdown. Vincent could see Emily and Mike checking their bindings, preparing to crash through the roof. They had identified the four heat signatures within the building and silhouettes provided by the Borescopes, so were going down back-to-back, with Emily taking the position facing the front door.

"Do you miss it, boss?" Antonietta interrupted Vincent avidly watching his team.

"No," he lied. "I prefer to be on this side of the fence these days. Better to leave it to the young ones."

"Alpha One to all teams. Show time in fifteen." She paused. "Ten… five, four, three, two, one. Green for go, I repeat, green for go!"

Within a few seconds, the flash bangs had gone off and, in the disorientation caused by the noise and the light, Saxby, Steve, Kerry and Jodie had all been cuffed with tie wraps, disarmed and had a dusty sackcloth thrown over their heads to then be dragged backwards through the hole in the wall created by Oliver and Amanda's explosion. None of them had seen any of it coming, although Steve had managed to send a round off, but had already been shot several times by that time, so his Kalashnikov had automatically deactivated, which meant none of his shots had hit home. All four of the 'hostiles' were dumped on the floor and the team shouted over their comms, "Hostiles down, clear hostages!"

For the next five minutes, there was a lot of communications chatter from everyone as they simulated moving the hostages over to the landing zone and then secured the entire area. When all of this had been done, Antonietta said, "Control to Alpha One, operation is a success. Final chopper away, prepare for your lift. Over." Before the team could do anymore, the lights around the complex were switched on, stunning half the team as they were still in their night vision mode. There was an audible groan.

"Why don't they warn us when they're going to do that?" Lee yelled.

"Sorry guys, my fault," Nikki said. "Oliver, come and see how your sister and Jodie are handling it!" She led him over to Saxby and Steve who lay quite still on the ground. Nikki cut their restraints and removed their bags. "You both okay?"

"Absolutely fine, well done! That was amazing!" Steve said, in obvious awe.

"You could have been so much more brutal with us, though; why weren't you?" Saxby asked.

"We didn't need to. We don't see the point in unnecessary violence," Nikki responded.

Oliver wandered over to where Kerry was sitting on the floor. "Never heard you quite so quiet, sis." He cut her restraints and removed the bag before doing the same for Jodie.

Kerry appeared, with her hair all over the place and her face bright red with anger. "Have you SEEN these marks on my wrists?! They will be there for absolutely WEEKS!" Kerry screeched at Oliver. "They're so not going to help my tan!"

“Sorry sis, nothing to do with me, take it up with Billie,” Oliver said, laughing, then said thoughtfully, “I think I’d prefer a real enemy to you, you’re a bloody nightmare.” He turned to Jodie. “How did you find it?”

Jodie had bright eyes and spoke excitedly. “Oh. My. God. That was amazing! I didn’t see any of you, I didn’t even hear you! One minute I was waiting, the next I felt someone tie my hands and drag me backwards!”

“To be honest we went pretty easy on you. We haven’t eaten yet, so our energy is down,” Oliver said, still laughing. “Glad you enjoyed it.”

“Okay everyone, gather round!” Nikki shouted, getting everyone’s attention. “Well done guys, thank you to our visitors, you made everything that little bit more realistic. Let’s go over to the debrief before we go and get some food.”

Saxby and Steve decided to join in with the debrief while Kerry disappeared to ‘go for bath to wash all the muck out of her hair’. Jodie had already disappeared off to the kitchens to make sure that the team had their last evening meal ready.

Vincent was just finishing his conversation with Antonietta and Damian, asking them what they needed in order to get around-the-clock surveillance and analytics for the next operations. Damian explained that they would need more analysts, but Toni thought that a recruitment plan might be more appropriate. Both are easier said than done, Vincent thought to himself, but he thanked them both anyway for their input. “Go for it,” he said to Damian. “But keep me in the loop.” He made his way down to the briefing room to find the team removing their body armour and battle gear when Jodie burst through the door carrying hot mugs of tea and shortbread biscuits.

Vincent could see Steve talking to Oliver, telling them that the level they had achieved was seriously impressive and, coming from the sergeant of the regiment, that was high praise.

"What do you think, Saxby?" Nikki directed the question at the newest member of their team. "Coming from your Seals and Delta?"

"You're way ahead!" Saxby said enthusiastically. "Your comms and surveillance is superior to everything I've ever seen; the way you took that building... Steve and I didn't even see you! Amazing!" Nikki grinned back.

"Well done, Nikki. It's honestly fantastic. Do that tomorrow and it's a done deal," Vincent congratulated her.

Nikki called for everyone's attention and congratulated them all on the slick practice. "But remember. The hostages will not be cardboard cutouts and our hostiles will not be people we share drinks with. It's going to be ten times harder. But I know you all can do it. Vincent?"

Vincent cleared his throat. He wasn't into big speeches, but neither was he into the Yankee style hollering and whooping that the rest of the team seemed to enjoy. "Guys, well done, I'm very impressed. Let's keep moving things forward; there's always room for improvement of course, but well, you were pretty darn good. Tomorrow. Do. Not. Take. Any. Chances. If something doesn't seem right to you, it probably isn't. Talk to each other, communicate, but most of all be careful. Make sure you are all back safe and sound by Friday. Don't come back as late as Saturday, because it's the new Doctor Who and I'm not missing it."

He saw Saxby look around with a confused expression and mouth at Emily, 'What's Doctor Who?'

"Thanks Vincent," Nikki said, taking control from Vincent who sat back down. "One last thing guys. The rescue has been moved forwards, so get to bed, because it's an early start tomorrow. I want you all up at 0400 hours to leave by five! Goodnight, team."

CHAPTER 12

SMELLY CAMELS

It was 0415 hours, still dark. The team was gathered around the Eurocopter, saying goodbye to everyone remaining at base. Their essentials were already packed, having been driven to the airport and pre-loaded into their plane to save the team valuable time this morning.

Nikki watched on as Vincent went around each member of his team, wishing them the best of luck and telling them one last time to just be careful. He took extra time over Oliver, holding onto him tight, as though he would never let go. Nikki thought she could see tears building in his eyes and looked away, knowing he would hate it if she had seen.

"Right everyone. On board, now. We have a tight schedule to stick to," she announced, the team obligingly climbing into the helicopter. Nikki was proud that not one of them was showing signs of the early morning start. Though sombre, as they always were before a mission, wondering what was going to happen, Nikki knew they were raring to go. This is what they had been training for all this time.

Vincent pulled away from his son and gripped him by the shoulders. "Be careful, Oli. I can't lose you. I can't lose anyone else." His voice broke as he said those last words.

"I'll be back, Dad. I promise." Oliver said awkwardly and gave him a slap on the back before pulling himself on board the Eurocopter.

Nikki climbed in and did a quick head count, though she knew everyone was there. "Right! Let's go!"

The helicopter lifted off the ground and the rotary blades thrummed seemingly much louder than usual, disturbing the cool, morning silence. The pilots, William and David, would be meeting the team at Malta Airport for the four-hour flight, which meant they would arrive at the Northern Chad airport at 0820 hours, local time. After the short helicopter ride, the team boarded the plane and, within a matter of minutes, were flying towards their most important mission yet.

Nikki had thought to use the time to go over all the intelligence one final time to see if any last minute amendments needed to be made, but instead found herself relaxing into her comfortable seat and taking the opportunity for an hour's shut eye. Most of the team slept the whole four hours, eager to be as awake and active as possible; today would be a long one. The lights had been dimmed in the main cabin of the GS550 to allow easy sleep, but as Nikki stirred she realised that they were making their final approaches to the airport. William had turned the lights on gradually to allow the team to wake naturally. She sat up and pulled herself out of her seat to make some coffee for herself, in order to fully awake before they landed. As she walked towards the coffee machine, she passed Emily, who appeared to be stirring. She gently placed a hand on her shoulder and said, "We're ten minutes to landing, Em. Want a coffee?"

"Cheers, Nikki. Yeah, please. I didn't get a chance to earlier, but I suppose I'd better go and put my face on," she replied, to which Nikki laughed.

"What's going on?" Oliver asked groggily, having woken up in the seat next to Emily at the laughter.

“Oh, Nikki and I were just discussing why we put ourselves up for this shit. We could be dancing the night away on a beach somewhere instead,” she lied prettily.

“I’m up for dancing the night away on a beach with you,” Oliver said cheekily.

“Oh my darling, is that your way of asking me out on a date?” Emily said.

“Might be,” he grinned.

“Love, you couldn’t handle me,” she said with a sigh, taking the coffee Nikki offered her.

It was exactly 0823 hours when William landed the GS550 on the short, disused, ex-military airfield. He followed Nikki’s strict instructions and taxied the plane over to the north end, leaving the engines running while she made contact with her foreign legion ‘friends’. She was sat in the cockpit waiting, when the radio burst into crackly life.

“Alpha Oscar Sierra One, do you copy?” a female voice with a slightly French accent asked.

“Alpha Oscar Sierra One, we copy. Over,” Nikki replied.

“Alpha Oscar Sierra One, landing zone is secure and code is five, seven, sixty-nine. Welcome to the desert!” the woman responded cheerily. Nikki quickly secured their confirmation and lowered the stairs so that the team could step onto the rough, dusty tarmac which had once belonged to the French military. Immediately the team had to shield their eyes from the strong African sun, which was bursting through the thin layer of clouds above them. Both Oliver and Scott immediately took off their hoodies once they felt the humid air that surrounded them. Once Nikki’s eyes had adjusted, she saw a tall figure covered from head to foot in the local African dress and carrying a Famas F1 Rifle striding towards them. Nikki covered the metres between them and stood. There was a short exchange of words before the figure removed her headdress to reveal an olive-skinned woman who was beaming at Nikki.

"How the fuck are you, Nikki?! No calls, no texts, not even a postcard! I haven't heard from you in two years and then you just send me a bloody email?" she screeched at Nikki, before flinging her arms around her for a brief hug.

"I've been busy, Freya!" Nikki responded, trying to maintain her composure in front of her team, who all stood watching, agog. "You look great!"

"Oh thanks," Freya shrugged off the compliment. "So I guess you're still working for that smooth, Italian-looking guy, right? What's his name, Vincent?"

"Yeah, why? Want a job?"

"No. Still working for myself. Always will."

The two girls caught up quickly and the rest of the team began to unload their kit from the plane. Out of the corner of her eye, Nikki could see Oliver trying to gain her attention. She turned to him. He pointed two fingers at his eyes and then one over to the north of the airport, as subtly as he could. Nikki followed his thoughts and looked over to the shrub he had indicated.

"Nikki it's fine, they're with me, though they're obviously not good at hiding. Pierre, George and Philip will protect your transport," Freya said. "I've also arranged what we planned. Two guides are going to meet us here. I've told them that we are taking some wealthy German hunters on some illegal safari, which luckily for you is pretty common around here. I'll stay with you until you're a few clicks away from the targets and then I'll... err... deal with the guides however I see fit."

"I know I said not to compromise the mission under any circumstance, but if you can contain them until the mission is over, do try to keep them alive. I hate wasted blood," Nikki said.

The team changed into local dress, with the girls making sure to cover their faces to prevent anyone from being able to recognise their feminine features. The boys had been working on growing stubble, or beards if they could, over the last few weeks in order to also protect their features from being recognisable. Usually, they were all clean-shaven.

Freya received confirmation from Pierre that the two guides were now approaching the runway from the east with a herd of camels in tow. "From what they can see, they're alone, so we don't have any unwanted visitors following them."

The guides arrived and everyone mounted their camels, speaking as little as deemed possible. The sixty-kilometre journey from the disused airport to the first staging point just outside of Kukawa would take just over four hours, if the camels averaged about fifteen kilometres an hour, provided they didn't meet any trouble on the way. The team all had their weapons and essential communications on underneath their native dress and two Peli cases attached to the spare camels contained the remainder of their kit.

Freya held her rifle close to her as she spoke fluent Sara Maba, a French Arabic dialect spoken only in this region, to the two guides. Nikki could tell from her tone that something the guides were saying was irritating her. At one stage, Nikki watched as she gripped her rifle and pulled it closer into her body, an indicator to the guides that she meant business.

Freya called out loudly. "The fuckers were trying to renegotiate their terms. I convinced them not to bother, though." Nikki nodded in response.

She glanced at her watch. The time was now 1100 hours local time. By 1600 hours, they would be ready at the first staging area. She gestured to the team to mount up.

"I hate smelly camels," Lee whispered to Scott. His camel grunted loudly as Lee gave it a sharp kick to make it stand up, which it did so jerkily, almost throwing Lee off in the process.

"I'm not sure that they like you much either, brother," Scott whispered back, eager not to give away their English, but laughing softly.

Before mounting, Nikki quickly went to say goodbye to their pilot. "Will. If anyone comes near this plane, the operation has been compromised, in which case I want you to get out of here as quickly as possible without a second glance. Freya has left Pierre, George and Philip over there to watch the plane. If someone comes, they will lay down cover fire and allow you to take off. If that's not possible, they're going to evacuate you from the plane and get you safely out of this area. Remember, control back at headquarters can and will reposition a drone which will have hellfire capability, so if necessary, you have that extra support. Clear?" she said rapidly.

"Clear, boss. Good luck," William said.

Some time into the jolted, uncomfortable camel ride, Nikki checked her Gargo watch. The time was 1330 hours. That figures, she thought to herself, as another droplet of sweat made its way from her forehead to her chin. The sun was beating down on them, if it wasn't for the climate controlled suits the heat would be excruciating. However, it would only be another two hours at this pace, then they would be able to rest up. Freya had taken the forward position behind the guides and the twins were flanking the group with Oliver taking the rear. So far, the ride had been almost silent.

Despite the heat, there was a carpet of green springs around, which seemed to disappear and then reappear as they made their way through the long expanse of desert. It was supposed to be the rainy season, though the team had yet to see even a small sign of it.

Chad measured over 500 square miles, over twice the size

of France and four times as large as the UK, and contained one of the largest lakes in the world, named Lake Chad, which had given the country its name.

As Nikki thought about all this, Oliver interrupted her, talking quietly on the comms, telling them all to check out their three o'clock. Before Nikki could turn and see, Freya had already interjected, telling them not to panic; it was only some herders pushing their cattle.

The team continued again in near silence for a further two hours, seeing nothing more than local herdsmen moving their cattle and camels. On occasion, they came across a herd of gazelles and once even a flock of ostriches passing just north of them. The midday heat had faded away to be replaced by a humid feeling as the clouds moved in overhead. Both Nikki and Freya were frequently checking their co-ordinates and, before long, they were almost upon the first staging zone. After a brief glance at Nikki, who nodded, Freya moved her camel forwards to attract the attention of the guides, telling them she wanted to stop for a rest. They shared a confused glance and told Freya in halting French that they were not yet at the campsite location that they had arranged. Freya waved her rifle in the air. The two guides immediately dismounted.

Lee and Scott did not need asking twice, quickly dismounting before taking up defensive positions, covering the team. Freya waved the rifle at the guides again and they both dropped to their knees with their arms above their heads. Nikki pulled out some tie restraints and quickly tied both of their wrists. "The illegal German hunter charade is going to be pretty hard to keep up," Nikki said to Freya, gesturing towards the girls who had taken off their nomadic dresses to reveal HK416s.

Freya spoke to them in their native language, explaining what would happen to them if they didn't follow their strict orders. They barely responded, obviously terrified.

Nikki quickly scanned the area. They were in perfect shrubland with a high vantage point, which meant that they could see for miles to both the north and south. Satisfied, Nikki announced, "This is where we will lie up for recon." The team jumped into action. Mike and Billie unloaded the Pelis from the camels and began to set up their temporary camp. Emily got out the satellite phones, dialling in some numbers before handing one to Nikki so she could contact base.

"Alpha One to Control, come in. Over," Nikki said down the phone.

"Control to Alpha One, go ahead," came Antonietta's voice immediately in response.

"Alpha One to Control, just confirming that we have reached the first staging point. Are we still green for go? Over?" Nikki asked.

"Control to Alpha One, we confirm. Status is still green for go. Over," Antonietta replied.

"Roger that, Alpha One. Out." Nikki signed off and handed the phone back to Emily.

Amanda and Oliver were helping Freya secure the camels on a long leash so she could take them back to the airfield along with the guides. They had decided that this would be the best strategy, keeping the camels close rather than letting them loose. If someone had found them, they may have begun to ask questions, so it would be simpler to take them in another direction, at least until the mission was over.

Nikki went over to Freya to say her goodbyes. "Thanks for your help, Freya. I will be in touch again soon, I promise."

"Be safe, my friend," Freya said with her French accent. "Invite me over when you're back, yes?"

"You be safe too. Of course you can come, Vincent would love to see you again. He really appreciates everything you do for us." Nikki kissed both of her cheeks before Freya mounted the camel to make the long journey back to the airfield.

"Bye Nikki. Goodbye everyone, good luck!" Freya shouted to the team. Oliver gave her a quick one-fingered salute and the girls smiled at her, giving a wave as she turned to go.

"What a woman," Oliver said. "Respect for bringing us all the way out here."

"Team, rest up for thirty before Amanda and Oliver start the recon."

The sun was nearly down by the time Oliver and Amanda had painted their faces with jungle camouflage, ready to make the short journey through the scrub to recon the terrorist camp. The sky was orange with the setting sun, the temperature dropping rapidly.

"Okay, you two. Do not take any chances. Just find an easy route in for the team, but do not engage at all, under absolutely no circumstances, unless you are under fire. Both our drones have been refuelled and the blimp will soon be in the air, so we will know if anyone is around and decides to take a look. Good luck," she said, sending them on their way.

Within a few minutes, Nikki was receiving pictures from their digital binoculars that Oliver and Amanda were relaying to her. They had managed to make the journey without a hitch and, from what she could see, they were now about 700 metres away from the camp.

"Alpha One to Alpha Two, receiving the live pictures, there's a slight delay but 10/10. Remain in your current position and we will make our way to you shortly, over," Nikki told them.

"Roger that Alpha One, staying put. Over," came Oliver's hushed reply.

It was now fast growing dark, as typical in Africa. It seemed as though one minute, the sun was up and beaming, then the next it had disappeared. Tonight was no different.

Soon, the only light that would remain to the team would be the moonlight.

Scott and Lee led the way. The Peli cases and all the other equipment that they didn't need for the operation had been hidden. Everything else had been loaded onto the team's backs in lightweight backpacks. Nikki did not believe it was necessary to weigh the team down with twenty days worth of food rations in case something went wrong. They each had what they would need for the next six hours and that was all that mattered. Mike covered the team's rear as they made their way slowly and quietly to join Oliver and Amanda, who did not move their eyes from the camp, while constantly relaying the images back to the operations room in Gozo. They were recording any relevant movements to see if any patterns were emerging amongst the terrorists but it appeared that, other than disappearing off for pisses and eating food from an open fire, there was a distinct lack of organised patrols. However, Nikki knew from past experience that you could never underestimate your opponent. Always treat them as if they had the same discipline and training as you, then they can never surprise you. The Kalashnikovs that they all carried had as much capacity to kill as the high-tech weaponry that the team held.

They all lay down on their stomachs, surrounding the two already in place, and asked for an update. The main thing that Oliver and Amanda had noted was that the guards on the front entrance were repeatedly opening the doors and making conversation with someone on the inside, without entering, which led the team to believe that there were hostiles inside the building, exactly as they had anticipated that there might be.

"They also keep throwing some things into a hole around the side of the building. I've tried to get a look at it, but because the light has faded I can't tell what it is. Looks pretty big. It's probably only rubbish, but might be worth a look," Oliver said to Nikki. She took the binoculars off him and tried to look at where he was pointing, but the hole was concealed by the building. She handed the binoculars back without a word. She had a bad feeling about that pit, which she immediately chose not to ignore. Her instincts had never let her down before.

The team started to take up their positions. "I'm cutting all communication, team. This is what all our training has been about. Good luck. Remember everything I've told you," Nikki said, cutting the communications. Mike and Emily began to pull their equipment out of their backpacks, ready for their roof descent. Nikki counted the guards and made it six in total at the front entrance, with four making irregular and brief perimeter checks. The remainder were in a small building adjacent to the main building, which would presumably be acting as Senaullah's accommodation. Though the mission would have gone ahead without Senaullah being present, Vincent felt it would be more beneficial if they could capture him alive, especially considering all the intelligence he would be able to provide them. Before a few seconds had passed, a three vehicle convoy was making its way towards the camp. Speak of the devil, Nikki thought. She gestured to the team to halt all preparations as she watched the scene play out before her.

About sixteen men climbed out of the three cars. Nikki's heart sank, thinking of more people to take out, sending up a silent prayer that they would leave. There were some initial greetings and customary shots were fired up into the air, breaking the silence. After some loud, rowdy chatter and more pointless gunfire, most of the men climbed back into two of the three cars and drove away from the camp, sending up a shower of dust and dirt. Senaullah himself, the leader of the terrorist organisation, along with three of his men, now made his way towards the little outbuilding. Nikki watched to see what would happen next when suddenly her attention was drawn back to the main building. A short scream had erupted from the main building as three small girls were dragged out by two of the guards. The scream was met with a cuff around her head by one of the guards. Nikki felt Amanda's body tense next to her. Please don't do anything to them, oh god, please. They were not in a position where they could bring the strike time forward. The five shadows disappeared into the outbuilding where Senaullah had made his residence and Nikki quickly gestured to the team to get into position.

The twins were soon in position on the high ground surrounding the camp, providing all-round sniper cover of both buildings, the campfire and the road into the camp. The only blind spots to the two snipers were the east and north of the hostage building, which would account for approximately three hostiles. Nikki's team would cover the north building, which was the breach point, and Emily was responsible for anything on the east. Nikki quickly ran over everything in her head one final time.

Everywhere is covered, she thought to herself. It's almost show time.

CHAPTER 13

SHOWTIME

Antonietta and Vincent stared at the large screens which made a 180-degree arc in the operations room which were all displaying live images of the team, the breeze block building, the GS550 parked in the disused airfield and the surroundings of the terrorist camp. Antonietta had been up early making sure all the satellite data was correct and also to make sure that the US Marines were in position to launch the aerostat surveillance blimp which was now hovering 10,000 feet above Ganye, giving everyone present in the operations room real time surveillance.

Vincent looked around at the people filling the room. Jodie was staring wide-eyed at the screen, having jumped at the opportunity to watch the team in action. Vincent knew she had barely slept last night following the excitement of the simulation; she had been training with Kerry and Gichin again all day, which she referred to as 'another episode of Karate Kid'. Kerry had declined, wanting to catch up with her friends over video chat. Vincent had known she wouldn't come, having found the simulation experience far too real. She had always preferred being told what had happened the next day, contrasting enormously with Jodie, who liked to be in the front seat for all the action. Gichin was also present, having accepted

Vincent's invitation to watch the team whom he had personally trained. Saxby and Steve had joined them too. Steve had made contact with the Delta 2.1 team in Diffa, Niger, who were only a thirty-minute flight from the hostages. This eight-man SAS unit were operating with two Eurocopters and at exactly 22.35 hours they would take to the air to provide escape for Nikki's team, then fly them across the border to the disused airfield to meet with the GS550 which would be fuelled and ready to go to bring the team back to Gozo. Steve was personal friends with the leader of the team, Mattie Smith, as they had been on several operations together. Mattie had assured Steve that the men were ready to go. Some of the screens also displayed live feeds from the Germans who were watching, as well as the PM and Tim who were logged on at Hereford.

"How we doing with the White House?" Vincent asked Antonietta.

"I just gave them the link, they're logging on now," she replied, keeping her eyes fixed on the screen. "They will be patching through in five."

Vincent had relaxed now that he knew the team were in position, having been uncompromised so far. This was the part that they were good at, the part that they had all been training so long for. Their communications were top drawer and the intelligence was all real time. Vincent knew he could be on the lookout for anything that might go wrong, in which case he could immediately evacuate the team.

Another screen fluttered into life and revealed the American President, Baker, who was now watching their live feeds. Vincent stood. "Good evening, all. No need for introductions I'm sure. Our team is now ready to go, so we are going to relay all the live images. We will have time for any necessary discussions afterwards," Vincent said in a business-like tone, knowing full well he wouldn't hear any response as

Antonietta had muted all audio. Vincent took his seat again and watched as the blimp, now in position above the terrorist camp, began to relay clear images. The operation was now underway; Vincent only had eyes and ears for his team.

Watching the screens, Vincent could see that they had moved in. He watched as his son silenced one hostile on the north side of the building with his knife, simply placing one hand over his mouth and allowing the blade to do the rest. Billie did the same with another hostile on the west side, two taken down with no shots fired.

Emily and Mike had taken out two hostiles on the east side before clambering quickly, but silently, onto the roof, ready for their descent. The twins were watching it all unfold from their vantage point and Vincent could see their fingers poised and ready on the trigger as they scanned the area incessantly. The six guards watching the entrance had now become five, as one had joined six others sat around the campfire just a few feet away from the entrance. They seemed oblivious to the fact that several of their friends were dead.

"Wait," Vincent said to Antonietta as she shifted one of the cameras to focus on a different part of the operation. "Go back." He exhaled. "Please tell me that that's not a grave." Antonietta zoomed in on the place that Vincent was pointing at and turned to Vincent, saying nothing. He looked away from her and felt a lump in his throat. Distracting himself, he turned to look at the small building where he knew Senaullah was. Nikki and Amanda were there and had positioned three canisters of sleeping gas just inside the doorway. Oliver and Billie had also placed two canisters each at the north-west side of the entrance and the north-east to allow for any sudden wind changes, which would most certainly take out the five guards. They had also placed the C4 for the breach and inserted the cameras into the side of the buildings to see where the hostiles were positioned.

Vincent could see that the campfire was going to be an obstacle, as they hadn't had one in their simulated practices. However, from the sounds of the minimal communication between the team, the twins and Mike would make short work of them.

"Drones are ten minutes out and the extraction team is in the air," Antonietta said to Vincent.

"It's all in Nikki's hands now," Vincent said, leaning back in his chair. All the team were now waiting for was the green light as they surrounded the building, unseen by any of the hostiles.

"This is Alpha One to all teams, status check. Over," Nikki's voice came over the monitor.

"Oscar One in position, campfire hostiles to the west are mine. Over," Lee replied.

"Oscar Two in position, campfire hostiles to the east are mine. Over," Scott said.

"Sierra Two in position and ready to breach, three hostiles on front entrance are mine. Over," came Mike's voice; Vincent watched on the screens as he tightened his bindings one final time.

"Sierra One, in position and ready to breach, two hostiles on the north wall are mine. Over," Emily replied.

"Alpha Two, charges in place for breach and I will cover Emily. Over," Oliver replied, with the switch detonator in his hand, ready to go.

"Alpha Four, in position, ready for breach. I will cover Mike. Over," said Billie.

"Alpha Three, in position for extraction of hostages. Over," replied Amanda.

Everyone was ready to go. It was now only seconds away. The time was now 2254 hours. The gas would go off in one minute.

"This is Alpha One to all team members, mask up and stand by. Wait for my signal."

Vincent had his hands clasped tightly together and was leaning almost out of his seat. Jodie gripped her knees with her hands and felt like screaming to break the silence. Antonietta and Damian continued tapping and zooming on their drone images and were busy checking the team's bios and making sure everything was under control. They didn't have time to feel nervous.

It was almost time to go. The screens in the ops room had a red tint bordering them, meaning that the team had red for 'hold' displayed on their watches.

The minute was up. "The gas has worked Vincent; the three hostiles on the entrance are down and the small building looks asleep to me," Antonietta informed Vincent.

"Alpha One to all teams, one minute to go. Over."

The final countdown began on one of the screens, which would be displayed on all of the team's watches.

Five.

Four.

Three.

Two.

One.

"Green for go, I repeat, green for go!" Nikki's voice screamed as the screen lit up green.

Vincent didn't know where to look as the team flung into action. The breach explosion caused a huge blast around the rear of the building; the phutt phutt sounds of Lee and Scott's snipers seemed to surround them, taking out the campfire hostiles before training their scopes on the small outbuilding. Nikki, Amanda and Billie breached the breeze block building and Mike had breached the roof, taking down two hostiles inside.

"Sierra Two, I have two hostiles down but one is missing," Mike yelled down the comms over the din, obviously frustrated.

"Sierra Two, this is Alpha Four, I took down your hostile for you. Over," came Billie's voice.

"This is Sierra One, I have two hostiles down but my bindings are stuck, I need someone to cut me down!" came Emily's slightly panicked voice.

"Sierra One this is Sierra Two, I've got you." And with that, Mike cut Emily's bindings and attempted to break her fall as she landed heavily in the building. The screaming from the hostage children was deafening, and the operations room were having trouble hearing the team over that noise added to the sound of the Chinooks landing outside.

Alpha and Sierra began trying to extract and calm the screaming and sobbing children from the main building through the enormous hole created by the explosion to evacuate them to the waiting Chinooks. The ceiling had almost completely fallen apart following Mike and Emily's breach, providing a little more light from the moon, which allowed Vincent to see slightly more of what was going on. He looked to the infrared images being relayed by the blimp and could see Billie, Oliver and Emily sitting the children down into groups, ready for a quick dash to the waiting Chinooks.

"The medics are now arriving, Vincent," Antonietta said. He saw Oliver raising his hands to make the children stand up, quickly ushering them in the direction of the medics. Some of the children were sobbing, but most of them were stunned into silence, following the orders given gently but forcefully by the team. Vincent could see Amanda doing a final sweep of the building, popping an extra round into each of the hostiles.

"Alpha Three, this is Oscar One, you missed one, to your seven o clock," came Lee's voice over the comms. Amanda turned quickly and fired off two rounds, taking down the injured man struggling to reach for his Kalashnikov. She gave a quick wave towards the vantage point where the twins were hidden in thank you.

"Alpha One to Alpha Three, come and take over from me with the children, I need to go and secure the package. Over," Nikki said, heading in the direction of the small building to check for Senaullah.

"Oscar Two to Alpha One, I will provide cover for you. Over," Scott said.

"Alpha One to Control, have you got some thermal images from inside the small building? I don't want to go in there unaware. Over," Nikki said.

"Alpha One, we have thermals on five targets and three non-hostiles we think, but cannot confirm. Assume they are hostiles, I repeat, assume they are hostiles. Over," Antonietta instructed.

"Copy," Nikki said as she booted open the door which landed with a crash and threw a flash bang which exploded immediately. She shielded her eyes against the sudden light.

The operations room watched as the first Chinook disappeared out of view into the air, carrying some of the one hundred children to take them into the safe hands of the Red Cross and then to their parents who had been long awaiting their safe return.

CHAPTER 14

THE PIT

After the flash bang went off, and her eyes adjusted to the darkness, Nikki entered the outbuilding, ducking low, covered by the dust which had erupted. She immediately identified Senaullah's unconscious body; without thinking she popped a round into each of the other sleeping men . Grabbing Senaullah by the scruff of his neck, she hauled his huge mass out of the small building.

"Oscar Two to Alpha One, need a hand boss?" Scott asked.

"Alpha One to Oscar Two, I'm going to dump this piece of shit near the fire, you can bring it with you when you move. Over." she replied, disgustedly. "If it moves, put a round in its legs. But don't kill it. They'll be wanting to surf him when we get back," she added quickly.

Nikki went back into the building, knowing that there were more people present than the ones she had killed, having watched the three girls be dragged into this building earlier. She squinted against the darkness and the dust. The smoke had almost disappeared; she could just make out a shape in the far corner of the room. She moved towards it, slowly.

The shape became three small bodies, which had been piled on top of each other. Blood was still seeping onto the ripped dress of the body on the top of the pile, which was lying awkwardly, as though it had been thrown. Nikki took a deep breath and swallowed the bile which had made its way into her mouth. She took a few steps closer and turned the body over. A small girl, perhaps only seven or eight years old, stared at her with unseeing eyes. Her black platted hair, stiff from dirt, hung limply around her face, her mouth open in a silent scream. Nikki took in the sight of her, swallowing another mouthful of bile and checking the girl's wrist for a pulse. Nothing showed. She placed her arms under the dead girl's body and lifted her small weight gently, placing her carefully on the ground. The girl underneath her still had a face wet with tears, but as Nikki checked her pulse, she knew that this girl too was no longer alive. Nikki's throat closed. She carried this girl from the third body, placing her next to the first girl, thinking that she couldn't take anymore. As she lifted the last girl's arm to check her pulse, she saw the girl's finger twitch. A small pump of blood was still making its weak way around this girl's body. Nikki felt herself go light headed, quickly picking up the girl and cradling her in her arms. The girl's eyes flitted open and she stared at the ceiling.

Nikki moved quickly out of the building carrying the girl, "Medic! Medic! I need a medic, now!"

"Alpha One, Sierra One, I'm on my way," came Emily's response.

The blood from the lacerations on the girl's body had covered her clothes and had spread warmly onto Nikki's arms. Emily arrived and glanced at Nikki, who could not meet her eye. She took the small girl off Nikki and gently set her down on the ground attempting to stop her wounds from bleeding, covering the small girl in bandages. "Nikki, she's going to be fine. She's lost a lot of blood, but we will be able to get her on a drip where she can be properly treated. She's going to be fine."

Emily took the girl once she'd done the best she could with her and sprinted away at full speed towards the waiting Chinook, giving frantic instructions for a drip.

The other two aren't so lucky. Emily returned and they both entered the small building, gently picking up one of the girls each. They took them to near the campfire, which was still burning itself away into embers, laying out some black, zip-up body bags. They had hoped they would not have to use them.

Nikki could faintly hear Antonietta telling her that their lift had now arrived. Looking up, sure enough, the helicopters circled the air above them. One thing stuck in her mind; she had to know what was in that pit behind the building, because she now believed she knew.

She stood in an almost dream-like state and made her way to the back of the breeze block building. She could not even get close, as the stink of death overwhelmed her. She retched. Eight, maybe ten, naked children's bodies had been flung into a pit. Her eyes watered as she thought about the body that they had watched the fuckers throw in, thinking that it was rubbish.

"Nikki," came Emily's voice from just next to her, though she hadn't seen or heard her approaching. "Vincent's on the Sat for you, says it urgent."

Nikki took the sat phone from Emily. "Vincent, what is it, what's wrong with the comms?"

"Come on Nikki. We have to go. There's nothing more we can do here."

"OK, it's your call Vincent. I'll see what I can do." Nikki tossed the sat phone back to Emily.

"Control to Alpha One, do you copy?!" Antonietta said. Nikki wondered how many times she had asked.

"Go ahead, Control," Nikki answered weakly, turning slowly to walk with Emily to where their lift had now landed.

"You have visitors approaching from the south. It looks like the same party from earlier, the two vehicles. They probably heard some noise and are coming back to check it out. I am deploying the drones now," Antonietta answered.

"Do we need to worry about them getting here?" Nikki asked, suddenly concerned for her team's safety.

She could hear Antonietta's smile. "No, Alpha One. Absolutely not."

"Alpha One to all teams, pack up. Our lift is here." She circled her arm around her head to indicate to everyone who could see her that it was time to go. The twins were already running down from their high ground.

"Thank fuck we don't have to go back on those shitty camels," Lee said to Scott.

"I honestly don't know what's wrong with you, Lee," Scott replied, voice dripping with sarcasm. "You get a nice mini vacation, with a few camel excursions, and all you do is moan! Civvies would pay a fortune for this shit."

"You're a wanker."

The second Chinook disappeared into the midnight air, taking the last of the kidnapped children with it. As it disappeared off to the east, Nikki saw flames erupting from the ground about four clicks south of them. Visiting time is over, she thought to herself, knowing Antonietta had deployed the drones as promised and that group of terrorists wouldn't be worrying them anymore.

She headed over to the helicopter waiting for her and the rest of the team and climbed aboard. "You okay, ma'am?" the sergeant said.

"Oh please don't call me ma'am," she said, though she had a smile on her face. "I'm Nikki." She extended a hand and he took it, giving an apologetic smile.

"Oscar team and Sierra team, chopper one, Alpha team,

chopper two. I want Senaullah on chopper two with me. I want some one to one time with this one."

Lee and Scott carried Senaullah's still unconscious body over to the helicopter where Nikki was waiting; she and the sergeant pulled his dead weight on board. "You sure, Nikki?" Scott asked her, sounding disappointed. "Lee and I were wanting to drag him through the trees all the way back."

"Scott, you're not funny. Chopper one, now!"

Emily, Mike, Scott and Lee boarded the other Eurocopter and Nikki could hear greetings and laughter as they saw friends that they recognised from previous missions. They all hugged each other, celebrating the success of another mission. Before long they were up in the air. Nikki slumped in her seat, staring at Senaullah who lay on the floor in front of her with pure revulsion. Oliver was chatting away to some of the SAS guys and Amanda and Billie were helping each other struggle out of their backpacks and headgear.

"Fuck me. Look at my hair!" Billie exclaimed, obviously trying to gain the attention of the two rather attractive SAS men. "You'd think Toni might design something we could carry as a brush after all the explosion and rubble shit."

Everyone burst out laughing except Oliver, who stared at the two guys with warning in his eyes. "Don't be fooled. She's hard bloody work."

Nikki sat, unable to join in with the jokes and laughter, wrestling with her conscience as Senaullah began to stir. She couldn't shake the images of the two dead girls, which had imprinted themselves in the back of her brain, the pit containing the bodies of too many innocent children. In one swift movement, she made her mind up, standing up and grabbing the last two grenades from Oliver's belt.

"Nikki, what you doing?!" Oliver shouted.

"A change of plan, that's all," Nikki smiled calmly. She

pulled Senaullah up to his feet and stared into his eyes, which had grown wide with fear. "Take us higher please!" she yelled to the pilots. She ripped the tape from Senaullah's mouth. "You going to tell us anything we need to know?" she asked him pointedly. When he didn't respond, she viciously thrust her knee into his crotch. He doubled over in pain and groaned. "Would you give us any information if we tortured you, you son of a bitch!" she screamed.

Senaullah didn't respond, apart from hurling spit right into Nikki's face. She wiped it away with a smile. "Just what I thought."

She dragged him over to the sliding door of the helicopter and pulled it open, allowing the cool air to enter the helicopter, which rushed around them. She stuffed the two grenades down the back of his shirt, but not before pulling the pins. She pushed them down and stared into his eyes. "This is for the little girls who won't be making it home." As he opened his mouth to scream, she violently shoved him over the threshold between him and the night sky. She closed her eyes after watching him disappear in the darkness, slamming the sliding door shut again and wiping the spit from her face with the back of her hand. The boom of the distant grenades exploding seemed to emanate around the silent helicopter for minutes. Then everyone looked away from Nikki and continued to chat, as though nothing out of the ordinary had happened.

Nikki slumped back in her seat and closed her eyes. It didn't seem long before they had disembarked the helicopter and were on the warm, comfortable GS550, heading back to base. The team were all tucking into Jodie's pre-packed flight meals of chicken penne pasta in a rich creamy sauce as Oliver was sorting through the well-stocked bar. It was only now that Nikki allowed herself to breathe a sigh of relief. After losing Becci on the last mission, she could not describe how good it felt to have her team safely around her. She stood up to attempt a debrief, but fatigue took her and she resigned to joining everyone for a beer.

"We just saved nearly one hundred young girls."

"I can't believe how well that went!"

"Emily, I was so scared when your bindings failed! Holy shit!"

"The way you took out that guy when he was standing just behind me, how did you even do that?!"

Nikki stood listening to the excited post-mission chatter. She simply turned to everyone, who immediately stopped talking. Silence fell. "To Becci," she said, quietly.

Everyone raised their glass. "To Becci."

CHAPTER 15

A LONG DAY

After terminating the live links to Germany and the White House, Vincent received congratulations from the PM.

"Fantastic Vincent! Congratulations! What a team you have there, aye, what a team. If only we could give you the recognition you deserve, but you want this to remain off the books, as usual?"

"Yes please," Vincent said respectfully.

"Of course, if that's what you want. And you'll return Senaullah in one piece so they can do some questioning at MI6? They seem to think they might be able to get some information out of him, though I'm not convinced. We will make it clear to the media, though, that he was killed at the camp, to avoid awkward questions."

"Yes, as soon as the team get back, we will get him on a secure plane headed straight for you. I'll keep in touch."

As soon as Vincent had said his goodbyes, Antonietta grabbed him by the arm and said, "Vincent, you have a missed call off Jen and a text saying it's urgent."

Vincent grabbed the phone off her, dialled the number and said, "Jen, what's up?"

"Please tell me you've seen the local news! I know you're

busy, and I want to know how the mission went, but I think you need to see what's going on!"

Antonietta heard and was already switching to the news channel on the biggest of the screens filling the room. A news reporter was standing at the sea front at Mgarr speaking Maltese, but the caption underneath read in English: 'TWO DIVERS TRAPPED IN XLENDI FERRY WRECK'.

It was so rare for there to be diving incidents around Gozo, though it was massively popular for both novice and experienced divers, being one of the top five destinations in the world. It was generally a very safe area... but this particular wreck had sunk in 1999, coming to rest seventy to eighty feet down, had rolled upside down before landing on the sea bed and had caused many of the few incidents that had occurred in the past.

Vincent quickly picked up his phone again, dialled a short number and spoke quickly to the person on the other end, asking for more information on the bulletin. He could hear Saxby in the background quietly asking Steve, "I don't get it, what does this have to do with Vendicare?" He hushed her so that he could hear Vincent's conversation.

Vincent listened to the person on the other end patiently, until at one point he couldn't contain himself. "You have to be joking?! Who do you think we are! Thunderbirds!?" he shouted down the phone, before throwing it on the table. He took a deep breath in an attempt to calm himself.

"Do you dive?" he said bluntly, turning to look at Steve.

Steve took a breath. "I'm sorry boss. I would have joined the SBS if I could," he replied apologetically.

Vincent turned to Saxby. "You?"

"Level Three Dive Leader. You had to be for the Seals," she said.

Vincent turned to Jodie who was still sat, pale faced, but

he could see her fingers crossed. She was staring hard at him. He knew she also had a Level Three and was a competent diver, having trained her personally. He battled with himself, before turning to Antonietta.

"Antonietta, get me a chopper in the air in five while we get our gear together. We're going to have to drop into the water from the helicopter. The divers must only have about twenty to thirty minutes of oxygen left." He turned to Saxby, then to Jodie. "You two are coming with me." He didn't need to ask twice. They both rose and all three ran as quickly as they could from the operations room to the stores to collect wetsuits and all the necessary gear, planning to change on the helicopter. If they didn't go now, their mission would become a recovery rather than a rescue.

"There's no time for equipment checks. Grab everything you need. Get spare tanks for the trapped divers. We need to go, now," Vincent instructed them. They took what they needed and ran to the waiting helicopters. A flight technician, one of Vendicare's longest serving, was waiting for them with the helicopter ready to go, explaining that all of the pilots were either on the mission or on standby for the team's return. Jodie, Saxby and Vincent threw their gear into the helicopter and climbed on board.

"That's absolutely fine. Get us to Mgarr, just off the ferry quay, where the old Xlendi ferry wreck is. Do you know where I mean?" Vincent shouted while putting in his comms and pulling his wetsuit on.

Wilson pulled the helicopter into the air and hurtled at full speed towards the wreck. "I sure do, I dive there often myself. It's a nightmare, full of subsidence. They need to close it off, it's always been too bloody dangerous. Only a matter of time before something like this happened." Maybe they will now. "We'll be there within three to four minutes, boss."

Vincent checked behind him and saw the girls almost geared up. Saxby was just helping Jodie put her comms in, as she had never used them before, and explained them to her briefly. Jodie was nodding her head feverishly and taking it all in. Once they'd finished, Vincent attempted to brief them over the noise of the helicopter and the wind rushing all around them. "A party of six divers went to check out this wreck. The instructor, some English lad apparently, headed to the surface for help after two of his divers, a brother and a sister, got trapped when the ferry wreck suddenly moved. By the time we reach them, they're only going to have five, ten minutes of air left, so we need to act quickly. Jodie, you haven't done a heli-drop before, I know, but it's easy. I'll go first, then you, then Saxby. Just step off backwards and hold your spare tank outwards." She acknowledged his instruction with a nervous smile. Saxby nodded.

"One minute to destination," Wilson shouted back at them.

"Follow my lead and under no circumstances go too close to the stranded divers until I give you my signal. They will be in a panic and might grab for you." He opened his bag and gave them each three Cyalume flares. He then turned the lights and comms on his face mask on and indicated for them to do the same. He looked out of the window. "That's great, Wilson, just where that buoy is. Hold it steady, here. Go as far down as possible. Okay, great." Vincent pulled the Eurocopter's sliding door open and instantly everyone was met with a sudden gush of salty air and water sprayed up from the sea. The swell was huge, the rotation of the air surrounding the helicopter turning the water almost into a whirlpool. They were only seven or eight feet away from the sea. Vincent stepped to the edge of the helicopter, pulled his mask over his face and dropped backwards. He hit the water and instantly felt the cold surround him. He took a deep breath as his body accustomed itself to the temperature of the water. His mask started to mist over but, when he put his head under the water, the heated plastic kicked into gear and the mist disappeared. Jodie landed with a loud splash next to him and made a short, sharp squeal at how cold the water was. Saxby jumped in immediately after.

"Comms check, is everyone receiving. Over?" Vincent asked.

"10/10," Saxby responded.

"Loud and clear," Jodie said.

"Let's go. Keep close," he said, disappearing under the water.

He couldn't see a thing. The water was pitch-black around them. He pulled a torch out of one of his side pockets and lit it up. They didn't have time to make a gradual descent; they needed to get to the wreck fast. Vincent wished that they had had time to set up some underwater transport, but they hadn't. This dive was going to be extremely taxing. Forty feet down, Vincent realised he could see a light in the distance and thought that the divers must have torches shining. He cracked the Cyalume flare and held it out as he swam towards the light, hoping that they would see it and know that help was on the way. The dive was hard going. Vincent could feel the pressure in his ears and the toll that the constant kicking was having on his legs.

Antonietta, Damian and Steve back in the ops room were listening to their comms and monitoring the bios on the screen, but had no visuals on the group as they had not had time to get them up and running. They all anxiously stared at the screen, hoping and praying that they would be able to rescue these two divers. Feeling utterly useless, Antonietta was keeping a close eye on Jodie, whose heartrate was far higher than her usual exercising rate. Antonietta watched, she heard Vincent say over the comms, "I have a visual on the two divers. One appears to be moving, but I can't get a lock on the other. I am going to circle around and come behind the one that is nearest to me. Jodie and Saxby, I need you to check out the other diver. Please be careful. Antonietta, if you can hear me, get the decompression chamber ready." Vincent knew that they would be monitoring their progress. They had two decompression chambers on the island; one at the main hospital and one at Vendicare's base. Vincent, knowing his team did a significant amount of diving, had installed a hyperbaric chamber, sparing no cost, and now sent up a silent prayer of thanks that he had done so.

He came slowly around to the side of the diver. She had seemed to be moving wildly from a distance, but now had slowed her movements. Vincent could see she was still breathing, but perhaps had fallen unconscious from lack of air, or was conserving her remaining oxygen by limiting her movements. All of a sudden, as he got closer to her, she opened her eyes and saw him, wildly making a grab for him, flailing her arms and legs, doing exactly what Vincent did not want her to do. He was not close enough to see her air gauge to tell how much oxygen she had left, but if she didn't calm down soon, she would use what little she had in no time. Knowing that sign language would take too long to mime out, and not knowing whether this girl would even be able to understand what he was saying, he pulled a purposely designed underwater LCD tablet from his belt and held it up in front of the girl's eyes.

"Antonietta, I need you to sign into my Ultra tablet and communicate with the girl. I need you to tell her to relax and breathe calmly to conserve her oxygen, then keep talking to her to distract her while I take a look at her feet and see what's trapping her," Vincent said over his comms and he handed the girl the tablet and pulled his gloved fingers into an 'OK' symbol. Her eyes were wide with panic, but she took the tablet and read the words on the screen.

Antonietta's voice came back over the comms. "I've written that if she understands what I've said, she needs to give you the thumbs up. Has she understood everything?" Vincent looked up and the girl was slowing her breathing and starting to take small, regular breaths. When she saw him looking, she gave him a thumbs up. Vincent relaxed and said, "Saxby, how's it going, how's the diver?"

"He's... barely alive, Vincent. I think he has run out of air. Jodie has connected the spare tank and I'm trying to free him from the debris. We need to get him out of the water as soon as possible."

"Get him up to the surface now; leave Jodie with me in case I need a hand," he said, checking the girl's air gauge, which showed only twenty bars. Only four minutes to work with.

"Roger that."

"Antonietta, keep talking to the girl. Tell her everything is going to be fine, she will be home for dinner, anything to relax her, while I take a look at what is trapping her." Vincent cracked another flare and rolled his body, kicking his flippers to get him down to the girl's feet.

Saxby's voice came over his comms. "I've freed the male diver; Jodie and I are just pulling together a surface plan."

"Okay great, keep it up." Vincent stared at the girl's legs, looking at the twisted way in which her ankle had got caught. It didn't seem as bad as he'd first thought. It seemed as though she had stood on some rotten wooden flooring which had given way and she was now trapped just below the knee. "Antonietta, I'm going to free her now. Warn her it might hurt a bit. Tell her not to kick at all; I will have her out within two minutes."

Jodie suddenly appeared at his side, telling him that Saxby was making her way to the surface with the other diver and asking him what he wanted her to do. Her Gerber serrated knife was already in her hand. They began to cut away at the rotten wood together, with Vincent trying to manoeuvre the wood around her knee. "I think if we can just free her by a few millimetres on either side, despite the swelling, we should be able to pull her free." Vincent left Jodie to work on the wood and swam up so the girl could see him. He pointed at her mouthpiece, then held two fingers in the air, indicating that she had two minutes of air left. He then showed her the spare tank that he had with him. "Antonietta, I need you to tell her that I'm going to switch the two tanks, so I need to swap mouthpieces without her panicking." A few seconds later, the girl gave him the thumbs up, obviously having understood what Antonietta had told her via the Ultra tablet.

"She should be free now," Jodie said over the comms. "I am going to try and pull her leg out. Keep her still."

Vincent took both of her hands and indicated that he wanted her to hold him tight around the waist. He could see in her wide eyes how terrified she was. He knew how she felt. The claustrophobic feeling when something goes wrong while diving was terrifying when there was little or no light... he shook off the feeling, knowing he needed to focus on this rescue mission.

"Okay, she's free, but she has a piece of splinter stuck right through her leg. I don't want to pull it out in case it's gone through the bone."

"That's fine, leave the splinter. We can deal with that when we are on land. It's time to go. We need to get to the surface, fast. Hold onto her tight and we will gradually let her up. We are going to need to stop every ten or so feet so that she can decompress." They began to make their way up and every time they stopped Vincent would give her the thumbs up and smile to try to keep her relaxed. The water around them was starting to turn a muddy-red colour from the blood seeping from the girl's wound; Vincent indicated to the girl to keep her eyes on the surface, hoping that she wouldn't see the blood.

A few minutes later, they surfaced and the cold wind hit them hard. Wilson was hovering just a few feet above them, with Saxby already on board. Vincent held the girl's chin so that she was out of the water, saying over and over again, "Everything is going to be fine, everything is going to be fine." Saxby lowered the winch from the cabin and Vincent clipped the hook onto his belt, holding the girl tightly to him. They lifted out of the water and Vincent could feel the girl shaking violently against him. Once she was safely on board, Saxby returned the winch down to the water and safely brought Jodie aboard. It seemed like an eternity before the Eurocopter's door finally slammed shut, stopping all the noise from the elements with such a sudden force that the world seemed to fall silent.

"Malta Hospital or base, boss?" Wilson asked as he pulled the helicopter upwards.

"Base. Let Antonietta know that we will definitely need the decompression chamber," Vincent replied, removing his mask and comms.

Jodie was holding the girl tightly in her arms, having removed her mouthpiece and goggles. Vincent took the few steps towards them and cut the girl's wet suit away from below the knee to get a closer look at the wound. The jagged piece of wood had not gone all the way through her leg and looked as though it may have just missed the bone. Vincent, not wanting to mess with it too much, took some bandages from the first aid kit and tied a tourniquet just above the wound to try and stop the bleeding until they could get her to their medical team. Jodie was holding the girl, who was deathly pale and breathing shallowly, whispering calm, soft words into her ear. Vincent turned away and said to Saxby in a quiet voice, so that the girl couldn't hear her, "Where's her brother?"

Saxby turned to him with tears in her eyes. Her voice shook. "I got him to the surface but I could tell he wasn't breathing. Wilson was here waiting, so I took him straight over to the ambulance crew that was waiting for us on the quay. I... I don't think he's made it, Vincent." A tear caught on her eyelashes freed itself, falling onto her cheek.

"Shit," Vincent said, putting his head into his hands.

"There's something else, Vincent. Wilson filled me in. The TV crews have been filming the whole thing. Damian was going to cut their studio feeds, but Toni thought that would make the lack of coverage all the more suspicious. She's monitoring YouTube and the other social media platforms in case someone links this rescue to Vendicare. Steve went down to the quay to stop them; he said he'd managed to pull their RF feed in the van so that they will be able to record, but won't be able to transmit their recordings. Toni is also putting in calls to the Maltese government to lean on the TV company. They told me to let you know as soon as I could."

Vincent was grateful that the team were already working on preventing any footage of the rescue from being released. It didn't matter so much if it was only Malta, but these sort of things tended to go viral and Vendicare could not be revealed to a worldwide audience. It would ruin everything. "Thanks for letting me know. I know Antonietta and Damian will do everything they can to stop any footage of us getting out."

"Steve also got some intelligence while he was on the quay from the dive group they had been with. This girl with us now, her name is Molly. She's twenty-two, a medical student at Preston Royal Infirmary. She was staying at the beach hotel Marsalform with her brother, who brought her on this dive with Preston Diving Club. He was twenty-seven... he brought her along because she needed cheering up after a recent split with her ex-boyfriend, who has apparently been stalking her ever since."

Vincent tried to take it all in. "Thanks Saxby." She nodded.

They touched down at base and the doors were being pulled open before they could even stand up. A medical team took Molly immediately to the decompression chamber, which they said was only a precautionary measure, and patched up her wound.

An hour later, Vincent, Saxby and Jodie had all changed out of their wet things into tracksuits and were waiting outside the decompression chamber to find out if Molly was going to be okay.

Saxby turned to him. "Do you want me to tell her about her brother?" she said, sombrely.

He sighed, knowing that they would not be able to avoid telling her. "If there's anyone for the job, Saxby, it's you. I'd really appreciate it. Try and let her down gently. I know she's going to be distraught, but there's nothing we can do." She nodded. "I want to thank you both. You were absolutely fantastic. If it hadn't been for you two, I know we would have been recovering two bodies on this mission."

CHAPTER 16

BLACK PUDDING

The sun was rising, illuminating the tiny island of Gozo. It was just after 0600 hours and the Eurocopter carrying the team from Malta airport had just touched down on helipad one. Vincent and Jodie were standing, having stayed up all night to welcome the team back.

Scott jumped out of the Eurocopter and saw Jodie standing there. "Jodie, get that breakfast on! I could eat my arm." Jodie simply smiled in response and ran over to Scott quickly, giving him a huge hug. "Oi, why so clingy?! I've been on loads of missions and never received a welcome like this before," he objected.

Oliver climbed out of the helicopter and looked around. "Don't suppose my dear sister is up and waiting is she?"

"Are you kidding? Haven't seen her since yesterday afternoon. She's probably still dreaming of My Little Pony," Jodie replied, laughing.

The rest of the team were climbing out of the helicopter. Vincent greeted them all with a quick embrace before telling them to all make their way to the main restaurant building as Mel had been preparing them a English breakfast buffet, knowing they would all be famished after the mission. Vincent stopped Oliver as he made his way towards breakfast and pulled him quickly into a wordless hug. Oliver pulled himself away gently and smiled brusquely at his father before they made their way together to the kitchen.

The twins and Mike had already piled their plates high with bacon, sausage, eggs, hash browns and black pudding.

"Top result, Jodie!" Lee said. "Black pudding is my favourite, where did you get it from?"

"Oh believe me," Jodie said with a touch of exasperation. "It wasn't me that got it. Sometimes I think I waste my time on my nutritional diets with you lot. Mel bought it from some town called Berry or something." She laughed.

Nikki came and sat herself down next to Vincent, carrying a lighter plate. "Everything been alright while we've been gone? I know everything falls into disrepute without us, but..." she said jokingly, but fell into silence when she saw the look on Vincent's face. "What? What is it?" she asked.

Vincent sighed and stood, knowing it would be easier to tell the team as a whole. He didn't want to go into the fine details, as he didn't want to overshadow their mission success or highlight the fatality. He gave them the headline version of the diving rescue, putting particular emphasis on how Jodie and Saxby had contributed so much to saving Molly's life. When he had finished, there was a big round of applause from the team, everyone crowding around Jodie giving her a hug. Vincent saw Scott grasp her hand and squeeze it and, for the first time ever, it seemed, Jodie was stuck for words.

"So, Molly is going to be staying on base for the time being. I know you all mean well, but please be sensitive. She is still in shock and is struggling massively with the loss of her brother," Vincent said solemnly. He sat back down, the chatter in the room rising as everyone discussed the new turn of events.

"Well done you," Nikki said to him. "Though I thought you'd hung up your diving gear?"

"Yeah, me too," Vincent said with a half-smile. Then something occurred to him. "Nikki, did everything go to plan after our chat on the sat phone?"

Nikki went quiet and drew her eyes away from Vincent's gaze, suddenly becoming engrossed with her breakfast. "He... err... I did exactly as you asked."

"Nikki? Did he give us anything?"

She looked up and stared him brazenly in the eyes. "I asked him if he had any information and he said he would never tell us anything. So I let him go, literally."

Before Vincent could process this, he felt his phone vibrating in his pocket. He looked on the screen and saw Tim's name flash up. He looked from Nikki to the phone and sighed.

"Hey, Tim. You're up early."

"So are you," he responded. "Listen Vincent. The wheels have fallen off the American mission, quite literally." It took Vincent a few seconds to understand what he meant and what he was talking about, before he remembered that their friends across the pond were mounting an operation to take out the Islamic State inner circle. He bristled briefly about the fact that he hadn't even been told the mission had started, but decided not to say anything, allowing Tim to fill him in while he sat listening silently. Nikki watched on. "I don't have all the facts yet, but at 0300 hours, several dozen US Special Operations Commandos mounted a seek and destroy mission in Northern Syria. Their intelligence suggested that a number of senior Islamic State officials, including the leader, Al-Baghdad, were meeting to arrange the overrun of the Kurdish part of Iraq. Unfortunately, this intelligence was flawed and two black hawk helicopters with fourteen Special Forces on board were shot down, killing eight, including the two pilots. There are six people unaccounted for, but Homeland Security believe Islamic State are holding them and will use them to taunt President Baker, or worse, get him to call off his strategic airstrikes. Just to make matters worse, it seems as though what brought them down was supplied by Gorelov, or the pro-Russian separatists."

Tim eventually paused for breath and Vincent took the chance to interrupt. "Is this all going to be kept under wraps, or will there be a news conference?"

"I'm under the impression that it's going to be kept classified for now while President Baker explores their options." Good, thought Vincent. That would give him a chance to take a look at the bigger picture. He saw that Oliver had now joined the table and was looking at him with an interested expression. "Tim, you'll appreciate that Nikki and the team have only just got back from the mission in Chad, so I want to debrief them and stand them down; they're still pretty wired up from the operation. But I have an idea which may work. I'll ring you later when I've slept on it." And with that, Vincent ended the call. "Oliver, get the team assembled in the briefing room in twenty minutes. That should give them a chance to finish their breakfast. Now is as good a time as any to give you all a heads-up on what's been happening in the world while you've been gone." Oliver nodded and stood up to tell the team. "Nikki, can you go wake Saxby and Steve for me and tell them the same?"

"Of course."

"Jodie!" Vincent shouted, beckoning her over. "Will you come with me to check on Molly?"

They wandered in the direction of the villa. "Have you been on your bike yet today?" Jodie asked, casually.

"Not yet. Not really sure I feel like it today."

Jodie smiled at him. "Not sure if it would be a good idea, considering what happened last time you took your bike out on the road." He smiled back.

They entered the villa where they had left Molly in one of the guest rooms to have some time to herself and get some rest, expecting for her to still be asleep, but surprisingly they found her sat downstairs on the large sofa with her knees up against her chin and her arms wrapped protectively around herself. Her hair was still wet and she stared blankly at the wall opposite her. Jodie looked to Vincent, then walked slowly over and sat next to her, putting an arm around the back of her thick white dressing gown and pulling her closely, whispering a greeting.

"Molly," Vincent said sombrely. She turned to look at him with a vacant expression on her face. "You don't need to do or say anything until you're ready, but if you want to contact anyone, just let us know. In the meantime, you're welcome to stay here as long as you need to, or as long as you want to." She turned back to the wall without a word and Vincent felt that she was more comfortable in Jodie's presence than his. He mouthed to Jodie that he ought to leave, turning. Just as he grabbed the door handle to leave the room, he heard Molly's small quiet voice pipe up for the first time.

"I don't have anyone. I don't have anyone anymore."

Vincent turned. Jodie mouthed at him, 'Just go,' and pulled Molly into a tight hug.

As he walked across the courtyard, the cold feeling Molly's words had left him with contrasted greatly with the warmth of the morning sun on his back. He knew that sensation of loss. He knew it all too well. The sympathy he felt for Molly was excruciating. His eyes began to sting; he couldn't tell if it was caused by the sunlight reflecting from the bright stones he walked on or tears.

He felt tired and emotionally drained as he entered the ops room where the team were sat waiting for him, while Saxby recounted the longer version of the diving rescue. The adrenalin keeping him awake had stopped pumping into his bloodstream; the only thing now keeping his eyes open were the double espressos he had been drinking all night.

"Everyone," he announced. They all fell silent and looked at him. "Apologies for dragging you away from your breakfast. But what I am about to tell you is something that I need you all to be on board with before Nikki and I move it up to planning." He then spent the next ten minutes giving a rundown of the current state of affairs involving Islamic State, the kidnapped news reporters and the missing Special Forces. No one uttered a word and no one moved a muscle. They all knew the exact consequences of failed intelligence; Becci's death came unbidden into everyone's thoughts. "No matter what happens, you guys are now on forty-eight hours of downtime; enjoy every last minute, as I have a feeling things are about to get pretty busy. That means no one working. Including you, Nikki!" Everyone laughed and Nikki blushed slightly. "Any questions?"

Saxby got there first. "From what you've said, it seems pretty clear that there are three specific missions and three different operations. Which one are we getting involved in?"

Vincent smiled. "All three," he said simply. Everyone's mouths dropped open, including Nikki's.

"How is that even possible?" she said.

"I'm really sorry Nikki, I didn't get a chance to discuss this with you first, I know it's all a little bit of a shock, but I've been having a really good think. Well, that's not strictly true, most of the time I'm making it up as I go along, but I think we can do it! My initial idea was that we could draft in a team from Hereford to rescue the journalist hostages, putting Steve in charge. And then we could draft in a Navy Seals team to rescue the US Special Forces hostages, putting Saxby in charge of them. And finally, but most importantly, Nikki and the team could take out Islamic State inner circle."

"Yes, I suppose that is possible, but when are we going to

find the time to do all these three one after the other?" Billie piped up.

"Well, that's what I'm saying. We do them all at the same time," Vincent said, dropping his biggest bombshell on them yet, watching their mouths drop open further accordingly.

It was Mike who ended the shocked silence. "I definitely think Hereford would go in for this; they wouldn't miss an opportunity to be involved in such a big operation. But the issue with this is the Seals. No disrespect, Saxby, but I just can't see them going in for it."

"None taken," Saxby said, before turning to Vincent. "He's right. I can't see it happening."

"Well, I don't doubt that there will be politics at play here, but they have absolutely no option if they want to come out of this saving face and saving their own hostages," Vincent replied.

"Why do we have to do the operations simultaneously? That just makes everything so much riskier," Oliver said.

Nikki interrupted Vincent as he started to explain why. She already knew the reason. "If only one operation takes place at a time, then the other two missions will already be compromised and would be impossible to complete. For example, if the American mission to rescue the Seals hostages succeeded, the journalist hostages would be put to death and vice versa."

"Couldn't have put it better myself," Vincent said, relieved, smiling that Nikki understood his train of thought. "Okay everyone, let's leave it there. Here begins your forty-eight hours of down time. Don't worry about what I've just told you, we will discuss it more in a few days time. Enjoy!" Everyone began to file out of the room, talking avidly about what Vincent had just suggested but also what they were going to do with a whole forty-eight hours of freedom. He heard Emily and Amanda mention something quickly about 'catching some rays', but smiled when he heard Oliver say something about going to go and see Kerry. "Oh, Saxby, Steve, could you just stay an extra minute or two?" he said quickly to their retreating backs.

They sat down. "Steve, once I've had a chat to Tim about what I'm thinking, I thought you could begin to pick out your team. You too, Saxby, once I've managed to put a call in to the White House. However, in the meantime, just assume that it's going to happen and brief Antonietta on what you might need satellites-wise and what chatter her and Damian will need to be on the lookout for, as we need to find the locations of each of the hostages and Islamic State before we can take any more steps. Make a plan and present it to me in the morning when we've all caught up on some sleep."

He stood up, thanking them, then made his way towards the villa. Before he collapsed onto his bed, he quickly checked in on Kerry, who was just coming round from a long sleep. Before he could say anything, she jumped up.

"How did the mission go? Is everyone okay? Is Oliver back?" she asked frantically.

So she does care, Vincent thought, though he felt immediately guilty for this thought afterwards.

"Everyone's fine sweetie. Oliver is going to come and see you at some point today, I heard him say. Everyone is fine. Jodie, Saxby and I also had to go on a little dive rescue yesterday," he said, playing down the drama of it to stop her from worrying. "There's a girl called Molly staying with us. I thought you could help Jodie keep her company. She lost her brother and she's feeling extremely lonely."

"Yeah, Dad, of course," Kerry said with downcast eyes. She knew that pain of loss too. She knew it all too well.

"Okay, great. I'm going to head off to sleep, I'm exhausted. Try to keep the noise down, yeah?" Vincent headed off to his room. Not feeling up to a conversation with Tim and the PM just now, he sent Tim a quick text.

‘Conference call at 1700 hrs GMT?’

He immediately got the reply. ‘Yes. Speak to you then.’

Vincent had intended on calling Jean to let her know how well Jodie had done on the dive mission, but then thought about what her response would be, which would involve panic and a slight scolding. He rolled over, thinking better of it, and within seconds was sound asleep.

CHAPTER 17

THE FALLEN

All was quiet around the villa and the complex. Emily and Amanda had fallen asleep by the pool, with the rest of the team hidden away in their rooms taking some well-earned rest. Antonietta and Damian had come in after lunch and were working with Saxby and Steve on locating all of the targets using the latest intelligence reports.

Saxby had been speaking with some of her contacts in Virginia Beach, where the main base for the Seals was located, but with every single one the door had been slammed in her face, so she had decided to try some of her contacts in the CIA. These efforts had proved to be slightly more fruitful, with some off-the-record comments, but she still had nothing solid to work with. It looked as though all the agencies were in the dark. You wouldn't think we were all on the same side, she ended up thinking repeatedly.

Steve had fared slightly better. He had already spoken to one of the NCOs at the newly formed SRU – Special Reconnaissance Unit – attached to the SAS and SBS, which had previously been known as the 14th Intelligence Unit, or the 'DET', whose main role had been to deal with the troubles in Northern Ireland but whose primary role now was to provide close target reconnaissance, surveillance and eyes-on intelligence to the regiment. Their state-of-the-art electronic surveillance equipment and satellite deployment with drone intelligence was almost up there with Vendicare's.

Steve put the phone down and shouted over to Saxby, "I think we might have something here! They haven't given me any information yet, but once the NCO has spoken to Tim it looks like they may have a location on the hostage journalists!"

"Steve, that's great news!" she replied.

"Well done, Steve, that's fantastic," Nikki said, surprising them both as she walked casually into the mission control room and pulled up a chair next to them. It was amazing how Nikki managed to look as though she could be on the front cover of Hello after only six hours sleep following a camel ride, a rescue mission saving a hundred kids and travelling goodness knows how many miles.

"We have something here as well!" Damian shouted excitedly from the other side of the room. They all stood up to look at what he was pointing at on his screen.

As Saxby, Steve, Antonietta, Damian and Nikki were busy doing their intelligence search, Vincent, over in his villa, came to. He stretched and sat up, blinking at the bright light that filled his room. He lifted his phone from the wireless charger and looked at the time, gasping loudly when he saw that it read 1500 hours. He hadn't slept past morning since he was a teenager, yet he felt so refreshed from having finally caught up on his sleep. He rested back against his pillows and switched the TV to the 24 hour news channel. He smiled to himself as images flashed up on the screen of the rescued children being handed packs of colouring books, sweets, juice and cuddly toys by the Red Cross and UNICEF teams. As he watched a particularly touching reunion between one of the children and her parents, he heard a soft tap on the door, which he almost hadn't heard.

He muted the television before shouting, "Come in, Kerry!"

She pushed open the door and said, "How did you know it was me?" before she ran and dived onto the bed next to him.

"I recognised your tap," Vincent said, laughing. She stared at the TV, so he turned the volume on again and they watched it together. Kerry snuggled up next to him and put her head on his chest. He kissed her gently on the forehead.

"I hope all those kids have someone to hold them like this when they get home," Kerry murmured softly. Then she sat up. "Molly's been asleep on the sofa all day, so Jodie was wondering if it was alright for us to go to the hotel together so we can collect hers and her brother's belongings."

"Of course, that's fine. Best get some money out of the safe so that we can settle their accounts for them," Vincent said amiably. It was always better to pay for things in cash, as having a paper trail by using a credit card made you traceable; you never knew who was watching. "Take the G-Wagon that's out front. There aren't any registration documents on it. I'll keep half an eye on Molly until you get back," he said. Kerry kissed him on the forehead before skipping out of the room.

It was four pm by the time Vincent emerged from his wet room. He felt fully revitalised, better than he had done in months, ready to catch up with all the latest developments on Islamic State. He made his way into the kitchen and waited for his Gaggia to heat up and dispense his coffee. He pulled out his phone and sent a short text to Jean: 'Alright if I ring you later on tonight? V x.' He then put his phone back into his pocket and looked up, only to be startled by Molly, who was stood by the large breakfast bar, staring at him.

He tried to recover from his shock so as not to alarm her, putting a smile on his face. "Coffee?" he asked casually, hoping that Jodie and Kerry wouldn't be too long. He wasn't very good at dealing with emotions.

"Yeah," she replied. "Milky. Please."

He poured the coffees and took them outside, where they both sat under the Pergola, which shaded them from the late afternoon sun. Molly, surprising Vincent, was talkative and asked questions about Jodie, the villa, wanting to find out more about Kerry and her London boarding school. Vincent felt himself relax and answered each of her questions, glad that she was opening up. A few minutes later, she fell into silence and Vincent followed suit, not wanting to fake conversation if she wasn't in the mood for talking. A few moments later she said quietly but earnestly, "Thank you for saving me, Vincent."

Taken aback, Vincent began to mumble together a response. "Don't worry about it... it was a team effort, I... it was nothing... I..." he took a deep breath. "Molly, I only wish we had heard the news a few minutes earlier. Then we may have been able to save your brother. I'm so sorry."

"Where is my brother?" she asked calmly.

"He's at the main hospital on Malta. If you want to go see him, that's absolutely no problem. Only if you feel up to it." He knew she needed to soon, as there was the matter of the formal identification and the police statements to sort out, but he knew that it would all take time for her to come around to being ready for that type of thing.

"Would you be with me?" she asked, studying the green and black grapes which hung all around them.

Vincent was startled by the question. "If you want me to be."

"I do, if that's okay," she said, leaning forward to grasp one of the grapes. "Are these for eating?"

Vincent took one of the grapes from the vine and placed it into his mouth before turning to her and nodding. A few moments later, as they both feasted on the delicious grapes that surrounded them, Vincent heard the screech of tyres from the courtyard. "That'll be Jodie," Vincent said to Molly. "She's a little heavy on the brakes." Molly smiled.

Jodie and Kerry appeared a few moments later and Vincent saw with relief that they hadn't brought any of the belongings in to show Molly. He feared that might trigger her memories and send her into grief again. Instead, Jodie came straight over to Molly, knelt in front of her and said, "We nipped into town. I've bought you some nice things that I thought might be your style! They're in your room if you want to go and have a trying-on sesh. If you want, we could go do a proper shopping trip altogether at some point."

Molly grinned in response. "Thank you so much! I'd love to!"

Vincent, already alarmed at the mention of shopping, decided to take his leave. "If you're all good, I'm going to nip over to the office. There's some paperwork to finish off," he said, getting up from the Italian solid oak table, quickly but oddly remembering the months it had taken to arrive from Naples.

"You work on Saturdays?" Molly asked, surprised.

"Mol, tell me about it, he works every bloomin' day of the week," Kerry said to a round of giggles.

"I'll be back soon, I promise. I'll cook tonight. See if you can get your brother over?" he directed at Kerry.

"You? Cook? There's something that doesn't happen every day," Jodie said and the girls giggled again.

Having taken enough of their teasing, Vincent bowed and said, "Later," before heading over to the ops room in preparation for his conference call with Tim and the PM. As he entered the room, he saw Nikki chatting away animatedly in French to a girl on the screen, who on closer inspection turned out to be Freya, while Antonietta and Damian huddled together with Steve and Saxby, looking at some data on the screens. As Vincent took a seat, waiting for Nikki to finish her conversation, Jen entered the room.

"Oh. Sorry to interrupt. Busy in here!" Jen said, waving at Nikki who quickly gave her a nod before carrying on with her conversation.

"Jen," Vincent said as she pulled up a chair next to him. "Tell me, is that Nikki's identical twin sister, or is she ignoring my request to take the weekend off?"

"Don't get me involved!" Jen said with a laugh, before winking at Nikki.

"Why are you in at the weekend anyway? You know you aren't supposed to be, I haven't called a meeting or anything, unless something's going on with VirtualTech?" Vincent asked.

"Nikki asked me to come in. She's asked for a million dollars. I'm intrigued to know what she wants it for, but I know she will have a good reason for it."

"That's news to me!" Vincent said, amused.

A few minutes later, Nikki ended the video call and Damian and Antonietta completed their satellite protocols, moving over to the board table so that they were ready for the conference link with Hereford and Number 10. As the clock counted down to going live, Vincent found himself watching the screen showing the twenty-four hours news channel. The news flashed across the screen, reading 'SECOND JOURNALIST EXECUTED BY ISLAMIC SECT, THREAT TO KILL A BRITISH THIRD.' Vincent's attention was then, mercifully, drawn away from the screen as Mike Delaney stood in the doorway caught his eye. He gave him a questioning look and Mike mouthed, 'Can I come in?' Vincent nodded and Mike pulled up a chair just out of the camera's range.

Just then the screen went blank and Damian said, "They're going to be five minutes late with the link up, Vincent. I guess they've just seen the news," he said, gesturing towards the news screen.

"I suppose it's only just happened," Nikki said.

"It's a nightmare. Social media and twenty-four hour news means that these terrorists can play their little act out in real time and our security forces can't dumb down any of the information," Vincent muttered.

Mike coughed. "My phone's been ringing constantly from MI6 this morning. They're in a real panic. My boss wanted to pull me back, but someone rightly said for me that it would never happen now that I'm here." He smiled at Vincent, who smiled back.

"Mind if I use these five minutes to just run a couple of ideas past you all?" Nikki said.

"Go ahead," Vincent said.

"Okay, so, here's the plan. We would give the illusion that we are going to give in to the terrorists and, using an intermediary, start negotiating for a hostage release just like the Belgians, French and Italians have done on several occasions. This would give us time to implement the next part of our plan. This is where we give the illusion that we are trying to rescue the hostages, but with a difference. We would pretend that we have been given wrong intelligence again and will attempt to rescue them, accidentally-on-purpose, from the complete wrong locations..."

"They wouldn't buy that though, would they?" Mike interrupted, before receiving a look off Nikki that made him wish he hadn't.

Nikki continued. "Islamic State would then be moving the hostages on a regular basis, for fear that our intelligence catches up with them. In the past, they have moved their prisoners every ten to fourteen days, so while we 'get our act together', we track all these movements. Once we are in business, we leak them fake intelligence that we are striking at one of their older locations. It doesn't matter, which, so long as it is a wrong one..."

"...so then they send all their best Jihads to attack us at the wrong venue while we hit the correct place!" Vincent finished for her enthusiastically, finally catching onto Nikki's train of thought.

"That's brilliant," Mike said.

"Does anyone have any questions?" Nikki asked, looking satisfied.

"The PM is ready for link-up, Vincent," Antonietta said, ending their discussion.

"Just, hold them for a couple of minutes if you can, Antonietta," Vincent said, wanting to finalise the idea of this plan in his head before he moved onto something else.

"How are we going to get our failed intelligence to them?" Saxby asked.

"That's where Freya comes into play; that's who I was talking to on the phone. Last year, she was responsible for negotiating the release of two French hostages and had some serious contacts on the ground. More importantly, she is trusted by some of the locals. So, we give her one million dollars to start the ball rolling, which she then offers to them. They will, of course, want more than that, as the French government through subsidiary companies paid out around a hundred million. A million will only be enough to buy us a seat at their negotiating table, but Freya will be able to gain their trust by giving them our 'intelligence', though it will be false. Then when the time would come for us to give them more money, we will already have taken all of the hostages."

"Brilliant, Nikki! Brilliant," Vincent said. "Antonietta, get the live link up now, we can't keep them waiting too long. We can discuss this more afterwards."

A few seconds later, Tim and Alistair Coombes appeared on the screen. The usual introductions ensued and the PM thanked them once again for the rescue of the kids. "Vincent, the German President has also confirmed that she will assist you in the child smuggling rings, whenever you're ready to take them out."

"Unfortunately, that's going to have to take a back seat for now, but I'm confident that it will be a top priority in the near future," Vincent said diplomatically. "Right, so Islamic State are now an immeasurable threat. I feel like the danger has now spread worldwide. I'm worried about what that might set off..."

"Also, there is of course this issue of the next execution, which is rumoured to be another American. President Baker and his band of trigger-happy generals will also be looking at all of their options."

"Don't quote me on this, Vincent, as it is classified to the highest level, but I wouldn't rule out some sort of retaliatory strike."

"That's exactly what I'm worried about, so..."

Over the next fifteen minutes or so, Vincent explained his idea of a three-pronged attack, but for the time being left out the more precise details that Nikki had just described to them. He would most likely explain it in more detail later with Tim, when he may need his assistance, but for now he was only testing the water. There was no point bogging them down with masses of information. The PM listened to Vincent's proposal with a small frown on his face, as though he was having to concentrate hard. Tim's face was far easier to read; he looked interested.

"The most important thing in all this is that you, Alistair, speak to President Baker and get the green light off him to use the Seal team that Saxby has recommended to us. Everyone seems convinced that we aren't going to be able to get American involvement, but I reckon we can do it."

"For my part," Tim put in, speaking for the first time, "I'm absolutely fine for Steve to pick and lead this eight-man team from the regiment. And if Baker buys into it, we can get this show on the road as soon as possible."

The PM was proving slightly more difficult to sway. "Excuse me, I will have to come back to you. There's a call I must take." And, with that, Coombes stepped out of the room.

"I'm pretty much one hundred percent that President Baker's National Security Council won't sanction this kind of operation, but we may as well let Coombes give it his best shot," Tim said in a quiet voice, looking contemplative on the screen. "Our best course of action with the Americans is either to get the Chief of Staff or the Defence Secretary on board. Then we may stand a small chance."

"We are of course going to run into trouble with them, but we need their co-operation. By the way, Tim, I could do with you lending me a couple of your best intelligence analysts from your new SRU team to help Antonietta and Damian out if we are about to take all of this on."

"Of course, Vincent, anything to help. I'll send you a few profiles tomorrow and you can pick who you think will be best." As Tim said this, Vincent looked to Antonietta who had a small smile on her face. He knew this would make her happy.

The PM returned back into the camera's vision. "Right. The matter is seriously escalating. The terrorist threat level to the UK has been raised to severe. I've had to call an emergency Cobra meeting tomorrow morning. Vincent, can I throw them a bone? I need to give them something good, rather than just pile the bad news on top of them. I need to let them know that we have a plan."

"Just make sure it's a tiny bone, nothing that tips our hand," Vincent replied.

"Oh Antonietta, before I go. The information you gave me regarding the multiple internet searches on Vendicare has led us to a journalist called Claire Ashcroft, working for one of International News Corp's major tabloids. MI6 have had her under twenty-four hour surveillance and have just been informed that she has purchased a ticket to Malta next Thursday. When they did a sweep on her internet devices, they found that she had been looking at the footage on YouTube of your little diving rescue. Do you want me to get "Six" to lift her? We can do it under the prevention of terrorism, if you want," the PM offered.

"Absolutely not," Vincent answered before Antonietta could. "Six are way too heavy handed. They will convince her that she's on the right tracks. Thank you for telling us, but leave her under surveillance for now. We will deal with it. Thanks, Alistair."

"Speak soon, Vincent. All the best," Coombes said quickly before signing off.

"Jen, please can you arrange the million dollars for Nikki and we will see about charging someone else for it?" Vincent said, thinking that the PM had never treated money as an issue previously.

"Of course. I'll get it from our New York office. It's less aggravation with cash over there," she said.

"Ah! Now that you've brought up New York, that reminds me, I'm thinking of taking Kerry for a few days; I wondered if you and Saxby would like to join me. I have a feeling we may need to sell our little plan to President Baker," Vincent said to Jen with a look at Saxby. If they went to New York, they could be in the country under the pretence of visiting the VirtualTech offices there, which would draw no attention to them; if they went to Washington, leaving a paper trail with no good explanation as to why they were there, questions would be asked.

"When?" Jen asked, simply.

"Let's go on Monday. I don't want this weekend to be over too quickly."

"Are we taking our own plane? And would you like me to book 'The Pierre'? We stayed there last time and you said you enjoyed it."

Vincent thought about it for a split second before answering. "Let's go on public transport, as the team may need the GS550 while we are gone. Book a British Airways flight from Heathrow, around nine am; with a helicopter transfer we can be downtown for lunch." Jen was still looking at him expectantly and he realised he hadn't told her what to do regarding booking the hotel. "Oh, right, no, no, that place is too stuffy for Kerry. Try 'Yotel'. Someone recommended it to me the other day and it sounds pretty nice. Book three large suites. I think she'll like it there." He stood up. "Are we all done here?" he asked and received several nods. Everyone stood up. "Nikki, do you want to join us for dinner? I'm cooking."

She laughed. "As much as I hate to turn that down, I've already agreed to go to Beppes. All of us are going."

"Ah! Good idea, keep 'em all out of trouble," Vincent said, with a laugh.

"Oh really? Keeping them out of trouble? Doesn't sound like you keep YOURSELF out of trouble when you go to Beppes, or so I hear."

"...Good night," Vincent said, flushing and turning to leave before he could receive a scolding for his incident with the guy who had nearly knocked him off his bike.

As he made his way across the courtyard, creating a long shadow in the evening sun, he stopped. He turned, not towards the villa, but towards a side entrance, which took him to the rear of the property, finding himself in the well-kept, secluded garden area. He stood, where he had stood many times before, as the sun set and stared at the three immaculately kept graves with simple hand-carved Italian headstones.

The headstones each had very few words engraved onto them, but the words were accompanied by a simple, black cross at the top.

The first read: 'Marie Natalie. A loving mother and wife.

She will be greatly missed.' The date written below these words was over three years ago now. And yet not a day goes by where I do not feel the grief as strongly as I did when I first lost her. Vincent felt tears burning in his eyes. They were always tears of grief, yet they were tinged with anger. He let them slide down his cheeks. I avenged her death. I did. I did what I swore I would do. I killed her murderer, Alhusain Moses. And yet it didn't bring her back. It didn't make the pain go away. He found himself wondering, as he had many times before, what she would think of him now.

'Peter Natalie. Son and brother.' read the inscription on the next gravestone belonging to his son, the date of death matching his mother's. The tears poured down Vincent's cheeks. Too young, Vincent thought, as he questioned for the millionth time what his son would be doing right now. Would he have followed his father into the world of business? Or entered the forces, as Oliver had done? Or would he, perhaps, be making his own way in life? The bitter thought that he would never know left Vincent numb, as he turned to look at the final gravestone.

'Becci Moore, daughter in all but name.' Another date that he would remember forever. Another day that he would never be able to forgive himself for. He knew that this grave was simply a monument. They had never been able to recover her body from the failed mission, the mission that had cost her life. It was after that day too that Nikki had insisted that Vincent stop and concentrate on the management of Vendicare, while she dealt with the boots on the ground. That was probably best for everyone, he thought.

He continued to stare at the graves until it was dark, until he could feel the cold creeping upon him. He turned away. I will never forget, he said to himself, as he headed towards his villa, wiping his tears from his face.

When he entered the villa, he thought for a split second

that he had been transported to 'The Cavern' in the centre of Gozo. The bass music being played was thumping so loudly that Vincent could feel it in his chest. The smell of whatever was cooking was delicious. He stepped into the kitchen and was met with chaos. The girls were attempting to shout to each other over the booming music. They didn't see him stood across from them, but he could see Jodie with a wok in one hand frying something while gesticulating wildly with the other. Molly was sat on the kitchen surface with her feet tucked up, giggling at Kerry, who was using similar hand gestures to Jodie and seemed to be mimicking Gichin's style of teaching, making martial arts movements and jabbing at the air with her hands. He could see one empty bottle of wine and one that was on its way out too. Every now and then, when Kerry paused to take a breath, Jodie would continue the story, using her arms to demonstrate some blocking movements and at one point almost knocked the wok off the surface. Molly had a smile on her face and, for the first time since she had arrived at the villa, looked completely and utterly relaxed. Vincent surveyed the scene once more, and thought to himself, well, if you didn't know the situation, you'd have thought they'd all been best friends for years. He smiled to himself before deciding to take his dad-and-boss role seriously. He crossed the few paces towards the surround-sound control panel, before switching the music off entirely.

The girls immediately fell silent and looked around them, confused. Jodie met Vincent's eyes first and he raised his eyebrows at her. She grinned back, knowing he was joking. Kerry turned around and saw him standing with his eyebrows raised and put her glass of wine on the work surface before looking at the floor. Molly turned around and yelped, jumping down off the table in such a hurry that she almost ended up in a heap on the floor. "Sorry Mr Natalie," she said as she pulled herself to her feet. "I almost forgot for a moment I wasn't at home." She looked to Kerry and Jodie for some support; they all looked at Vincent, who laughed. Within a few seconds they all followed suit and all four of them were giggling.

"Molly, you ARE at home here. Get back up there and I'll top your glass up. And by the way, it's Vincent. Only people who don't like me call me Mr Natalie," he said, smiling, before he picked up the half-empty bottle of wine and topped everyone's glasses up before filling one up for himself. He saw Molly visibly relax as she pulled herself up onto the work surface once more. "So, what are we eating? That smells delicious!"

"King prawn stir-fry," Jodie said, grabbing the wok and flipping the contents. "Molly's favourite."

"Good choice," Vincent said, smiling at Molly.

They all ate the delicious food, chatting and laughing away. Vincent listened to them all discussing music and movies and was able to relax for what felt like the first time in ages. Once they had finished, Vincent took all the dishes off the table and carried them over to the sink; Jodie came with him to help.

"Jodie, I'm going to be taking Kerry to New York on Monday for a few days, and I was wondering if you would mind looking after Molly while we are gone. She seems to get on so well with you and you make her feel so at home."

"Not a problem, Vince, I like her company. Just make sure you bring me back something nice."

When they all took some coffees to drink outside, Vincent informed Kerry that she would be going to New York in a few days and that she had best start packing. She squealed with delight, running off to her bedroom, muttering, "Oh my GOD, I have NO CLOTHES!"

They all laughed at her before Vincent drew Molly's attention. "Molly, I want you to know that you're still welcome to stay here as long as you want to. If you still want me to come with you to the hospital to give the police statement, I'm more than happy to do that when I return." She smiled gratefully and Vincent excused himself, thanking Jodie for the lovely meal before heading to his room, switching on the television to find the latest episode of Doctor Who on his system record. There were three things that Vincent watched religiously on television: Saturday Breakfast, Doctor Who and Formula One. Oh, and when Marie had been alive, he had been forced to watch Strictly Come Dancing every Saturday night. But he hadn't watched that for some time.

His phone was ringing and he looked at the screen which showed a picture of Jean in Rome. He paused the TV and answered the phone. They chatted for about an hour as Vincent filled her in about the diving rescue and the success of their latest mission. He had expected her to be worried sick about Jodie, but she seemed to trust Vincent's judgement, telling him that she knew he would never let anything happen to her. Once they eventually ended the phone conversation, Vincent felt exhausted and decided to leave his programmes until tomorrow to get some much-needed rest.

CHAPTER 18

THE HEN PARTY

Beppes was packed.

It didn't help that the team took up most of the outside area, managing to cram all twelve of them around two tables intended for eight, which made things rather cosy.

Nikki, for the first time in months, had let herself go completely and was actually beginning to feel rather light-headed. She ordered some water to attempt to flush the alcohol out of her system and sat back in her chair, watching the proceedings as the team enjoyed their night out.

Billie and Amanda were organising party games and shouting over everyone. Oliver and Saxby were separated from the group and seemed to be having a pretty heavy conversation, as it was clear they had both had too much to drink. Nikki wondered briefly if there was some sort of spark there, as she had always thought that Emily and Oliver had some kind of connection. She tried to listen into their conversation and could hear Oliver assuring Saxby that his dad was generally quiet and reserved, but since what happened with his mum and his brother there could occasionally be 'red mist'.

Saxby laughed at that and raised her glass before shouting over everyone, "Oh well, here's to red mist!"

Everyone drunkenly raised their glasses, shouting, "Red mist!" "Yeah, red mist!"

"What the fuck is 'red mist'?" Billie asked.

Saxby and Oliver fell about laughing, as Oliver tapped his finger to the side of his nose. "Mind your own."

"By the way, Saxby, did I tell you he's my husband?" Billie said, jumping onto the table and staring at them with an accusing yet joky expression on her face.

She had barely finished her sentence before she was met with a chorus of, "SHUT UP, BILLIE!"

Scott and Lee had already moved onto another table full of girls enjoying a hen party. They had already ordered two rounds of the most expensive champagne Beppe had in and were now ordering their third. Nikki shook her head, knowing that they would be ordering it on Vendicare's pay check. She knew it wouldn't matter. When the team partied, they partied hard and cost didn't come into it.

Mike was chatting to Antonietta and Damian about their jobs and he was evidently impressed by what they managed to do, despite being half the age of the majority of the intelligence team at MI6 and 5.

Nikki smiled genially, before pulling out her phone to send a text.

'Hi, hope ur good, ur bus will be on time tomorrow so dnt be late. C u soon. Nik.'

"Who you texting?" Emily asked in a sing-song voice as she sat in the chair next to Nikki.

"Just texting Freya to make sure she knows we are sending the bus for her tomorrow," she replied and picked up her water. "Anything else you'd like to know?" she said cheekily, sipping her water.

"I really like that Freya, she's a top girl. Wouldn't want to fuck with her though," Emily said, slurring her words as she did. It was obvious she'd had too much to drink, though by the looks of them, who hadn't?

"I feel exactly the same," Nikki said, offering Emily some water before throwing an arm around her shoulder.

***

For an island roughly the size of Manhattan with a population of only 37,000, there sure were a lot of churches on Gozo. When Sunday came around, they sure as hell wouldn't let you forget about it. Every hour, from six in the morning, they would ring their bells. You could hear them echoing all around the island. After a boozy Saturday night, these bells would not be received well, Nikki thought.

It was eight in the morning as Nikki listened to the third round of bells, finishing a light breakfast of a brown toasted bagel with scrambled egg. She had already been to the gym and had even had a swim. Other than the private security on the gate and the flight technicians milling around, she hadn't seen a soul. I'm not surprised after what I saw last night. From the state they were in, Nikki didn't expect to see anyone surfacing before lunchtime. The only reason she was up early was because she knew William would be in the air now after picking Freya up from Tunis, where she had been on business since the mission. Nikki knew that she actually lived in Morocco, in a beautiful villa just north of Marrakesh, which used to be her parents'. Nikki had spent a lot of time there when she was on leave, enjoying the lovely country in Freya's company. They hadn't seen much of each other over the past few years, which Nikki regretted, but their work had kept overlapping; while one had down time, the other would be on operational.

The flight time from Tunis to Malta was only fifty minutes

or so, but Nikki had decided that she would pick Freya up herself in the Eurocopter. She was waiting at the airport and watched as the GS550 came to land. Freya stepped off the plane a few moments later and Nikki ran over to her, giving her a huge hug. She truly did have feelings for her, wishing they could spend more time together.

William carried Freya's bags over to them as they quickly caught up. "Do you want me to put these straight on the Eurocopter for you, Nikki?" he asked.

"If that's alright, Will, that would be great."

"Thank you so much for the flight, I will hopefully see you again," Freya said.

They both climbed into the waiting Eurocopter and Nikki set to with all the pre-flight checks. "I think I'm going to give you the tourist version of the flight home," Nikki said.

"Sounds good," Freya responded with a smile and, with that, Nikki pulled the Eurocopter into the air and flew back around the whole coast of the island; she even did a quick fly over the Azure Window, the most famous landmark on Gozo. It was created after two limestone sea caves collapsed a few hundred years ago and made a very popular spot for divers. Freya watched quietly, occasionally laughing or gasping at something Nikki said or a particular view that took her breath away. It took them over an hour to fly over the scenic route before Nikki pointed out the base.

"Andddddd next on our left is home sweet home," she said, banking left before quickly swinging to the right and then gently caressing the pedals, lowering the stick to land smoothly on pad one. Nikki switched off all the instruments and they both pulled off their headphones, climbing out of the helicopter and running away from the blades rotating quickly above them. One of the waiting flight engineers ran past them to move the Eurocopter into the hangar.

Vincent was walking towards them from the direction of his villa. His hair was wet from a recent shower and he was carrying his morning glass of orange juice in his hand; it was clear he had only just gotten up. He had a hand outstretched towards Freya, who ignored it with a smile.

"In France, we don't shake hands with people we like," she said warmly before kissing him gently on each cheek. "Bonjour, je m'appelle Freya, et je suis très heureux de vous rencontrer."

Nikki knew Vincent's French wasn't up to much, but he appeared to have understood the greeting and replied, "Bonjour Freya, je suis Vincent, et vous." He continued in English. "The team say that my French is on a par with Delboy's, but I understood what you said!"

"It was very good, Vincent," Freya said with a smile.

"Shall we go get a cup of tea?" Nikki suggested.

"Yes, let's go," Vincent said, picking up Freya's bag and leading the way.

"Ever the gentleman," Freya whispered in Nikki's ear. Nikki smiled back, not wanting to laugh out loud.

They made their way into the canteen area, seeing both Lee and Scott sat on one of the tables making their way through some breakfast. Both looked a little bit worse for wear and, in case Nikki was mistaken, appeared to be wearing the same clothes they had been wearing the night before.

"Well, hello boys!" Freya shouted to them. "Come, give your Auntie Freya a hug."

Nikki saw them both exchange a look, before standing up and giving her a brief hug.

"Now then lads. Care to explain why you're both wearing the same clothes that you were wearing last night and why you're up so early?" Nikki asked in her school teacher tone.

The twins exchanged another look and remained silent.

"WELL?" Nikki said expectantly, putting her hands on her hips.

"You know those girls we were talking to last night?" Scott said.

"The hen party ones?"

"Yeah. Well, we, er, ended up going back with them. They were staying on this yacht moored of Xwejini Bay and invited us back for some more champagne."

Vincent hooted. "Seriously?!"

"It's the first time I've had to do the walk of shame; it's usually the other way round," Lee said with a grimace.

"I wouldn't call it a walk of shame, as you can't quite walk on water. SOMEONE forgot to tie the dinghy to the boat last night, so we ended up having to swim ashore," Scott said, whacking Lee playfully around the head.

"I don't believe it," Vincent said, laughing.

"You boys!" Nikki scolded, but laughed anyway.

"Oh Nikki, before I forget, we have a conference call this morning with Tim and the PM. I woke up to a missed call off Tim, so I arranged it for ten am," Vincent said.

"Well it's almost ten now, we'd best get up to the comms room!" Nikki said. "Boys, we will see you later."

Vincent, Nikki and Freya ran up to the communications room to find Antonietta and Damian there, as always. They immediately set up the call to Mr Coombes and, after a few moments, he and Tim were on the other line.

"Hey there Vincent. We may as well get straight into it. I've got some bad news. I've spoken to the President and his advisors won't go for the plan at all, especially with the fact that Vendicare would lead the team. What he did say, though, was that Vendicare as a private contractor is free to take on any mission it wants to. Obviously, the British government can't sanction the taking out of Islamic State or the negotiations with the terrorists to free the hostages... as much as I want to assist you with everything, it has to be off the books."

"I've already made arrangements to fly out to New York to visit our VirtualTech headquarters. I was planning to sell it to the President myself," Vincent objected.

"There's no harm in him giving it one last shot," Tim said, agreeing with Vincent.

"Well, alright. I suspect he will at least give you a chance to explain. I'll make the arrangements," the PM said, eventually resigned.

Once the call was over, Freya said, "What a smooth operator you are, Vincent. I didn't think that call was going anywhere." Nikki silently agreed, impressed.

He smiled back at them. "I think he is still pissed with me over how we handled Senaullah."

Freya looked at Nikki for an explanation.

"Apparently he didn't fly well."

"Anyway, enough of that, have you sorted Freya out some accommodation, or do you want her to stop at the villa? I am sure we still have a room or two left somewhere."

"She's going to share my accommodation. She's only going to be staying a day or two before getting straight on the job, so I thought she may as well," Nikki explained. "Emily's already made the arrangements for Freya to fly into Israel and then make her way up through Amman in two days time."

Vincent jokingly shuddered. "Oh dear, don't mention Emily! I rang her this morning, forgetting you lot had been out on the town, and I didn't exactly receive a warm welcome."

"I wouldn't lose any sleep over it Vincent; she could barely remember her own name last night; I doubt she will remember this."

"Speak of the devil," Freya laughed as Emily came sauntering into the room. It was fair to say that she looked a bit worse for wear. Her hair was pulled into a messy bun on top of her head and looked as though it had sand in it; her face was pale and only half of last night's make-up seemed to have been taken off. She sat down with a thump and looked, bleary-eyed, at the table in front of her before focusing in on Nikki sat across from her.

"I thought YOU were looking after me last night," Emily said accusingly.

"Aren't you old enough to look after yourself?" Nikki asked with a coy smile.

"Looks like someone needs some coffee," Vincent said, standing up to get her a mug of strong black coffee, accompanied by a glass of water. He put them on the table before and received an evil look. "Em, I'm really sorry about waking you up this morning! Forgive me."

"Whatever, Vincent."

"Can we discuss something important?"

"Go for it," Emily said, stifling a yawn.

Vincent looked nervously at Nikki, who smiled and gave him an encouraging nod, which seemed to give him confidence. "Okay. You know the help that you've pulled in to transit Freya from Amman into Syria? Are they private contractors, or is it Mossad?"

"You know you aren't supposed to ask me that," Emily said, casually sipping the coffee,

"I will take it from your answer that it's the latter," Vincent said. "Don't apply for any spy jobs."

"Are you going to continue taking the mickey, or can I go and lie by the pool?" Emily said, obviously annoyed.

"Just one more thing!"

"What?" she snapped.

"If the Americans don't come on board I want you to use your contact in Israel to set us up with a Mossad hit squad in their place."

"And what 'contact' would this be? I'm not aware of any special 'contact' that I have."

"Well, when I say contact, more specifically, I mean your father."

Emily's eyes snapped to Vincent as the colour quickly came back to her face. "How the bloody hell do you know..." she said weakly.

"Stop panicking. I've always known Avraham is head of Mossad. Ever since you joined the squad, he's been ringing for regular updates on you. Every now and then we swap intelligence."

"SERIOUSLY?!"

"Who did you think gave him the information about Hezbollah at the hotel?" Vincent asked, smiling.

"Well, if you two are such good buddies, why are you asking me to do all the negotiating? Do it yourself."

"I thought it would be nice for your dad to see how far you've come and how much you've progressed. Please?"

"Fine!"

"Oh, one more thing..." Vincent said, delicately.

"Vincent I swear to GOD..."

"I know you dealt with some cases of Post-Traumatic Stress Disorder when you worked with Mossad. You know our girl Molly, who lost her brother in the diving accident? I wondered if you might be able to check her out for it. I'm worried about her."

"Fine. On one bloody condition."

"What?" Vincent asked curiously.

"You leave me alone for the rest of the day so I can recover from this bloody hangover."

"Done!" Vincent said triumphantly as Emily stormed out of the room.

"Wow," Nikki said, having surveyed the entire scene and being forced to hold in her laughter at several points. "I wish I could say you handled that one deftly, Vincent, but it was like watching someone waving a red flag at an angry bull."

"Car crash TV," Freya said, unable to stifle her laughter any longer.

CHAPTER 19

NEW YORK, NEW YORK

"Good morning, sir. May I have your boarding pass please?" came the sing-song voice of the overly polite British Airways Customer Service Representative.

Vincent handed over his boarding pass and executive card to the immaculately turned out woman. "Thank you, sir. You are flying with us today to JFK airport; your flight is on time, Mr Natalie. Welcome to the British Airways Concord lounge. If you would like to take your group through and make yourself comfortable, I will come and collect you when we are ready for you to board. Thank you," she said, finishing her pre-rehearsed yet faultless speech with a beautiful yet fake smile.

Jen and Vincent were regular flyers with British Airways and Vincent did secretly rather enjoy the luxury airline travel. In all honesty, he preferred this type of flying to even their own private planes, particularly on the long-haul. Kerry, he knew, had only travelled first class once or twice when she was younger, but he could see her appreciating it far more now. Even Saxby could barely contain how impressed she was, evidently only being used to economy class.

As they made themselves at home in the comfortable lounge, Vincent and Jen helped themselves to a glass of champagne that was on offer to them, along with the delicious canapés. Saxby leaned over to Jen and said, "Look at this room full of people! What do you reckon they all do? Do you think they're famous? Who can afford to pay $8000 to travel seven hours to New York? Oh, you could buy a car, or a deposit on an apartment for that!" She was utterly in awe.

"Honestly, Saxby, I promise you get used to it. It's true though. Most people in this lounge have more money than they know what to do with," Jen said.

Kerry, meanwhile, was texting on her phone. "Who are you talking to, Kerry?"

Kerry looked up, saw Vincent looking at her and pulled her headphones off, flushed. "Huh? Oh, I'm just texting Sarah."

"Are you showing off?" Vincent asked.

"...maybe. She's in Cornwall at the moment with her Dad, showing that they support some British Tourist Board or something, I'm just... light-heartedly rubbing it in!"

Vincent rolled his eyes, but decided to leave it, instead becoming engrossed in a conversation with Jen about a soldier's charity, suggesting that she ought to take a seat on the board and that perhaps they ought to increase their annual donations. "I've had another idea too; what do you think of recruiting one or two disabled soldiers? Both for Vendicare to help Antonietta and for VirtualTech to help you?"

"Good idea! Who better to work on intelligence than people who have trained all their lives to do it?" she said, nodding in agreement. "What made you think of that?"

"It was actually Oli's idea."

A different immaculately dressed British Airways woman appeared in front of them. "I apologise for any interruption I may be making, but I just wanted to let you know that as First Class is fully booked today, we have been unfortunately unable to seat you all together. I hope this is acceptable. We have put

Miss Lawrence in seat 5A which is on the left aisle of the galley, Miss Natalie in 5E just across from Miss Saxby, and Mr Natalie one seat in front in 4F," the lady simpered.

"That's absolutely fine, thank you very much. Don't worry, it was a late booking; we weren't expecting seats together." Vincent smiled and took the boarding cards from her.

"I don't mind swapping with you Vincent, or you could move Sax so that you can be with Kerry?"

Vincent merely pointed over to Kerry and said, "Really? She's going to have to have those headphones surgically removed before anyone will get any conversation out of her!"

They all laughed. Vincent thought briefly about sending Nikki a text to see how planning was going, but thought better of it. He knew that she would be getting on with it without any reminders from him; anything he said wouldn't make it happen faster. In fact it would only make it seem as though he didn't trust her.

They boarded the plane a few moments later and Vincent headed over to his luxury seat in front of all the others. A petite woman with striking, strawberry-blonde hair was trying to reach the overhead locker. "Oh, let me help you with that," Vincent said, taking the small, overnight luggage bag off her and placing it in the locker before doing the same with his own. "I'm Vincent, by the way."

"Aloma. Thank you very much," she said with a shy smile. Her voice was British, but had a slight twang to it. Vincent found himself immediately endeared to her.

The cabin crew were finishing off their pre-flight service of hot towels, magazines, drinks and toiletries as the captain came on through the speakers to give his formal announcements, introducing his team before they completed their safety checks. As the crew began to show the passengers how to fasten their seatbelts and use their oxygen masks,

Vincent thought about the times he'd been in the cockpit for take-offs and landings. The most memorable had to have been the time he had flown into Kai Tak, the Hong Kong airport, before they had built the new one in 1998. He hadn't been able to believe the flight path, which ran straight through the high-rise flats, almost letting you see what people were having for their lunch before the plane would bank left to land on the short, sea runway.

Two pinging sounds went off to inform the cabin crew that the plane was about to take off and immediately the 747 400 began to gather pace as it rumbled down the runway. The expensive crystal glasses clinked together softly as the plane began to lift off the ground and then with maximum thrust climbed to take the northerly route for the seven-hour flight to JFK. When the seatbelt sign switched off and the plane was cruising, Vincent turned around to see what his companions were up to. Jen was already studying the numbers from the New York office so that she could highlight some pointers for Vincent when they met up with Huber, the CEO of their American operations. Vincent knew she was excited about him seeing the team for the first time since he'd started Vendicare. She'd said, more than once, that it would be great for team morale and thought that Vincent could congratulate them on their twenty per cent expansion in this year alone.

Saxby was studying the first class menu. "What you thinking?" Vincent said to her.

She looked up, surprised to see him looking at her, and then looked from the menu to Vincent. "Oh, right! I'm torn between the mint, dill and lemon-cured Shetland salmon Gravlax or the cream of carrot soup infused with orange and star anise... though for the mains I've already decided on the salad of seared tiger prawns."

"Sounds good! Kerry, what about you, darling?"

She saw him looking and pulled off her headphones again. "Huh?"

"What are you going to eat?"

"Oh, it's all a bit fancy for me Dad, so I'm having the British beef burger with Monterey Jack cheese and chunky chips from the Bistro menu."

"I see. I'd best take a look myself," Vincent said. He could feel his stomach rumbling and immediately decided upon the Meze plate for starter and the fillet of beef for main course, plus an old burgundy to go with it.

"So, are you on business or pleasure?" Aloma asked from next to him.

"We have an office in New York that I haven't been to for years, so my CEO suggested that I show my face," Vincent replied. "How about you?"

"Oh, business of sorts. I write music," she said.

They chatted for a little while. Vincent didn't usually enter into conversations with strangers, but he immediately felt she wasn't a threat in any way. She filled him in on her music career, explaining to him that she was a solo artist who played soul and jazz and that she was going to be in New York to work on her second album.

Once they had finished their lunches, the stewardess cleared away their things, removed the table and reclined Aloma's seat into a completely flat-bed before providing her with a quilt and a pillow. Vincent declined the sleeping accessories as he rarely closed his eyes on flights, instead opting to watch some of the in-flight entertainment. Before he got comfortable he turned around to look at Kerry, who was laughing out loud at something she was watching on her screen. Saxby looked equally engrossed by something on her screen, while Jen still had her nose deep in her numbers, so he quickly plugged in and selected a series called 'The Vikings', which he was immediately hooked on.

What felt like no time at all later, the cabin services director was doing the rounds, informing them that she would be putting the lights back on soon. "Would you like a tea or a coffee, sir?" she asked, politely.

"Tea, please."

Vincent's neighbour looked a little dishevelled as she woke from under the quilt into the bright cabin lights, attempting to find her bearings. She gave him a small smile as she squinted, trying to find her wash bag and collecting her clothes before heading to the restroom.

Jen was already up having her afternoon tea and ploughing through her notes once again while Kerry and Saxby were waiting at the engaged bathroom doors.

A few minutes later, Aloma arrived back and sat in her seat, which was now upright. "You didn't sleep at all?" she asked.

"Can't sleep on planes, especially going stateside."

"Where are you stopping in New York?"

"Ah, this new place on Tenth Avenue called Yotel. It's supposed to be fashionable and boutique-y, so I thought my teenage daughter might like it there rather than the pretentious hotel we normally stay at. What about you?"

"Well, snap! I'm staying at the same place. Tell your daughter they have some great DJs playing there; the music is amazing."

"Thanks, I'll tell her, she's so into her music."

The plane made its slow descent, eventually landing on the runway at JFK airport. The captain came on the overhead speaker once more. "Welcome to New York everyone, the local temperature is twenty-seven degrees Celsius, expect thunderstorms please, I hope you have your umbrellas! Now, if everyone could just remain seated, the tower has just informed me that the police are about to board."

Vincent was just wondering if the PM had fixed up their

diplomatic entry as promised, so they didn't have to endure the horrendous queues synonymous with John F. Kennedy airport passport control, when Vincent spotted two men wearing all black boarding the plane. Well, these aren't local police officers, Vincent thought to himself as the two guys in dark suits and sunglasses had a brief conversation with the cabin services director before pointing directly at Vincent.

They walked straight to him and Vincent felt his heart catch in his throat, but remained calm and collected. "Mr Natalie, would you like to come with us, please," the dark suited young man flashing his badge asked Vincent. It wasn't a question.

"Show me the badge again," Vincent said sharply. "Bloody Secret Service, I might have guessed," he muttered to himself. All the effort that they had put into being here under the radar had been wasted now that the Secret Service had decided to do a bloody meet and greet. They may as well have held up a great big sign, Vincent thought. He indicated quickly to Saxby and Kerry to grab their things, as Jen was already reaching into her overhead locker, pulling out her bag. From the expression on her face, she was feeling the same as Vincent about this intrusion.

Vincent could feel several eyes on him. He turned to his neighbour, wondering what she was thinking. He pulled a quick, awkward smile. "Sorry about my security. They're a little bit clingy." And he turned to follow his new friends off the plane, with Kerry, Saxby and Jen in tow.

CHAPTER 20

THE PRESIDENT'S MEN

Vincent and Saxby leant against the door leading from the airport bridge onto the tarmac talking to Agent Josh Privy, the Team Leader of the Protective Detail. Jen had pulled Kerry to one side, telling her that nothing was wrong to put her mind at ease.

"What exactly is going on here?" Vincent demanded.

"Listen Vincent, I trained with the Counter Assault Team attached to the President, they're only doing their job..." Saxby tried to reason.

"I want to know why it was necessary for us to be manhandled off that plane!"

"We were asked to, Mr Natalie, sir. The President himself told us that your safe passage is extremely important and so has allocated you the greatest level of security," Privy tried to explain.

"Vincent, it's more than what would be given to normal distinguished foreign visitors, or even heads of state. It's a high honour coming from the President himself," Saxby said.

"President Baker also asked me to inform you, sir, that he is due to address the nation tonight; he believes he needs to come clean about the failed Special Forces mission, sir. But he wanted to give some time to you today and hear your viewpoint before doing so."

Vincent pulled his jacket straight. "Great. Good. That's fine. Jen, Kerry, I hope you fancy an out-of-hours tour of the White House. Let's go," he said, appreciating that Josh was only a messenger.

"I'm up for that!" Jen said, excitedly.

"Whatever. Some trip to New York this is turning out to be," Kerry said, pulling her headphones back on.

Josh led the way down the steps to the large black SUV that was waiting for them. They travelled only about two-hundred yards before exiting the vehicle to board the waiting GS540 jet, the earlier model to Vendicare's own GS550. It would only be a short flight to Dulles, then less than thirty minutes by car if using outriders, or ten minutes by helicopter to Pennsylvania Avenue. Vincent was just about to ask which mode of transport they would be using as they neared Dulles when Josh said, "We have one of the Presidential choppers warming up and ready to go for you, sir. I have made arrangements for the rest of your group to have a tour of the White House with one of the President's Press Officers, Kristie."

"Saxby comes in the meeting with me," Vincent said, matter-of-factly.

Josh's eyes flicked between Saxby and Vincent. "I would need to clear that with the Chief of Staff, Mr Natalie, sir."

"Not a problem," Vincent said airily. "Oh, but if you can't clear her, book four people on that tour of yours." He turned away from Josh, who now appeared to be sweating. They disembarked the plane and quickly climbed into the waiting helicopter, a VH3D. Vincent started pointing out the Washington landscape to Kerry, who had now decided to get interested and had removed her headphones as she pointed with her mouth open to the South Lawn, one of the most famous landmarks in the world.

"Are we on Marine One?" Kerry shouted excitedly to no one in particular.

"Actually no Ma'am, we only refer to it as Marine One if the President is on board, but this is one of the fleet of nineteen that we currently have," Josh answered with a standard Secret Service smile.

"Dad," Kerry said with a mischievous grin. "Please can I tell Sarah I'm here?"

"Sure you can sweetie, but chances are she's already been here, so I'm not sure how many points it will score you. Her dad is the PM, if you remember rightly."

The smile disappeared from Kerry's face as she realised he was right. Saxby and Jen were both attempting to hide their smiles and she sat back in her chair with a huffy look on her face.

"Well, so much for under the bloody radar," Vincent said to Jen, but loud enough that Josh could hear him too.

"Oh, who cares," Jen replied. "I can tick this off my bucket list now."

Once they were off the helicopter, they made their way into the Roosevelt Room, met by the cheerfully excited Press Officer Kristie. "Hi guys, my name's Kristie, I'm the Deputy Press Officer to the President, and I'm going to be giving you a little tour today," she said in an accent which Vincent couldn't quite place. As Kristie gave a smile to Kerry, a side door opened and the Chief of Staff, Bill Bolton, entered the room, extending a hand to Vincent.

"Apologies for the cloak and dagger treatment at the airport, Mr Natalie, but we were up against it with time and needed to get you here as soon as possible, what with all the new developments. I cleared it with your PM's office first, of course," Bill said in a deep, booming voice.

Vincent was about to respond curtly, to inform him that he

didn't work for the British government and therefore clearing it with the PM meant absolutely nothing to him, but decided that it was useless starting an argument at this very moment. Jen and Kerry were already following Kristie on their tour.

"Miss Saxby, is it quite alright if I have a private word with Mr Natalie here?" Bolton asked.

"Of course," Saxby said, following one of the Secret Service men into the West Wing reception room.

"Mr Natalie, I'm sure you will understand, the Chairman of the Joint Chief of Staff, Mr Peter Konwinski, and the Director of National Intelligence, Mr Josh Gaspard, in attendance feel that Miss Saxby should not be involved in the meeting with the President as we have decided that she does not have the correct level of clearance. Now if she would like to join the others on the tour..."

"She has the same level of clearance as me. Now, are we going to this dance, or shall I join my daughter on the tour you have running?" When Bill's expression was unchanging, Vincent added, "May you thank the President for his very kind hospitality, I'll be on my way."

He turned away from Bolton and began to walk in the direction of the doors, before he heard from behind him, "Fine! Fine!" He turned back around and smiled at Bolton, who sighed and frowned before walking into the West Wing reception room to collect Saxby.

He took them both through his own office and into the grand Oval Office where President James Baker was sat in one of two brown leather chairs, wearing a smart navy blue suit. Two large cream sofas were adjacent to these chairs and were occupied by the Chairman of the Joint Chief of Staff, Mr Konwinski, and the Director of the National Intelligence, Mr Gaspard. When Vincent and Saxby entered the room, all three men stood up quickly. Bill Bolton made his introductions, starting with the President, who greeted Vincent with a, "Nice to see you again, Vincent," and a firm handshake. Mr Gaspard, dressed in a dark suit, having worked his way up through the CIA gave Vincent an equally firm handshake and a rough smile. Mr Konwinski was dressed in full uniform, adorned with the many ribbons and medals that numerous Presidents had bestowed upon him.

"Gentlemen, we are running short on time, but the President has asked if he can present a gift to Mr Natalie and his team for their recent successful mission concerning the rescue of the children from Nigeria," Bill said, standing up as everyone else took their seats.

"Vincent, I have ten medals here for you to take back with you. Of course, we can't do a photo shoot or any publicity concerning it, but we appreciate everything your team did. Please accept out thanks on behalf of the American people," the President said, shaking Vincent's hand once more.

"Thank you, Mr President," Vincent said, feeling humbled, gracefully accepting the ten Presidential Freedom medals. "I'll make sure these get to the right people."

Saxby had taken a seat next to Vincent and he could tell how uncomfortable she was. Hell, she was sat across from the President of the United States; something that Vincent didn't even really think much of anymore.

Peter Konwinski took a glance at the President, who nodded at him, indicating that he could start the meeting, and launched into it. "Mr Natalie, we might as well get straight down to it. The American government cannot and will not allow a private military contractor to get involved in our internal security measures." He paused to cough but continued in a determined tone. "We understand that your team, albeit competent, is only a small operation and cannot possibly handle something as significant as what you are proposing to undertake." Vincent felt himself bristle, but knew that arguing would not be the way to win over these men. He hated being talked down to, especially by a man who felt the need to pin more medals to himself than Michael Phelps in order to prove his authority.

Josh Gaspard then took over, talking in a less condescending manner. "Perhaps we could instead offer you the opportunity to advise us, or maybe even have a small part to play in the actual operation?" Vincent said nothing, very purposefully picking up his cup of coffee to take a sip, indicating that he was in no hurry to talk.

Bolton picked up the Director of National Intelligence's thread. "We could base you and your team out here in Washington to allow you to link up your intelligence network to our own." Vincent could now see that they were attempting to sell him a joint operation; a complete wind back from Peter Konwinski's original outlined plan of being able to give the Americans some advice.

Vincent did not respond, instead taking another sip. "This is excellent coffee, Mr President," he said casually, putting his cup back on its saucer. He could feel them all looking at him and decided that now was the time to strike. He cleared his throat. "Gentlemen, I am shortly going to join my daughter on the tour of this lovely building as I feel it may be far more interesting and informative than the conversation taking place in here, but before I do, allow me to just leave you with one thought. When I left London this morning, I had an open mind for discussion with yourselves and had already had a meaningful conversation with our own PM. Now, he seemed to believe that this 'special relationship' between the UK and USA is becoming more of a 'dog and his master', with him being the dog and you the master, in case you hadn't guessed." He held his hands up as he saw Konwinski's mouth open to deny this. "His words, not mine. Anyway, as I was saying. Vendicare does not work for any government, including the British. Occasionally, we ask for assistance on tasks which have overlapping interests and, respectfully, we share when we need to share, but we never work for, nor take payments from, anyone unless it is relevant to hostages. I allowed you, Mr President, and Bill to watch our latest mission rescuing those children so that you could be safe in your assumptions that we are highly competent," he said with emphasis, looking at the Chairman as he did. "Now, my plan is three-pronged, with the intention of rescuing the hostage journalists, the captured Special Forces and taking out the Islamic State central command." He paused for effect before throwing his hand grenade. "Mr President, gentlemen, I refuse to go into more detail, nor discuss this any further, because, quite simply, you have an intelligence leak."

Immediately Konwinski stood up, outraged and red in the face. "Mr President, sir! We do not need to sit here and be lectured by some..." Before he could finish his sentence, Baker raised his hand firmly to stop him.

"Do you have any evidence?" the President asked calmly.

"I say this respectfully, sir. We lost an important member of our team when acting on your intelligence while trying to rescue hostages. This was followed by your own mission, where your intelligence was once again compromised and you lost several of your own Special Forces." No one, including the President, moved. They were hanging onto his every word. He pulled a tablet from his briefcase and, after pressing the screen a few times, handed it to President Baker. "Sir, we know for a fact that, two days ago, your Special Forces hostages were being held in that exact building showing on the screen. Our operatives on the ground are keeping tabs on their current movements." He paused to allow the strength of their intelligence to sink in. "Let's be frank. You guys cannot afford another screw up, your people won't accept it and neither will anyone else. The might of the world's superpower can't even rescue their own troops safely? Is that really the impression you want to give out? We are offering you the opportunity to have a win-win situation, which does not – I apologise for the forthright comment sir, but it's true – leave you with your pants down."

It seemed as though Konwinski was about to burst a blood vessel, but Vincent looked to Saxby; all he saw on her face was utter triumph. Konwinski took a breath and looked to Vincent. "So you're telling me that, at this exact moment in time, you know where our missing servicemen are?" he said, obviously agitated.

"That's exactly what I'm saying, sir."

Before Konwinski could pull together a response, Baker had turned to Gaspard, the Director of National Intelligence. "How is it that we have no idea where anyone is located, yet Vincent and his people can have an exact location with eyes on the target, live?"

Gaspard was stunned into silence, unable to pull together a response. Baker got to his feet as his face turned red. "How is it that the American taxpayer spent nearly seventy-five billion dollars in one year alone on gathering intelligence, yet we have none whatsoever?"

No response.

"What exactly are my people getting for their buck?!" The President nearly screamed, pointing a finger in Gaspard's face.

"Mr President, sir..." Konwinski attempted to say.

"No, Peter. I think I've heard enough. Gentlemen, give me the room." He waved his hand at them dismissively and sat back in his chair, seemingly exhausted but also embarrassed by his outburst. The two men turned to each other in mute horror and rage and stood up defiantly, stalking from the room.

Once they had left, Baker stood and looked through the oval window with his back to the room, his arms folded across his chest. No one spoke, an eerie silence ensuing. After a few moments, he said quietly, "Did the PM really say that?"

"Yes, Mr President, he did." Vincent then looked to Bill Bolton and Saxby, beginning to question whether he had gone too far with his plan, and whether or not they were about to be shown the door, when Baker pressed the intercom on his desk.

"Jane, could you come in please?" He then walked towards the sofa and sat down next to Saxby.

"Well, Miss Saxby, what do you think?"

"About what, sir?" she asked; Vincent could see her hands shaking as they lay in her lap.

"About this plan. I assume you know all about it?"

"Why yes, sir, Mr President, sir, I think it's an excellent plan. Though... it would have a far better chance of success if our Navy Seals were on board. I've seen what they're capable of first hand, sir, and know that they can only be an asset to the team that Vincent has put together."

"Good answer," he replied. A personal assistant, whom Vincent assumed to be Jane, came into the room silently and handed the President a notepad before promptly leaving again. "Well, if you ask me, it's time for a stiff drink. Would you care to join me?" he asked Vincent and Saxby, who both nodded enthusiastically. Bill took a small Blue Label which was apparently 'Scotland's finest export' and they each took a glass.

"Bill, what do you think? Reckon we can get away with letting Vincent and his team run the show?" Baker asked.

"Well, sir, you're the Commander in Chief. You can do whatever you want to. Obviously within reason, though." He lowered his voice. "However, there may be a fallout between your speaker and advisors like the two who just left the room. But this plan entirely works in our favour. We could always completely deny involvement. Although, in tonight's address, you mustn't mention the failed Special Forces mission, to allow Vincent time to put his plan into action."

"How long before you will be ready to go in, Vincent?" the President asked.

"About two weeks tops from the time I have Seal Team Six at our base," Vincent replied positively.

"Bill, how long before we can get Seal Team Six to Vincent's base?"

Bill looked confused by the question and was about to respond when Saxby jumped in. "They're on constant twenty-four hour standby for this exact reason. Sir!" she said, an afterthought following her outburst.

"So they are, Miss Saxby." Baker smiled and stood up. "Vincent, thank you for making me see sense. However, for now, if you could, keep only me and Bill in the loop. Good day," he said, shaking Vincent's hand.

There was a light knock at the door, Jane entering with Kerry and Jen behind her. Kerry ran over to her dad, telling him how amazing the tour had been. "Dad! Did you know the press office used to be a swimming pool? Ooo, ooo, and there's a flower shop! AND a family theatre! We gotta get one at the villa! I can't WAIT to tell Sarah all about this, she's going to be sooooo jealous!" It was only then that Kerry appeared to realise that she was in the presence of the President of the United States of America. She went bright red and stared at her shoes. Baker gave a quick smile to Vincent and stepped forwards, extending a hand to Kerry. "Good afternoon, Miss Natalie, it's a pleasure to meet you," he said kindly.

Kerry looked up and gave a shy smile. "It's nice to meet you, Mr President. Thank you for my pen," she said, showing him the Mont Blanc White House pen she had received as a memento of her tour.

"That's no problem. We're all done here, so I sure hope

you have a nice day," Baker said and nodded at Vincent, who gathered his daughter into his arms for a quick hug before giving her a gentle pat and pointing in the direction of the door. He turned to Baker and nodded his head slightly, before leaving the room.

On the helicopter back to New York, Saxby turned to Vincent and asked in a very quiet voice, "How did you get the location of those Special Forces hostages? I know you didn't have that information before we left and I haven't seen you talking with base since we arrived."

Vincent gave a quick sigh. "There are two things about today that you need to know," he said. "When outnumbered, as we were in the Oval Office today, your tactic is to divide and conquer. We did that, splitting the group into two." He paused. "The second thing is that fighting your battles is kind of like playing poker. It's fifty percent truth and fifty percent utter bullshit. I gave him the facts and, luckily for us, the President bought the bullshit." He gave her a quick glance and saw the horrified expression on her face. He laughed. "Don't worry Saxby. By the time we get back to base we will know the exact location of the Special Forces hostages, and so the bullshit will become fact. Therefore everything we said in that room, really, was the complete truth."

CHAPTER 21

BINGO

At base, Nikki was in the control room with Freya working on some data, which would hopefully contain something to give them a lead on the whereabouts of the missing hostages. They were now running a twenty-four-seven Kaleidoscope on all chatter relating to the hostages and Islamic State, with Vector searches filtering out all useless social media information, leaving only anything relevant. The Kaleidoscope looked for differences in speech patterns on all communication platforms, highlighting them to the operator. Antonietta had expressed that she felt certain that twenty-four hour monitoring would soon bring them the results they needed. The SRU unit at Hereford had managed to provide some very useful intelligence on both the journalists and the Special Forces hostages. Antonietta had allowed them to use the servers at Vendicare, which connected and trawled through the world's social media networks, allowing them to track any comments or blogs which these terrorists may use to glorify themselves for a home audience. This method had allowed them to reveal several new suspect British Islamic State members. One in particular had, under a pseudonym, been leaving messages for his wife on Facebook and Twitter, the footprints he had left behind suggesting that he could have something to do with the executions which had been broadcast.

His name was Salma Mahmoud, a twenty-eight-year-old radiographer from Manchester, with evident ties to Al-Baghdad, the leader of Islamic State or, in his own words, the 'CEO'. Even before leaving for Syria, the team had managed to discover that he was responsible for recruiting at least five hundred British men and women to the Islamic State cause.

Freya and Nikki had also been able to sort out Freya's flight and infiltration plan for her arrival in Israel. Emily's father Avraham had offered them Mossad's full support and back-up for Freya, which made Nikki feel far more comfortable with the mission.

Instead of flying Freya into the main airport, Ben Guiron, Avraham had made arrangements to use Ovda airport, which was some 40km further north and used by the Israeli military, which allowed Avraham to guarantee that they would not have any eyes on them. He had also offered them several operational vehicles with all the care packages and supplies that they may require.

Back at Hereford, Tim had managed to speak with the Saudi prince and had permission to set up a temporary operational base at Turaif on the northern border with Jordan. This would provide easy access into Syria, to the north-west of this base, with Iraq over to the north. The prince had also allowed them to have the SAS and Vendicare personnel on the ground with absolutely no interference from Saudi Arabia or Jordan. Furthermore, he would provide his own military guard to set up a security perimeter of twenty kilometres surrounding the new base.

It was more than they could have hoped for; Nikki felt herself grin that everything was falling into place.

Antonietta, with the help of the SAS Special Reconnaissance

Unit, was providing Freya with early intelligence data which had current locations on the journalist hostages, Special Forces hostages and some sightings of the Islamic State inner circle, who seemed to be currently based at Najaf.

Nikki had also sent all the details and clearance papers to their pilot, William, who would fly Freya into Ovda airport the next day, where she would be met by one of Avraham's contacts. They would provide her with the necessary papers and a briefcase containing one million dollars, which Jen had managed to wangle from the New York VirtualTech office under the pretence that they were paying for a new software design.

That morning, Nikki had also briefed Emily and Oliver to provide cover for Freya in Israel until Avraham's team could take over. Nikki also arranged for Emily to have at least a day with her father, as she had not seen him for over twelve months. She had told Emily that she could stay as long as she wanted, as long as she was back for the briefing when Vincent returned from New York.

Vincent had called her on his return flight from Washington to New York to let her know what had happened and to give Steve the green light to go ahead and pick his team from Hereford. Saxby had also informed her that she would make personal contact with Seal Team Six's commander and start the ball rolling on choosing a top-notch team.

Nikki knew it was going to be a struggle housing these guys at base, which was a shame, so Nikki had Jen's PA block of some rooms at a local hotel on the island under the guise of film extras.

Antonietta was now working around-the-clock, receiving full support from Hereford's SRU unit and her two new tech officers, Jamie and Carl, who were settling in well. These two had been at SRU since its conception and were top intelligence analysts with at least a year's undercover experience.

Nikki sat back in her chair and yawned. She felt exhausted, but happy that everything on the planning front was going well. She looked at her watch, shocked to find it was getting late. She quickly said goodnight to Antonietta, who was always ploughing away dutifully, and headed off to her room. As she was crossing the courtyard, she saw Amanda and the twins lazing around outside the main restaurant building.

"Hey guys, what's going on?" Nikki asked.

Scott sat up. "I'm so BORED of R and R. I need to be doing shit, man."

Amanda laughed. "It sounds like you've been doing plenty if you ask me, Scott."

Lee laughed too and Scott punched her arm. Nikki looked to Lee for some explanation.

"Oh, he's been spending quite a bit of time on that boat with the hen party chicks."

"Right, okay then!" Nikki said, with a laugh. There was an awkward silence as Scott found somewhere to look that didn't involve meeting Nikki's eyes.

"So when do all the newbies arrive?" Amanda asked with a little anxious giggle, eager to diffuse the awkwardness.

"Aren't they coming once Oli and Em have gone to Israel to set up that base?" Scott asked.

"Yeah that's about right," Nikki said.

Amanda grinned mischievously. "Now then Nikki, why those two? You know Emily has a soft spot for Oli and there you are, sending them off on a romantic trip to... Israel... who knows what's going to happen?"

"Ha, he wishes," Scott laughed. "I've got a soft spot for Jodie, but that doesn't mean it's ever gonna happen around here."

"No seriously!" Amanda said. "Emily's had a crush on Oli since she joined Vendicare."

As they argued it out, Nikki quickly dismissed herself

and took off to her room. She didn't really have time for all the discussions about love and crushes. There was too much work to be done. She quickly did her evening reps, then climbed into bed, becoming unconscious almost immediately.

***

BEEP, BEEP, BEEP. BEEP, BEEP, BEEP.

Nikki was pulled back into wakefulness, fumbling around in the darkness as she tried to remember what day it was. She pulled her phone off the bedside table and had to shield her eyes from the light it emitted. It was 0432 hours and her phone was ringing. It appeared to be a Hereford number. She quickly coughed to clear her throat and answered.

"Hello?"

"How's my favourite girl?" came the voice on the other end of the phone.

Nikki sat back against her cushions and yawned. It was Shaun from SRU. "Shaun. What's up? Why so early?"

"Nikki, sorry! It's just we've been using a web crawler to monitor all the social media outlets connected to the hostages. Well, one of the hostage's families tried to contact the kidnappers themselves and bingo! We have a hit." Nikki sat bolt upright, suddenly awake.

"Shaun, are you being serious?! Give me half an hour, me and Antonietta will be back at base, then give me everything you have," she said, quickly hanging up and jumping out of her bed.

She dialled Antonietta's number, who groggily picked up. "Toni! Hi, I'm really sorry to wake you so early, but you gotta get to the comms room as soon as you can. Shaun's found something. Alright if I meet you there in thirty?"

"Yeah, sure," Antonietta said before hanging up. Poor Toni, Nikki thought, but that girl's work ethic was like nothing she'd ever seen before. Though Antonietta did have a room at the base, VirtualTech had bought several villas on the north side of the island facing the Mediterranean and Vincent had suggested a while back that she have her own place so she could have some privacy and could invite friends and family over without the restrictions back at base. Though this was of course a good thing, it would mean that she would have to set off almost immediately in order to meet Nikki in thirty minutes.

Nikki ran to her bathroom and jumped in the shower, fully awake by the time she jumped out again.

Thirty minutes later, Nikki was in the comms room with Antonietta on a live link up with Shaun's office in Hereford. Nikki and Antonietta were trawling through the hit which they had traced back to Tadmur City, in the region of Palmyra, located in the middle of the Syrian desert. The city itself was flanked by a local airport and large prison which had been used to house Al Assad dissidents in previous years but, following the uprising, provided shelter for displaced families.

Shaun was unable to confirm whether or not anyone was being held at this location, but he was certain judging from the video footage of the first execution and the subsequent communications to the hostage's family that it had definitely come from downtown Tadmur.

"Do we have any co-ordinates?" Nikki asked.

"I'm trying to pinpoint them now; we have two drones flying a search grid pattern with locked in co-ordinates as we speak. We will hopefully have images in a few minutes," Shaun replied, a slight frown conveying his level of concentration.

"What about assets on the ground?" she asked.

"No one's got anywhere close. It's a bit of a red zone, this one," Shaun said. "We've previously had a four man recon team studying the airport, but they got pulled out when things got a bit too hot."

"This is great. I will pass these co-ordinates on to Oliver, Emily and Freya," Nikki said, a feeling of excitement building again in her stomach. Nikki checked her watch, thinking about her team going to Israel once she'd mentioned them. They would now be on board the GS550 heading towards Ovda airport with William and David at the controls. Their flight path and clearance had all been arranged yesterday with Emily's father, Avraham. They were due to be on the ground in forty-five minutes, where they would meet with Avraham and his team and then take Freya up to the forward staging point to check the facilities. Once everyone was up to speed, Freya would cross into Syria to meet up with her contacts to begin 'negotiations for the hostages' while trying to locate Islamic State.

Nikki had already dispatched all the comms and satellite equipment, which was due to arrive later on that day on the new A400M Atlas transport aircraft that had replaced the RAF'S old fleet of C-130 Hercules. Avraham had promised to personally clear the customs paperwork and oversee the delivery by Chinook directly to Oliver and Emily once they were at the Main Operating Base in Turaif, so that they could set up all their kit.

"Oh, Nikki, look. I've got something interesting up here." Antonietta had carried on with her research as Shaun was attempting to place co-ordinates. She looked studiously at the data before expanding the information on the 70" VPro monitor, which automatically began highlighting the numbers she had been looking at.

"What does it all mean?" Nikki asked, curiously.

"If all of these numbers are accurate and correct, they are a series of bank accounts in the Bahamas, Caymans and in Switzerland, with an electronic trail leading all the way back to Islamic State," Antonietta said.

"That's insane, Toni. Quick, send it to Julie back at MI6.

She'll get one of the forensic accountants on it and follow the trail to see if they can verify your findings. If this information is right, it could lead it us all the way to the money men!"

"And even more importantly, it will mean that we would be in a position to control their accounts," Antonietta added.

Nikki's mouth dropped open as she stood with her hands on the back of Antonietta's chair, staring at the screen. "This could be a game changer," she whispered. Could this be the breakthrough we've been looking for?

CHAPTER 22

VIRTUALTECH

It had been late when he, Kerry, Saxby and Jen had eventually arrived back in Manhattan. By the time they'd had something to eat in the restaurant and Vincent had made his necessary calls, it was the early hours of the morning and so everyone had decided to get some sleep. Vincent had asked Saxby if she minded sharing with Kerry, as he felt nervous leaving her in a suite with a fully stocked mini bar. Saxby had been fine with it, telling Vincent they got on well. The suite was so large they probably wouldn't even see each other, she had joked. It had a stunning 180-degree view of the Big Apple, from the skyline all the way down to the Hudson River, with a view of the Empire State Building.

One of the calls Vincent made that night had been to Jodie, who had informed him that she would be going to the mainland with Molly that day to do the formal identification of her brother and give a police statement, then Jodie would see if she was up for going back to the UK.

Vincent was exhausted by the time he got into bed, awaking a few hours later when his phone rang. It was Jen, telling him that their car was waiting downstairs to take them to the VirtualTech Head Office.

"Oh, I'll be five minutes Jen," Vincent said, running to the shower. He wanted to check on Saxby and Kerry before he went to find out what they had planned for the day. He quickly dressed and went to their room.

Amazingly, Kerry was up, laying on her bed, pressing switches to make it rotate 90 degrees, allowing her to see the entirety of Manhattan.

"Morning, Kerry."

"Morning, Dad, this hotel is SO COOL! Our billiard table is REVERSIBLE?!"

Vincent grinned, proud he had managed to do something right. "What are your plans for the day, Kerry?"

"I was thinking we could go shopping!" answered Saxby, who was standing in her bedroom doorway, still wearing some short pyjamas.

"Oh my GOD, we HAVE to go shopping! Do you know, I haven't spent a single penny since the end of term," Kerry said with wonder, before jumping out of her bed and running to the shower.

Vincent grimaced at Saxby, before saying, "At least it gets her up. Thanks Saxby, I hope you have an alright morning and Kerry isn't too much of a hassle. How about we meet for lunch at Del Posto? It's one of my favourite restaurants in the city."

"Sounds great. Don't worry, Kerry and I will have a great time," Saxby said with a smile before Vincent quickly left the room and ran to the lift. Jen was waiting in reception for him, holding two takeaway coffees in her hands, knowing how long it could take to travel the four miles to the offices.

"Did those Secret Service guys stay on guard outside our rooms all night?" Jen asked as the car pulled away from the hotel and into the hustle and bustle of the packed city in rush hour.

"I'm guessing so. I told Saxby to get them a coffee or

something, but you know how professional they are," Vincent said with a smile, before he laughed.

"What's so funny?" Jen asked, smiling, as Vincent descended into non-stop laughter. When he eventually pulled himself together, he attempted to explain his outburst.

"I don't know! I guess it's this whole American experience. Yesterday the White House, having a meeting with the President, today New York City with Secret Service standing outside your door. It all just seems so... surreal."

"If I didn't know any better, I'd say it was like a film," Jen said and they both started laughing again.

Their main offices were on Madison Avenue, a prestigious part of the city only four miles outside of Manhattan. The forty-six storey high-rise glass-fronted building was one of the first big deals Jen had completed for VirtualTech some five years ago. Since then, the property had doubled in price, now housing over 860 front line staff and operating twenty-four hours a day.

Vincent and Jen had managed the journey in only thirty-five minutes, which according to their driver Greg could be a new world record considering the rush hour traffic. Greg worked for the New York office and, as well as being their driver, he also provided low level security for Huber, the CEO of VirtualTech.

"Greg, can you just tell me if we have been followed at all from the hotel?" Vincent asked inquisitively.

"Certainly have, Mr Natalie. Black SUV. Registration GEK 4563. Two occupants; got a look of FBI or CIA about them, if you ask me, sir," Greg replied happily, with a quick glance in his rear-view mirror.

"Mind if you introduce yourself once we arrive at the building? They're going to need a car parking space; if it's possible to arrange a security clearance for them, that would be much appreciated. Also, here's mine and Jen's schedules for the next few days. Just give that to them, if you would. It will make their lives a heck of a lot easier," Vincent said, knowing the men who had been set to be their security were only doing their job in following them.

"Sure will, Mr Natalie," Greg replied before pulling to a stop outside the headquarters and jumping out to open the door for Jen as Vincent let himself out. He and Jen walked together to the front of the stunning glass-fronted atrium which served as one of the two entrances.

The renovation of this amazing building had been completed by architect and designer Robert T Wiser, who was responsible for the new T6 airport terminal in London. The glass entrance, which had been added to the 1934 shell of the building, stood forty floors high with six eighty-foot Chi-Chi Gingko Trees flanking the elevators and escalators which took you to the first floor – 'Mission Control' as it was called. Each floor of the building had breakout rooms and a coffee bar station with natural lighting covering the whole space. Vincent had felt especially happy with it when the renovations had first been made, but seeing it with fresh eyes after so long made him feel proud of the building that had been created; it was almost a work of art.

"Welcome, Vincent Natalie," came the robotic voice of the bio security system as it registered Vincent walking through the swing doors. They had installed the same software back at base, which meant that not one member of staff required access cards, including visitors, as the bio system was scanning every person in the building at the same time. If it identified anyone without access, the doors in that area would automatically close and only open with security clearance.

Huber, the CEO, hadn't seen Vincent in over two years and, recognising the significance of today's visit, had decided to meet them in Mission Control. After the initial formalities, he showed them up to the tenth floor where his office and the main boardrooms were. He then launched into an hour long presentation, using all the latest high-tech visual aids to present the company's next two years' planned growth strategy, which included a rollout of fifty-six new casinos in Asia, the current largest growing market in gambling. Vincent was aware of this rapid growth. In 1990, when he had first visited Macau, there had only been one casino on the entire island. Now, there were over seventy top class Vegas-style casinos. Jen had already prepped Vincent with a Q&A so Huber would think he was up-to-date with everything going on and still a huge part of VirtualTech when, in reality, Vendicare was where his heart now truly belonged. He did swell with pride, however, when he found out his original business idea – the VirtualTech system – was now in eighty-two percent of the world's major betting operations, including all current casinos.

Vincent's interest significantly intensified when Huber announced that the tech team were now beta testing the new MSIA – the Malicious Software Intruder Alert –

which Antonietta and Vincent had begun work on over two years ago. The MSIA's sole purpose was to detect any unauthorised access on their gambling servers, shutting it down immediately if there was. It would then track the location of the attempted hacker by sending a proxy hunter. This would then sit on the hacker's servers until such a time as it was activated again. It would then turn into a proxy assassin, taking down the server, as the name suggests.

"And how is the beta testing going?" Vincent asked.

Huber explained that it had been on test for over twelve months and that it had successfully detected and blocked over 300 malicious attacks and, other than some minor upgrades, they were planning to upload it onto all their systems within the next month.

"Huber, would you like to join us for lunch? It won't be enough to thank you for the time you have given us today, but it's the least I can do," Vincent said graciously.

Huber seemed flattered. "Why thank you, Mr Natalie. Allow me to just check I'm free for lunch with my assistant." And with that he left the room.

Vincent leant over to Jen. "Make sure we get full access to that beta version. I'm convinced that this software, with a few tweaks, will be able to help us locate Islamic State."

Jen smiled and winked. "Already got it."

Vincent grinned and Huber entered the room again saying that he would be more than pleased to join them for lunch.

An hour later, Vincent, Jen and Huber were sat having a drink at Del Posto when Kerry and Saxby arrived with security detail in tow. Vincent did quick introductions before saying, "Well girls, how's your morning been?" eyeing up the bags that Kerry was holding.

"Have we got a story for you!" Saxby said with a laugh before going on to tell them about a pushy male store assistant in the jewellery section at Bloomingdales who had 'taken Kerry under his wing'. But not before the Secret Service guys had given him a fright, according to Saxby.

"Oh dear, I know what that means, Kerry. What's in those bags?" Vincent asked, wearily.

"Well, I got this for Jodie," Kerry said, pulling some Meira T14k yellow gold single stud arrow-shaped earrings out of one of the bags. "And this for Sarah," she said, holding out a David Yurman bangle, which Vincent honestly thought could have been simply a Pandora for ten times the price, but he said nothing.

"Did you get anything, Sax?" Jen asked.

"Yeah, just a couple of nice work suits and tops, though our delightful assistant had been pushing me to buy some Prada goodies. I managed to avoid spending a whole month's salary eventually." She then looked mischievously at Kerry. "Kerry, why haven't you shown your dad your other purchases?"

Kerry looked at the other bags, which had been conveniently hidden behind the first. "I don't know what you're talking about," Kerry said lightly, though with a slightly angry look at Saxby.

"Come on, Kerry, let me see," Vincent said, telling himself to be understanding.

Kerry slowly pulled out some lug-sole lace up booties by Alice & Olivia, which were actually quite nice. She then pulled out the skinny jeans which the assistant had told her she 'just couldn't not buy'.

Vincent kept quiet for a few moments, before saying, "Kerry, darling, you're going to need to take those jeans back. They're ripped."

Kerry rolled her eyes and said, "Dad, if you're going to try and be funny, try some new jokes please." The group met each other's eyes and burst into laughter.

CHAPTER 23

ALOMA

It was beautiful New York evening, still in the late twenty degrees, when Huber arrived in the reception area of the hotel before making his way to the terrace on the ninth floor. Vincent had invited Huber and some of VirtualTech's top developers and staff to join him for drinks on the private area of the 7000 square foot terrace, which transformed into one of the most engaging outdoor bars in New York at night, complete with beautiful skyline views and some of the best up-and-coming DJs.

Vincent, Saxby, Jen and Kerry were already on the terrace, sipping from glasses of delicate champagne. The hotel had arranged a roped-off area at the far end of the terrace which overlooked the sidewalks of 42nd street and the breathtaking views of the regenerated Hell's Kitchen area of Manhattan. The city was lit up and sparkled; everywhere seemed so alive. A temporary private bar had been set up with two waiters serving them canapés, with the Secret Service detail watching the movements of everyone in the group and everyone around them.

"What have you been doing all afternoon, Vincent?" Jen asked him. "You seem to have been locked away in your room."

"I've been on a conference call with Nikki," Vincent replied, but decided not to go into further details seeing as they were in a public place and may well be overheard.

"Oh, Vincent, while I'm thinking about it, I've arranged a breakfast meeting with Sam Thomas, the Lieutenant Commander of Seal Team Six," Saxby said.

"Have you ever met him before?" Vincent asked.

"No, that team were never around when I was there. I think they were actually looking for Bin Laden at the time," Saxby said, before adding, "I did meet Admiral William North, who was in charge of all Special Forces operations. He was a pretty stand-up guy."

Just as she finished her sentence, Huber, along with about ten of his team, arrived. He introduced each of them to Vincent, including Roland and Davey, whom Huber said had done most of the work on the MSIA software. Vincent greeted them all with a handshake then offered everyone a glass of champagne, which they all accepted. As Vincent was chatting to the group and finding out more about VirtualTech from the people who ran it now, something caught his eye. He quickly beckoned over one of the waiters.

"Please could you kindly send a bottle of champagne over to that table at the far end of the terrace? Yes, that group of three near the entrance."

"Any message, sir?" the waiter asked politely.

Vincent quickly scribbled a note on the back of one of his business cards, handing it to the waiter along with a folded bill for his time, who then bowed before disappearing in the direction of the small group. Vincent turned back to his crowd in the sectioned off part of the terrace and decided to join his daughter and Saxby, who were looking out over the terrace towards the Statue of Liberty.

"Hello, what are you two chatting about?" Vincent asked, leaning against the side of the terrace, joining them.

“Nothin’ much Dad, Saxby was just telling me about where she grew up and what she was up to when she was my age,” Kerry said, slightly startled by his sudden appearance.

“Sounds like you two are getting on really...” Vincent broke off when he heard one of the Secret Service men behind him asking someone for some identification. He turned around to see a young woman with a glass of champagne in her hand standing next to the security men, smiling at Vincent.

“Why, thank you for the champagne Vincent, though I see you haven’t managed to lose your clingy staff.”

“Hey Aloma. I didn’t want to disturb you; just wanted to make sure you were aware that we haven’t been arrested or anything,” Vincent said to his neighbour from the British Airways flight. He gave a quick glance behind him to where Saxby and Kerry were. His daughter had a look of utter amazement on her face as she looked at the woman standing in front of her. He could hear her frantically whispering to Saxby and suddenly felt bad for not introducing Kerry.

“Kerry, darling, I’m so sorry. Aloma, this is my daughter Kerry and my American partner, Saxby,” Vincent said.

“Pleased to meet you, Saxby. Kerry, I love your boots! Where did you get them?” Aloma said with a smile.

“I... I got them this morning from... from Bloomingdales. Oh my GOD! Aloma, I love your music! I absolutely love it. I have your first album!” Kerry blurted out.

“Kerry, thanks! That means a lot,” Aloma said, with a slight blush; it was clear she was not used to such attention from her fans. “Hey, do you want to come and meet the DJ and a few of my friends?” She glanced at Vincent to check it was okay and he nodded, smiling, knowing it would make Kerry giddy with happiness.

“Woah, seriously?! This is better than meeting the President!” Kerry shouted before Vincent drew a surreptitious finger to his lips to show her to keep it down before they started attracting too much attention. Kerry gave an apologetic smile before Aloma linked arms with her and took her off to the other section of the terrace, with two of the Secret Service men quickly following behind.

"I wish I was still sixteen," Saxby said, mournfully.

"No you don't. You wouldn't be working for me and killing the bad guys if you were sixteen," Vincent said and Saxby smiled at him.

"You've got a point there."

They then both grabbed two bottles of champagne from the waiters and began to top up everyone's glasses, re-engaging in conversation with the VirtualTech workers. Vincent smiled and realised that, here in New York, he felt the most relaxed he had felt in months. Enjoy it while it lasts, he thought to himself grimly, knowing that what was to come could change everything.

CHAPTER 24

COUNTRY GIRLS

Saxby awoke early the next morning, considering she hadn't retired until late following their night on the terrace. After a quick shower, and a check that Kerry was still sound asleep, she decided to take a walk. She left the room quietly and got in the lift, walking out of the still sleeping hotel and into the brisk morning. The streets were quiet by New York's standards, which was almost unnerving, but Saxby revelled in the quiet, having never been much of a city girl.

She headed towards the Lincoln tunnel and down 12th Avenue towards Pier 66, walking with no particular hurry about her, just enjoying the sounds and smells of the city and the company of her own thoughts. She bought a coffee from a street vendor and walked to the edge of the Hudson river, leaning against the wall as she slowly sipped her coffee. The morning view was stunning. The early sun, having only just risen, was attempting to break through some stubborn clouds which hadn't blown away with the cool breeze, and the calm orange light that had fought its way through lit up the city that never sleeps.

Considering how quiet the streets were, Saxby noticed that it was busy on the river. Several small yachts were out for a morning sail, making the most of the breeze that filled their sails. A couple of barges were also slowly making their way towards Governors Island and a dredger was tied up on the riverbank as its crew had made its way for their breakfast.

She stared at the river, thinking back to the day when the breaking news had been about the United Airlines plane which had been forced to land in the river. They had called the pilot a hero after he had managed to save all the people on board. It made her smile. She loved those kinds of stories.

Her phone vibrated in her pocket, indicating someone else was up early. She pulled it out of her pocket and read a message from Vincent:

'Morning. Hope you slept well. Wondering if you wanted to get some coffee before Sam arrives for breakfast meeting.'

Saxby smiled to herself at Vincent's long-hand method of texting before remembering the meeting she had arranged with Lieutenant Commander Sam Thomas, the leader of the Seal team they were attempting to get on board. She checked her watch quickly, wondering if she was going to make it back in time, but breathed deeply when she saw that she still had an hour or so left.

'B back in 15' she replied.

She stared out at the river for a few more minutes, drinking in the first peace and quiet that she'd had in what felt like ages since her life had been turned upside down that day she had met Vincent at Hereford. It hadn't mattered to her. She was doing what she loved.

She found a bin for her polystyrene cup and wandered back towards the hotel. She found Vincent waiting in the lobby for her and they both went into a private breakfast room together to wait for Sam Thomas to arrive. As they were sipping their coffees, Vincent opened the report document on their visitor.

"Wow. This guy is only thirty-four and he's completed

three tours of Afghanistan, along with several covert missions attached to the CIA. Impressive," Vincent said, skim-reading and flicking through the document.

"Yeah, from what I know of him he's very good at what he does. Obviously the big mission was the one for Osama; I know he led one of the two assault teams into the compound with no loss of life," Saxby said, recounting the information.

"Amazing. Says here he's married too, with a four-year-old daughter, and graduated from Naval Academy with a Bachelor of Science in Mathematics." Vincent grinned. "Don't you just hate those people who seem to have it all?"

Saxby couldn't tell if he was joking, knowing he was a guy who really did have it all. She decided not to comment.

"What do you think of this guy?" Vincent asked when Saxby didn't respond.

"Apparently he's the talk of all the agencies and destined for a big career. I say he's the business."

"I agree. You don't get two bronze stars unless you know what you're doing." Vincent pulled his phone out of his pocket, frowning at a text he'd just received, then smiled. "Oh, it's only Jen. She says she's just picked Kerry up and is off to VirtualTech before they join Aloma at her recording studio downtown. I had no idea my daughter was such a huge fan; it was great to see how fantastic Aloma was with her last night. She introduced her to the DJs and now she's invited her to watch her record some tracks for her album."

Saxby smiled. It was adorable how pleased Vincent was that his daughter was having a good time.

There was a knock on the door and one of the Secret Service guys entered to show Sam Thomas into the room. He was a tall man, standing at about six foot, well-built and, although he was obviously intimidating, there was something very likeable and modest about the guy. Saxby warmed to him immediately.

Vincent gave quick introductions before offering Sam a seat, which he took. They all ordered some breakfast, Vincent launching straight into explaining the proposed operation to Sam, emphasising that until they had all the information to hand and one hundred percent confirmed intelligence, the mission was on standby.

Vincent grabbed the coffee pot and began pouring, before saying, "Although we don't follow an official military command structure, overall control goes to Nikki. She will give the green light on the operation. And I want you to know that no one goes into action who doesn't believe fully in this mission and its objectives."

Saxby could see Sam frowning slightly. Knowing this type of discussion would be one he was not used to, she jumped in. "This team has a very different attitude and ethos to agencies like the CIA, but I've witnessed their capabilities first-hand and believe that they are as good, if not better, than everyone I've ever worked with before."

"Well, I have to say your attitude intrigues me, but I have seen enough to know that even America doesn't always get it right. I was assured by Admiral North that this command came all the way from the President. I believe y'all will know what you're doing," Sam responded.

"So, what's the current position your team are in?" Saxby asked.

"We are flying out tonight to Brize Norton. Someone there is arranging transport to your base," he replied.

"Great. We should all get back there at roughly the same time, as we are leaving tonight too," Vincent replied. They chatted some more for just under an hour, discussing the kit, electronics and weapons that would be provided so that Sam and his team were fully aware of what to expect. "Thank you so much for coming to see us, Lieutenant Thomas. If you have any needs, or questions, get in touch with Nikki back at base on your arrival; she will be able to sort you out with absolutely anything. It was nice to meet you; I'm very glad to have you on board," Vincent said, extending his hand once more.

Saxby also shook Sam's hand with a smile and left the room following a quick salute to them both. Saxby grimaced at Vincent, who was shaking his head. "Some habits die hard, you know," she said with a laugh.

CHAPTER 25

RED EYE

The overnight British Airways 0172 'red-eye' flight was fairly uneventful, containing no famous faces or celebrities. Everyone other than Vincent took advantage of the flat, comfortable beds to get some sleep, so he decided that it would be a good time to catch up on his emails, all of which would send once he locked onto a satellite. He decided that the first email he needed to send was to the PM, with Tim copied in, to let them know the result of his meeting with the President.

From: vincent@vendicare.com
To: pm@10d.gov.uk
Copy: tim.smith1@reg.gov.uk

President meeting with Baker went very well. It looks like we have the green light to go ahead.
Seal Team Six now on secondment, arriving at base shortly.
Will brief you both in person on my return if possible, may be worth getting some dates to Nikki for a visit.
Thanks for your support,
Regards,
V. N.

His mind then wandered to Jean, as it often did, and he pressed the 'compose message' button once more, knowing he could use his offer of taking Jodie with him to Turaif to take care of all the catering as an excuse to message Jean.

From: vincent@vendicare.com
To: jean.panaro@skyit.com

Hey Jean, I hope you're well and not working too hard. I'm sorry we haven't spoken much these past few days. I've had my hands full with a few issues and, believe it or not, I've been in New York! But it looks like it's all settling down now, fingers crossed.
Those dates are still good for the Seychelles for me, the girls are really looking forward to it I think, I hope you are too.
I just bought Jodie the new Xbox One, just in case you were thinking of getting her one, although I'm sure you weren't!
Just in case Jodie mentions an upcoming job that I may have talked to her about, let me tell you first! I am thinking of taking her with me on a little business thing, but please don't worry about her. It's very low risk, unless she manages to do herself some damage whilst in the kitchen.
By the time you get this, I will have landed at London Heathrow, then I'm going straight back to the villa. I will ring you tonight.
Lots of love,
Vincent xxx
PS, Kerry asked me to say hi.

Vincent let out a small sigh and put his tablet back into his briefcase. He leant back against his chair and switched on his in-flight entertainment, plugging in some earphones as he did so. He browsed through the available films and found one he hadn't already watched, yet was being raved about by everyone. Something about some high-flyer on Wall Street. He clicked on it, letting his mind be taken over by the storyline for the next few hours while everyone around him slept.

A few hours later the plane landed at Heathrow airport. Vincent and his party disembarked the plane and were escorted to the private part of T5 where William was waiting with the GS550 ready to take them on the short flight back to Malta. Kerry had slept the whole way from New York and was now curled up on the leather director's couch, breathing lightly as she slept. Saxby was making some notes on her tablet and Jen was sending a few emails, thanking the staff in New York.

Vincent could feel how dry his eyes were from lack of sleep, but he brushed the feeling away as he heard a ping on his tablet, notifying him that he had an email.

From: jean.panaro@skyit.com
To: vincent@vendicare.com

Morning Vincent, I guess around about now you should be on your way back to Malta?
Glad your trip went well and that things are settling down – I think you need a decent break from your work!
Give Kerry a big hug from me, and Jodie too when you get back, although I do wish you'd stop spoiling her!!
I can't wait for the Seychelles - I've already packed!!!!
(only joking)
Ring me later if you get a chance, I've got the day off today.

Love and hugs
Jean xoxo

Vincent smiled as he read the email that she had sent. He missed her a lot and couldn't wait to spend some time with her in the Seychelles. He saw that everyone around him had dropped off back to sleep, so decided to go to the flight deck to see William and catch up with all the gossip. He took a seat next to him and Will turned to glance at him.

"Good trip?" he enquired casually.

"Pretty good, apart from all the politics," Vincent replied, giving him a half-smile, half-frown.

"I'm doing back-to-back flights today. I'm flying Molly and Jodie to Manchester Airport later on today. I'm going to stay over at the airport, if that's alright with you, and then bring Jodie back tomorrow morning."

"Yeah that's fine, best to keep up on your sleep." Vincent was glad that Jodie would be flying with Molly. It meant that she would have some support when she got back, someone to settle her back down into her normal life at home. Vincent put on the spare pilot headset and dialled some numbers into the instrument panel, receiving an instant ringing tone.

"Hello?" came the voice on the other end.

"Morning, how are you?" Vincent said.

"Oh it's you! I'd forgotten what your voice sounded like seeing as you haven't spoken to me since forever," came Jodie's scathing response.

Vincent caught William's smile and returned it as he attempted to apologise to Jodie. "I'm sorry Jodie..." he tried to start, but as usual, he couldn't get a word in edgeways.

"I can't believe you've been to the FLIPPING White House! And Kerry getting to meet ALOMA. What is all that about Vincent? I tell you, you've got a lot to answer for when you get back. I'm not happy. No, seriously! Not happy! I never get to go anywhere!"

"Have you finished?" Vincent asked when she paused for breath.

"Well, did you bring me anything back?" Jodie asked in a voice that meant she was fishing for something.

"You'll have to wait until I get back," Vincent said. "How's Molly doing?"

"She's good. I think she's ready to go home to be honest. I'm going to offer her some support, if that's alright."

"Yeah, of course, that's fine. Make sure you see Antonietta about sorting her out a new phone, with our safety tech programmed in, and teach Molly how to use it." With the tech that Antonietta could load onto the phone as well as the direct link to the operations room, it would act as a personal attack alarm and a GPS locator. He rang off once Jodie had agreed to sort out Molly's phone and rang Nikki.

"Hey Nikki, are you alright?"

"Vincent, hey! I'm good, are you?"

"Yeah, I'm good thanks. Are you still okay to meet us as soon as we land?"

"Yeah, I'll see you in a couple of hours, just text me when you've landed in Malta."

Vincent went back into the main cabin, thanking William, and helped himself to a coffee. He wandered over to where Kerry was fast asleep and gently nudged her back into consciousness, knowing that they would be landing in about twenty-minutes time.

CHAPTER 26

MURDER ON THE NILE

Freya leaned on the balcony of her room in the Hotel Zenobia and looked out at the town of Palmyra which lay before her, breathing in the fresh air of the morning and feeling the sun on her face. Nada al Husain, the self-proclaimed press officer for Islamic State, had organised this room in the hotel for her and she was treated to not only an overlooking view of the city square but also a clear view of the prison situated on the crossroads.

The Hotel Zenobia had apparently been built in the 1930s, made famous when Agatha Christie and her husband Max visited to take part in archaeological digs. The locals claimed that she was inspired to write Murder on the Nile whilst standing on her balcony in this exact hotel. Freya's accommodation was in the old Oasis Wing, which had all the latest modern facilities and had been decorated to seemingly resemble a Bedouin tent.

The ancient Aramaic city of Palmyra was once the crossroads of the Greek, Roman, Persian and Islamic cultures and had been used for hundreds of years by camel herders as a stopping point. The World Heritage site, Freya thought, was looking a little bit worse for wear, with abandoned ordnance and pockmarked walls from the constant barrage of shelling and light machine gun fire.

Freya had left Emily and Oliver in Israel and made her way here to Palmyra in Syria alone. It would have been easy for her to come in under the radar, but she had decided that as she needed to meet with these people from Islamic State, it was easier to just announce her arrival and let them be her travel agent. She had arranged to meet with Nada al Husain later that morning on the pavement café owned by the hotel and was merely counting down the hours she had left before their arranged meeting time. The Mossad team secretly looking after her had asked if she would try and keep all meetings outside if it were possible, as they could then provide extra cover in case something went wrong. She scoffed again now as she had done when they had first asked. This is why she hated working for other people, why she had decided to go freelance. Nobody seemed to get that she could look after herself and that she didn't need backup, or cover fire, or help in any shape or form. But she was doing this mission as a favour to Nikki, so had informed the Mossad team not to interfere unless they deemed it to be a life or death situation. She felt confident, however, that the terrorists were more interested in her money than capturing some lone woman negotiator who held little benefit to them as a hostage or a corpse. Hell, she probably wouldn't even be worth much of a ransom. But that was exactly why she was so good at what she did.

Freya made her way back into her room and lay on the comfortable bed, facing the ceiling, realising that she never truly felt nervous; though she supposed she now had backup and thus knew that nothing truly awful was going to happen.

She waited for the rest of the hour to pass by and then stood up, checking her comms equipment one last time before leaving the room.

Twenty minutes later, she was sat at the small café table, sipping a cup of coffee.

"I don't suppose you're going to give me a receipt for all this money, are you?" she asked Nada al Husain sarcastically. He looked up at her without moving his head to better see her and stared at her for three seconds before ignoring her comment and continuing to count the money in the briefcase before him.

It was over thirty degrees, the humidity unbearable, as Freya sat at the outside terrace café. Though she was dressed in European clothes, consisting of trousers and a tank top, she was wearing a dark, patterned headscarf and a loose shawl over the shoulders, which was hiding her Famas F1 machine gun. She held it nestled under her arm and could raise it in a millisecond if she felt something was amiss. She had two guests sat opposite her. The first was Nada al Husain, the 'press officer', and the other was a mysterious colleague who had not spoken a word throughout the exchange. Though Freya was extremely curious and intrigued as to who this man was and why he was there, she knew that if she asked too many questions she would draw attention to herself, so she had resolved to keep her mouth shut. Once she had handed them the briefcase containing the million dollars, she knew she was in business; all that was needed now was a little bit of patience and perseverance to see this meeting through.

She hoped that her Mossad team, who had promised to have eyes on her the whole time, had managed to take some photographs to allow them to identify the mystery stranger.

After several minutes of counting the money over and over again, Nada al Husain looked up from the bag of money and nodded at his guest, who nodded back. Without saying a word to Freya, they both stood up and left, taking the bag with them. Freya frowned and sat back in her chair, sipping the rest of her coffee. they hadn't given her a receipt after all.

A few minutes later, she pulled out her phone and began typing.

CHAPTER 26

A NEW FRIEND

Antonietta, with the help of Julie at MI6, had worked through the night studying the money trail left by Islamic Sect and both were puzzled, not only by the amount that Islamic State had in funds but also with what they appeared to be doing with it.

Over a hundred million dollars worth were in bonds, with another hundred and twenty million in stocks and shares. That was only one account. It appeared that they were trying to mask their operation as a legitimate business and the banks were facilitating their notions, albeit unwittingly and unknowingly.

Antonietta felt sure that if they could just hack the servers, then they would be able to attach an invisible watermark to all the transactions, which would follow them around. This would let her know instantly where all their money was going, even if they moved it from one account to another. The only time that they would lose track of the trail was if the money was turned into cash, but by the looks of their previous transactions that hadn't happened before and was unlikely to happen in the future.

Antonietta guessed that Islamic State would be using their cash, like the kidnap cash that Freya had just dropped off, for paying bills and donor donations and other illegal funds such as trafficking, oil revenues and self-imposed taxes, whereas their bank accounts revealed no such trace of any money laundering.

"Very clever..." Antonietta said quietly. Just then, the Vendicare email symbol flashed up on the screen. Antonietta clicked on it and saw that they had received an email from Freya. "Nikki! Get over here, I've got something from Freya!"

Though the Mossad team had 5g virtual satellite cameras monitoring her, the team were only able to monitor Freya's movements through her standard GPS watch. They were unaware of how the meeting with Nada al Husain had gone, whether he had taken the bait.

From: fry@vendicare.com
To: Nikki@vendicare.com

Hotel is just as I remembered it, but the tea is still too sweet.
I've made a new friend. I hope you like the look of him.
Meeting with Agatha went well! Have spent all my holiday money though, I hope dad will send me some more.
Think I will be meeting up soon with my three brothers and two sisters, but I'm slightly worried; I think I may have another sister!
Will try and find a post box to send you a card later.
Lots of love,
Fry

Antonietta read the email three times over, and on the third time made no more sense of it than on the first.

"Toni, what's she said?" Nikki said, appearing behind Antonietta's shoulder.

"I actually have no idea," Antonietta said, bewildered, as

she enlarged the email and put it on one of the screens so that Nikki could read it. "I think you may need to translate for me."

Nikki read the email once or twice. "Well, the tea is still too sweet is the phrase she will always use to confirm that she hasn't been compromised, so that's good. Meeting with Agatha means that she has made contact. She's spent all her holiday money, so she's handed over the money, but she wants some more just in case. Three brothers and two sisters will be referring to hostages; we know there are five, three male and two female, but she says something about a possible other female hostage, which would be news to us." Nikki looked studiously at the email for clues before shaking her head. "The post box means she will ring later when she's sure she's alone. I've made a new friend.... what does that mean? Damian, could you get some images up from the Mossad team?"

"Sure thing Nikki, got them open here now. I can see Freya sat across from two men at some terrace café."

"TWO men?" Nikki asked.

"Yeah, two."

"Run facial recognition on the one that isn't Nada al Husain, now. We need to know who that person is."

Damian set to work on scanning in the images. A few moments later there was a light ping, meaning that the machine had finished running the facial recognition on the pictures which Freya's Mossad team had uploaded.

"Okay, we have facial recognition on Freya's new friend," Damian announced; Nikki and Antonietta both rushed over. "It's Salma Mahmoud."

Suddenly the door of the room opened and Vincent and Saxby entered. The room was full. Antonietta was at the monitors with Nikki and Damian, staring at the profile of Jihadi John. The two new recruits from SRU, Jamie and Carl, were transferring information on the big screens and Steve was on the phone talking to Tim, making arrangements to fly over to Malta to pick the boys up from Hereford when they were due to arrive at 1700 hours. Steve came off the phone with Tim as Vincent entered the room and so was the first to greet him with a handshake. Then Nikki walked over to Vincent. "Good trip?" she asked.

"Would have been better if you were there," Vincent said, smiling, then he announced to the room, "Well kids, that was a pretty successful trip to the States!" and with that he filled them in on his trip, including a meeting with the President at the White House itself and being manhandled off a plane by the Secret Service.

Saxby cut in. "The President dismissed his Chief of Staff AND the Director of Intelligence with just a wave of his hand," she said, grinning.

"Ohhhh, I wish I had seen that! Priceless!" Nikki said, laughing.

Antonietta then saw Vincent looking at the screen behind them, which was showing the picture of Salma Mahmoud. He turned to Nikki with a questioning look on his face.

"Sit down; let's get some coffee and we'll explain what's going on," Nikki said by way of explanation, pulling out a chair for him. Everyone else took a seat too. Antonietta gave a quick briefing explaining about the money trail that she had caught up on and Vincent looked thoroughly pleased with their progress.

"If we can keep an eye on their finances, we will be able to keep an eye on their movements and also their motives. Great, Antonietta, brilliant!" he said.

Then Nikki launched into her finding of Salma Mahmoud and the meeting with Freya. "It was a success; they took the money, but there was an extra person at the meeting. We did a facial recognition scan on him and found out that it was Salma Mahmoud, the guy that we suspected was behind the executions. Unfortunately, it means that this British national, who was brought up in Manchester, is part of Islamic State; he apparently recruited many British people to their cause. MI6 have been looking at this character since the first execution, but I think it's time to let the PM know that it was indeed who they have been suspecting. I don't think he will take the news too well, but it's our responsibility to tell him, I think. Also, Freya seems to think that there are more than five hostages. She believes that they are holding an extra female that we didn't know about, but she has no idea who she is or where she has come from."

"An extra hostage? And the guy behind the executions is British?" Vincent sighed. "As much as this news is disappointing, and disturbing, it's news nonetheless, so it's progress. Well done! I'll tell the PM once this meeting is over and I think I'll also put in a call to the President. Now, how is everything going with preparations for our SAS and Seal teams coming in tonight?"

Antonietta was slightly astonished that Vincent had taken the news as well as he had, but Nikki took it in her stride. "Amanda is going to collect the boys from Hereford at about 1700 hours, then pick the Seals up at 2000 hours."

"And what do you think regarding housing them all?" Vincent asked.

"Well, Jen and I have made arrangements for the teams to be housed in a hotel."

"Really? I wonder if it might be more beneficial to have them on camp. It might be better for them getting to know each other for general team morale? What do you reckon?"

"I think that's a good idea, but where exactly are we going to put them all?"

"Well, we only have four rooms left in the main building... what if some of the team move into the villa? We've got twelve rooms and only three are currently in use. Then the rest of the rooms in the main building can go to the new team members coming in," Vincent suggested.

Nikki thought for a couple of seconds and then said, "Yeah, great! I'll have a word with the teams at lunch and see who's happy to move. Good idea, Vincent."

"I also thought that tomorrow night at The Club on the mainland we could have dinner with everyone so that the guys can let their hair down, then we can start work the following morning."

Nikki readily agreed. "It will give me a little extra time to go through a plan for a work-up of our next operation".

Everyone started to stand up and gather their things, as the meeting was deemed to be over. Antonietta started to make her way back over to her computer when she heard Vincent behind her. "Shit!" he shouted.

"What?!" she said, turning back around quickly.

Vincent looked at her apologetically, then pointed to one of the smaller screens. "McIlroy has just missed a putt."

Antonietta scoffed loudly. "I thought for a second it was something serious!"

Vincent looked shocked. "It IS serious! The yanks are one point up in the first four balls!"

CHAPTER 28

COOK LIKE YOUR MUM

Oliver and Emily were at the MOB (Main Operating Base) for Operation Houdini, which was located in Turaif, checking out the facilities and relaying any new information back to Nikki. Oliver wanted to make sure that they had everything ticked off before they left.

The building itself was just a shell. Apparently it had been earmarked as a new communications centre by the Saudis to keep an eye on the Assad regime but, after Syria fell into disarray, the plan was abandoned. The major advantage to using this building was the fibre optic infrastructure which had been installed and linked to Sabre communication dishes mounted on the top of the three-storey building. Antonietta, having seen the blueprint to the structure, had already told them that she felt sure she would be able to patch into the system. Emily even suggested that seeing as this base wasn't actually under any direct threat, Antonietta could run the tech operation from here.

As they didn't want to open up the circle of trust to the Jordanians and the Saudis, Emily had got her father to agree to send a small team of engineers up from Mossad who could start getting the base into operational readiness. They would also need temporary living quarters setting up for up to forty personnel, but more importantly, an operation centre with emergency generators and a signals mast for point-to-point and satellite communications.

"Well, Em, what do you think? Reckon we can get this place operational in three to four days?" Oliver said, wandering around the building with Emily.

"I don't see why not," she said. "As long as you pull your finger out."

Oliver turned to look at her. It didn't seem as though she was joking; she hadn't looked at him or spoken to him properly since they had left base. Oliver hated talking about feelings, especially with women, and most of the time attempted to ignore anything that might be wrong. But he felt he needed to know what was bothering Emily. She was never usually like this. "Em. What's going on? You've been funny with me since we left Gozo."

She glanced at him, then looked away. "Nothing, Ol. Forget it."

Oliver would have gladly left it at that, but he pressed on despite himself. "Come on, tell me."

"No."

"Please."

She turned to him abruptly with a sharp look on her face, as though she wanted to hit him. But he watched her face crumple as she whispered sadly, "Do you like Saxby?"

Oh god. Was Oliver's first thought. He couldn't deal with emotions like this. And his second thought was, Do I? He thought Saxby was great, and really easy to get along with, but did he like her...?

"Wow, that's a bit random," he said with an embarrassed expression on his face. "Why would you ask a question like that?"

Emily looked at him for a few more seconds with a sad expression on her face before she pulled herself together.

"Ignore me. Let's get all this crap sorted out, then we can get back to base," she said, walking away and pulling out the satellite phone. She typed in some numbers before starting a conversation in Hebrew with the person on the other end, whom Oliver assumed to be her father, Avraham. He breathed out slowly, praying that would be the end of it.

***

"Thank you very much, Mr Aaron," Oliver said respectfully as Emily's father handed him an ice-cold beer. They were sat in the thirteen acre gardens of Avraham Aaron's old, Italian-style villa. Olive and lemon trees grew all around them, but dispersed towards the north side of the garden, revealing an incredible view over the pastoral Naphtali valley and the round hills of the Galilee. There was also a fully floodlit basketball court, football pitch and volleyball court, which Oliver thought might look good back at base, but that looked somewhat out of place in these beautiful, delicate gardens.

He had not failed to notice the security personnel surrounding the property when he had first arrived. They must have exceeded thirty personnel. When Oliver had whispered "why?" to Emily, she had responded saying that her father was the highest valued target on the Hezbollah hate list, after the Israeli PM. Oliver watched one of the security personnel wander around the garden with a machine gun gripped tightly in his hands. It seemed as though the Aaron family were so used to it that they didn't even notice their presence.

"Oliver, please, call me Avraham," the man said with a genial smile. "Now then! Tell me. What's going on between you and my daughter?"

The question was so out of the blue that Oliver choked on his beer. He coughed loudly, spluttering.

"Father, stop it!" Emily said, giving him a small slap on the arm and glaring at him while she looked to her mother to intervene, though Oliver couldn't help but notice that her cheeks had flushed. "Don't try to embarrass me."

"Well, she likes you Oliver!" Avraham said with a wink before standing up abruptly and inviting him to join him in the alfresco dining area. Oliver threw a quick, embarrassed glance at Emily, who was avoiding his eye, before standing up and following Avraham.

The four of them settled into the alfresco area in the grounds of the villa. Oliver chatted away easily to Emily's mother Avigail, or Abby as they called her for short, as they tucked into the food that was being served to them by a waiter. There were many things that Oliver did not like about the Middle East, but the cuisine was most certainly not one of them. He had a taste for their amazing spices and Abby's cooking certainly did not disappoint. He tucked in eagerly to the Shakshooka in front of him – a concoction of tomatoes, onions, garlic and sweet paprika topped with a poached egg – and could barely contain his ecstasy.

"This is absolutely delicious Abby, thank you so much!" He wiped some pitta slices around his plate to get up all the juices. "Can you make this, Em?"

Before Emily got a chance to answer, Avraham bounced in. "I told you Emily! The way to a man's heart is through his stomach!" He gave a jovial laugh, tucking into his meal.

Emily looked at her father with a half-smile, half-frown. "As I was about to say, Mother taught me how to cook when I was little. But then I joined the military, then Vendicare, and I never really need to cook anymore. Or rather, I never get the chance," she said.

Oliver sensed that she was upset by this. "Well, when we get back you could do a special Israeli night for the team. They'd love it," he said, trying to give a sweet, meaningful smile.

She looked up at him and frowned. "Whatever," she said, shaking her head. Oliver opened his mouth to respond but realised he had no idea what to say.

Fortunately, Avraham jumped in. "Oliver, when you get back, if you would have a word with your father about meeting up with me that would be very much appreciated. I would like to work more closely with him in future; I feel that we make a good team."

"Yeah, no problem. I think he may actually be considering coming with us on this op, so you will have a chance to see him then, if you'd like," Oliver replied.

"That's even better!" Avraham replied. The housekeeper began clearing their plates, but Avraham held up a hand. "No don't worry about that; Mo, Abby and I will do it. We need something to keep us moving. Or rather to stop us drinking!" They began clearing the plates and took them off to the kitchen, leaving Emily and Oliver sat opposite each other at the table.

"More wine?" Oliver asked.

"Yes, please," Emily said, not meeting his eye.

He topped both of their glasses up and leant back in his seat, sipping the drink. After a few minutes of silence, he leaned forwards again. "Emily, why did you ask me about Saxby?" he asked, eager to find out what was going on in her head, whether she might be thinking what he was thinking.

"Honestly, Oliver, if you need to ask, I really shouldn't have said anything," Emily replied.

Oliver gently took one of Emily's hands, looking at her for what felt like the first time ever. They both stared into each other's eyes. Emily took a breath and was about to say something when Oliver's phone began vibrating on the table before them. They both gave little nervous laughs.

"I... er... I probably ought to get that. It's Nikki," Oliver said and Emily waved her hands in the air in exasperation, but smiled to say it was fine.

"Nik, what's up?" Oliver said.

"I'm just wondering what you want me to arrange for you transport-wise tomorrow. Why? Are you particularly busy? Sorry if I'm interrupting something."

"No, no, don't... er... don't worry, you aren't interrupting anything," Oliver said, glancing at Emily as he did so, who gave him a rueful smile. "Could you sort us out a flight at around ten tomorrow morning?"

"Yeah, that can be arranged. See you tomorrow." She ended the call.

Oliver sat back down, not taking his eyes off Emily. She was running her fingers nervously through her thick, long, blonde hair. "Everything okay at the office, dear?" she asked jokingly. But Oliver knew her well enough to know that she was putting on a front to try and hide the fact that she was scared.

He gazed into her blue eyes. She looked at him nervously, waiting for him to speak. After a few more moments he whispered, "Are you sure you can cook like your mum?"

It seemed like an eternity before Emily registered what he had said, but the moment she realised he was making fun of her, she raised her hand and swung it in the direction of his face. It would have been a hard slap too, if Oliver hadn't quickly raised his hand to block her. Catching her unawares and vulnerable, he put both hands on her face and pulled her in to kiss him.

She melted underneath him as they kissed. He pulled away from her and smiled. She grinned back at him. Wordlessly, he took her hand. They began to walk around the garden together. It was a mild evening, the sun beating down gently on their backs as they strolled, looking at the flowers and occasionally stopping to exchange a small kiss.

After a few moments, Oliver squeezed Emily's hand. "So,

what now? What's the plan?" He could feel how happy she was. He had never been truly sure about his feelings for Emily, whether or not they were really there. He knew they had been strong, but hadn't been sure if it was just because of the type of work they did, watching each other's backs, the bond that develops from that. But now he knew that he wanted to be with her.

"I don't know," she replied, then smiled. "I never truly thought it would ever happen, so I never planned what we would do if it did."

Oliver thought back to his father's unwritten rule about relationships within the team and, although he wholeheartedly agreed with the principle of it, he felt that it was different with him and Emily.

"How did your parents know there was something going on?" Oliver asked, curious.

Emily smiled apologetically. "Well, I've always told Mother everything, so I guess she will have mentioned it to Father. Sorry."

"No need to apologise!" Oliver said quickly. "It's me that needs to apologise for being so damn slow on the uptake."

"If only you were as sharp with understanding emotions as you were on missions, eh, Oli?" Emily said, grinning. She stopped under a lemon tree which was shading them from the sun and pulled him to her once more. Oliver kissed her back, but pulled away, noticing a flash of binoculars from a few hundred metres away. He pulled Emily behind him and then relaxed when he realised it was just the security wandering around the garden, keeping an eye on them and making sure they were safe.

"Not much bloody privacy around here," Oliver complained.

Emily pulled away from his grip and looking accusingly at him. "And why exactly would we need privacy?"

"What! I... I don't mean that!" Oliver said, flustered at the accusation. She raised her eyebrows at him, folding her arms across her chest. "You know what I mean! Em!"

She burst out laughing and punched him in the arm. "Now it's my turn to wind you up!" Oliver grabbed her and picked her up, spinning her around as she squealed at him to let her go. He tickled her and they began wrestling, ending up in a heap on the floor, giggling and out of breath.

"Hey, I have a question," Oliver said, sitting up.

"What is it?" Emily said, following suit and turning to look at him.

"When do we tell our parents?"

"Hmm. Maybe it's a little early yet. I guess we should wait and see what happens."

"I suppose we have only been together a matter of hours."

"If you ask me, I feel like it's been years," Emily said, covering her face with her hands. "Oh dear, no, that was an awkward thing to say. Oh shit, I take it back, forget I said that!"

Oliver pulled her hands off her face. "No, Em, you're right. I feel the same."

"You must remember how perceptive your dad is though," Emily said. "It won't take Vincent long to read into it and realise what's going on."

"Yeah, I guess you're right," Oliver replied, wondering how it would be best to handle the situation that they were in. "I suppose if everything goes wrong and Dad won't change his mind, we can always get jobs with your father and Mossad!" he said.

"No way! You can work for my father and I'll work for yours!" she said before she pulled him to his feet and they made their way together back to the villa.

CHAPTER 29

FAITH

"Anyone in?" Vincent shouted as he entered his villa for the first time since returning from New York. There was no reply, so he shrugged. He made his way up to the terrace and found the three girls sat around the pool chatting. Kerry was talking animatedly to the other two, who were both leaning up on their arms with their sunglasses covering their eyes. As Vincent neared, he heard Kerry mention Aloma's name and smiled. Aloma had obviously made a lasting impression upon his daughter.

"Boungiorno!" Vincent shouted, greeting them all. They all turned around to look at him, smiling.

"Hi Mr Nat... I mean Vincent!" Molly shouted, correcting herself.

"Ciao!" Jodie screeched as she threw down the magazine she was holding and rushed to give him a kiss on the cheek. Kerry looked on, shaking her head at her, knowing that Jodie was only interested in what Vincent had brought her back from New York.

Vincent handed Jodie a huge bag. She clapped her hands together and bounced around in delight, opening the bag. Inside was a new Xbox One. She squealed again. "I ordered one!! But they said it would take MONTHS to come, oh yay, Vincent, thank you so much!" Vincent then handed her a small package, exquisitely wrapped. When she opened it, she pulled out a new Tag Heuer Formula One ceramic ladies watch. Jodie jumped up and down, shouting, "Thank you, thank you Vincent!" Vincent grinned. He loved making other people happy. "Kerry, check it out!"

Vincent could see that Kerry was about to tell Jodie that she had in fact picked it out, but Vincent shook his head at her discreetly and she closed her mouth again, giving him an evil look. "Yeah, Jodie, it's awesome," she said, unenthused.

Vincent turned to Molly. "Mol, I know Kerry will have been going on about her a lot, but do you like Aloma?"

"Yeah, of course I do, who doesn't? I'm waiting until she comes to Manchester on tour, I was going to book tickets to see her," Molly replied. "Why?" she asked, suspiciously.

Vincent pulled out a gold-cased CD, Aloma's first album called 'Faith', which she had signed, 'To Molly, lots of love, Aloma'. Molly freaked out at the gift and gave Vincent a huge hug. They both thanked him hugely and Vincent told them it was absolutely no problem.

"Molly, I'm going to go and disappear off to my room now. I want to wish you a safe flight, alright? Jodie will look after you, I know it. You're welcome back any time," he said.

Molly smiled at him. "Thank you so much for everything you've done for me, Vincent. You've made this all so much easier for me and... without you, I don't think I'd be standing here now. Thank you... and I will definitely take you up on that offer of coming back!"

Vincent laughed and gave her a quick hug. "Then I'm sure I'll be seeing you soon."

He made his way to his room and jumped onto his bed, switching on the television to begin watching the afternoon session of the Ryder Cup. It hadn't gone well that morning, but things seemed to be picking up somewhat for the Europeans. He watched intently, then noticed a strap line running across the bottom of the screen, representing the twenty-four hour news channel. It read: 'MI6 HAVE IDENTIFIED JIHADI JOHN TO BE MANCHESTER MAN SALMA MAHMOUD.' Suddenly, all Vincent could think about was this Salma Mahmoud and what Nikki had said about there being an extra female hostage being held by Islamic State. For some reason, he couldn't get the thought out of his head that this hostage discovery was a big deal and that they needed to do something fast. He couldn't shake the feeling that this was really, really important, but didn't know why.

He shook his head in an attempt to clear it and turned off the television. He climbed out of bed and wandered around the villa. Jodie and Molly had left and Kerry was in her room, listening to music. It had been decided by Nikki that her, Oliver, Saxby and Emily would move into the villa, which had released four rooms for the American Seals Team, meaning everyone was now able to stay at the base.

Nikki and Saxby had obviously already settled into their temporary rooms, as Vincent found them sat by the pool, enjoying the last few hours of sunlight of the day. He sat down next to them and began chatting, saying he wanted to make sure that the new people arriving were made to feel welcome and thanking them both for moving out of their rooms to help that become a possibility.

Nikki looked at him suspiciously. "Vincent. What's up?"

"Nothing, Nik, nothing..."

"Tell us."

Vincent put his head in his hands. "I don't know, it's just that something about this upcoming operation feels a bit... fuzzy. I haven't quite got a clear picture in my head yet."

"That's good, Vincent. It means you're thinking it through as thoroughly as you always do," Nikki replied.

Vincent sighed. "Yeah, I guess you're right." He clapped his hands to snap himself out of it. "So! Do you two fancy doing something a little different tonight? I need a distraction."

"What did you have in mind?" Saxby said.

"I fancy going to The Club on the mainland. I know we will be going there tomorrow anyway with all the Americans and boys from Hereford, but maybe it would be nice for our team to go before everyone else arrives."

"I'm up for that," Saxby said.

"Ah, what with everyone arriving, Vincent, and Freya in the thick of it over there, I think I'll stay behind and look after the shop," Nikki said, smiling apologetically, though Vincent knew she was doing the right thing. "Why don't you see if the twins and any of the others want to go?"

"Good idea. I'll send them all a text. Should be a fun night!"

CHAPTER 30

FISH 'N' CHIPS

It was raining slightly. Jodie and Molly had cleared passport control on arrival at Manchester airport and picked up the hire car which had been booked by Jen with Hertz across from the terminal.

"Is it always this bloody miserable?" Jodie asked under her breath as she programmed the satellite navigation for the twenty-mile journey to Ribchester, which was located in the stretch of countryside between two places called Preston and Blackburn.

Molly laughed. "Pretty much!" Molly was still laughing at Jodie over the customs incident. The customs man had asked Jodie to step back behind the line while he was checking Molly's passport, which had rattled her and, then, when he asked Jodie why she was visiting the UK, she snapped and told him to 'mind his own fucking business'. She had almost got into serious trouble for it too, until he scanned her passport and an alert flashed on the screen. He had then apologised and allowed her on her way. She was feeling particularly smug about that. All travel documents for Vendicare staff had an embedded chip in them as well as tracking which alerted immigration officers never to challenge or delay them.

"He really should mind his own business though. What is it to him what I'm doing in the country?"

Molly merely laughed in response and Jodie smiled. She had gotten quite close to Molly over the past week or so. She felt that even if they hadn't met under the unfortunate circumstances that they had, they could have quite easily become good friends.

It took them forty-five minutes in the new Jeep Cherokee 4x4 to get to Molly's house. Jodie stopped where the sat-nav instructed her to, pulling up outside a stone-built terraced house on a road called Church Street. She stared at it for a moment. "This is your house?" Jodie asked disbelievingly. It was strange for her. She had been brought up in a large Italian house surrounded with acres of wildlife, then lived in the villa back at base. She wasn't used to tiny houses in rows.

Molly looked slightly confused. "Yeah?" Jodie shrugged and started to look for somewhere to park, manoeuvring the enormous car this way and that. "Might be best if you park on the pub car park," Molly said after a few moments of enjoying Jodie's evident struggle.

They entered the house a few moments later. It was cold and damp, to Jodie, though she supposed the heating hadn't been on for a few weeks while Molly had been away. Besides, if the weather was like this all the time how could you ever be warm? Why you would choose to live in this cold country I have no idea, Jodie said to herself with a shiver. She had a look around as Molly rushed to turn on the thermostat to get some warmth into the old, stone building and shivered again, finding this tiny, terraced house almost claustrophobic.

"I... Jodie, I think someone has been here," Molly shouted nervously from upstairs.

Jodie ran up the tiny stairs in a matter of seconds, seeing Molly standing in one of three rooms at the top of the stairs, which she presumed to be Molly's bedroom. She was standing staring at a partially open drawer. "I would never leave a drawer like that," Molly said; Jodie immediately believed her. It was obvious, even from the short time that they had spent together, that Molly was very particular; the rest of the house was immaculately tidy.

"Does anyone else have a key that you're aware of?" Jodie asked, keen to find out who it could have been.

"Well, my ex-boyfriend did, but after what happened, the police told me I should change the locks. No one but my brother had a key after that," Molly said, her voice shaking.

Jodie gave her a quick hug and said, "Don't worry, it's probably nothing. Anyway, I'll be here tonight, so if anything is amiss we can report it straight to the police."

Molly took a deep breath. "Yes, you're right, of course you are. Let's get something to eat, I'm starving!" she said, running back down the stairs to the kitchen. Jodie followed her and found her with her head in the fridge. "Mmm. We may have an issue. There's no food in the house. Do you fancy going to the White Bull?"

Jodie shrugged. "Yeah sure, why not?"

They put their coats on and walked the fifty or so feet across the road to the White Bull. Jodie had never seen a pub in her life. In Italy and Gozo, there were either trendy bars or restaurants. Molly laughed at her when she told her that she'd never seen anything like this before when they walked in.

"Are you crazy?! It's a pub! You can't go anywhere in the UK without finding one!"

Jodie looked at one of the display signs. "What the hell is 'Fish 'n' Chips'? What kind of fish?"

Molly looked astounded. "It's fish and chips! White fish, in a beer batter, served with chips and mushy peas!"

Jodie pulled a face. "Sounds like something the twins would eat."

Molly looked at her as though she was from another

planet, then burst out laughing and wouldn't stop until they had ordered. She ordered a stuffed chicken for herself and a Caesar salad for Jodie, who had no trust in any English food whatsoever, which was made worse by the speed with which the dishes arrived at their table.

They had both probably had one glass too many when they eventually stumbled through Molly's front door a few hours later. They decided not to bother with coffee as they were both exhausted, plus Jodie had an early flight in the morning at nine am.

Molly's spare room was already made up, so she wished Jodie goodnight, promising she would see her off in the morning. Before Jodie switched off her light, she decided to message Vincent.

'Hi V. Missin me? Got here okay with Molly. Everything's good. Not nice here, raining all the time. Had dinner… ew, in a pub...! See you tomorrow. Jod x'

Jodie also decided to send a quick message to her mum. She felt bad for leaving her alone in Italy for all this time. 'Hi mama, missin you loads. In Manchester at the moment. I wish I was with you its so miserable here. Smells of fish and chips tbh. Love you mama, Jodie x She then curled up in the bed with her phone next to her, waiting to see if both would reply, but sleep took over her.

She awoke feeling disorientated a few hours later. She looked around her in the pitch-black, trying to gain some awareness of her surroundings, when she suddenly heard voices. She closed her eyes in the darkness, allowing herself to listen more intently. The noises had stopped. Jodie shook her head. It was probably just Molly talking to someone on her mobile. She groped around for her phone on the bed and found it. It said that it was midnight. She climbed slowly out of bed, gripping her phone tightly in her hand. She padded gently to the door, leaving the light switched off, as it might alert someone that she was awake if she turned it on. She remained cautious.

The traditional, solid oak door had cracks in it and so she pressed her face against it and peered through, hoping to see or hear something that might give her a clue as to why she was suddenly so on edge. Slowly, she released the latch and pulled the door towards her. It creaked loudly. She stopped it, listening again in case the noise had sparked any reaction. Silence. She pulled the door again, making sure it didn't creak, and stepped out onto the landing when the gap was just big enough for her to fit through.

Again she stood, still and alert, listening. The wooden floorboards beneath her creaked with even the slightest weight change, so she tried to keep her body as motionless as she could. She still couldn't hear anything, but she felt on edge. Something wasn't right here. She took a few steps towards the stairs and peered over the banister. A light was on downstairs that definitely had not been on when they had gone to sleep. Jodie placed her finger over the alert button on her phone, which, if it was pressed, would activate an alarm signal back in the ops room at Vendicare. She edged towards the stairs and pressed her back to the wall before kneeling and gently slipping down the stairs to make as little noise as possible.

She eventually reached the bottom of the stairs and stepped into the light of the living room. Her mouth dropped open in horror.

Molly was sat in one of the dining room chairs facing her, dressed in her shorts and a T-shirt. She had rope wrapped around her body and there was thick black tape over her mouth. When she saw Jodie standing there horror-stricken, her eyes opened wide and she began to struggle against her bindings.

Jodie took a small step towards her, then felt a blinding crack around the back of her head.

Everything went black.

CHAPTER 31

PROOF OF LIFE

Freya had been in contact with Nikki by satellite phone from a secure location. She had been extremely pleased to find out that the base team had identified her mystery stranger. But they had an issue with letting any of the other agencies become aware of this. Vincent had made it very clear that Nikki was to trust no one. The last thing they needed now was an off-the-book agency trying a snatch and grab with this Jihadi John, or worse, a drone strike while Freya was still in the vicinity. The situation needed to be handled with caution.

Nikki confirmed to Freya that they were looking at a window of two weeks for the planned three-prong attack and rescue; with the other teams arriving that night, it looked like a realistic target, providing that the hostages' movements could be discovered. Freya had signed off assuring Nikki that she would take care of everything and would report back later after her meeting tonight with Nada al Husain.

It was a few hours after that call and Nikki was sat in the canteen area at base surrounded by men from Hereford and the Seals team. She, along with Antonietta, had done all the introductions and informed them where they were going to be sleeping and what their training programme was generally going to consist of. As she looked around, she was pleased by what she saw. They all seemed highly competent and, despite the hours of travel that they had sitting on their backs, they were listening to her attentively. Once Nikki had finished, Mike Delaney stepped in, informing them all of their first briefing tomorrow and about the dinner tomorrow night back at The Club casino that they were all welcome to come to as a team building exercise, but also for some downtime and to relax and settle in.

"So! Now you're all acquainted, I think it's time for some food, what do you reckon?" Mike said, smiling. His suggestion was greeted by a roar of approval from the assembled men and they all jumped up.

Nikki smiled, but then felt her phone ringing in her pocket. "Sorry, I need to take this," she mumbled quickly to Antonietta, who nodded, before she left the room and pressed 'answer call'.

"Hey Freya, how did the meeting go?"

"Er, yeah it was good," came Freya's voice on the other end of the phone. She sounded anxious, a little distracted.

"Freya, what's going on?" Nikki asked quickly, a sense of worry crawling over her.

"I've... I asked for proof of life for the five hostages. They gave me six DNA samples. I asked for the sixth name, telling them that we were unaware of a sixth hostage and all they could tell me was that she was female. They refused to give the name."

Nikki was silent on the other end of the phone. Her mind was playing tricks on her and she couldn't register anything.

"Nik, you still there?" came Freya's nervous voice down the phone.

"I... How can they have another Special Forces hostage? They haven't been able to come into contact with anyone who could class as a hostage since the Special Forces failed mission and no one else has been reported missing..." Nikki stumbled over the thoughts. "Thanks Freya, thank you, I just need to think this through. I'll speak to you soon." Nikki ended the call and put her head in her hands, her brain whirring.

She looked around the ops room, forgetting how she had even got there, and began to pace up and down the room, muttering to herself. A few minutes later, Antonietta appeared in the doorway, breathless and frantic.

"Nikki! What are you doing?!" she screamed.

Nikki looked at her, confused, her mind numb. "What?"

"Look at the bloody screen!" Antonietta yelled. Nikki turned around, seeing the control screens flashing up red alerts. "It's Jodie's alarm!" She sprinted to the computer and immediately began to frantically type in codes. A few seconds later, pictures began to materialise on the screens and they were transported into what looked like someone's kitchen.

Nikki quickly shook her head, pulling her brain back in gear. "What's going on? Where is she?" she asked desperately. Antonietta began to zoom and pull at the camera to change the angle; they could now see Molly tied to a chair, tugging against some bindings, with her face covered by black tape. "Where's Jodie?! What's happening? Change the angle again, Toni!" Nikki shouted. The camera moved down and the screen showed an image of a body slumped in front of Molly, with the shadow of a figure standing behind her holding a shotgun. "Zoom! Zoom!" Nikki instructed Antonietta, desperate to find out who it was, praying that it wasn't Jodie and that it wasn't what it looked like.

"I can't do anything else with the camera angle, something's blocking my movement!" Antonietta shouted.

"Keep working on it!" Nikki shouted as she pulled her phone from her pocket and began to dial numbers as quickly as she could.

She got through to Hereford immediately and managed to speak to the duty officer, who readied a four-man unit based on another op at Manchester airport. "We'll send them to Ribchester right away ma'am!" the man said after a few minutes. "They'll be in the air in ten minutes, scheduled to land on a playing field behind the house. I will inform the Manchester Armed Response Unit to be in attendance and provide backup," the man said. Nikki hurriedly uttered her thanks before she hung up.

"Toni! Check Jodie's bios! She might be wearing her precision biometrics wristband, in which case we can find out how stable her condition is!" Nikki shouted. Antonietta immediately searched through the computer to find Jodie's bios. Nikki didn't say it out loud, but she thought she had seen a pool of blood by the side of Jodie's head. She prayed it was only from the butt of the shotgun that the man in the background was holding, not the barrel. She prayed with all her might.

Her thoughts suddenly turned to Vincent. Should she call him? What would his reaction be?

"She's alive, thank god!" Antonietta yelled. "Her heart rate is low, but nothing major!"

"Toni, I gotta go! I need to get over to the mainland to see Vincent; he's at The Club, and this is not the type of message I can give over the phone. If you need any assistance, grab Steve, he'll be down in the canteen with the new people here. In fact, I'll tell him to come up here when I go down."

Antonietta nodded and turned back to the screen immediately to monitor the situation as Nikki bolted from the room, running for the canteen and then the Eurocopter.

CHAPTER 32

WE HAVE A PROBLEM

"Good evening Mr Natalie and Miss Natalie. Cara is expecting you on the first floor," the security guard at The Club said as Vincent and Kerry walked through the open glass door. Vincent nodded his thanks. Kerry linked her arm through his as they made their way up the traditional oak staircase to the first floor, where The Club's Director of Guest Relations Cara Simone was waiting for them.

She greeted them with a beaming smile and walked over towards them to kiss them both on each cheek. "Bonsoir Vincent, êtes-vous bien?"

Vincent had first met this thirty-two year old French national on a visit to the Paris Vegas Casino a few years ago. He had watched the style and ease with which she dealt with the high flyers of the casino world, who spent a million or so at a time, and knew that he wanted her to run The Club for him. She hadn't needed much persuading. She told him she was getting bored of the Vegas scene and running The Club came with not only less problems, but also more upmarket guests.

Vincent smiled back. "Do we have time for a quick, private drink?" Vincent asked.

"For you, always," she said with a typical French drawl.

She then looked behind Vincent and Kerry at their assembled team of Saxby, Billie, Amanda and the twins and handed them each an envelope, which contained five black square chips with a value of $1000 on each. "Ah, Mr Natalie, I have one prepared for your beautiful daughter also, if that is okay with you?"

Vincent nodded, before asking the twins to keep an eye on her.

"No problem, boss," Lee said. "Come on Kerry, let's get some shots." Vincent shook his head, knowing, or at least hoping, that Lee was joking.

He and Cara made their way to a private lounge and sat on one of the plush leather sofas and began a discussion about how The Club was functioning, how he thought Cara may have improved the relationships with their high-stake gamblers. They then moved onto the dinner plans and table reservations for the following evening; Vincent said he would appreciate her joining them if she didn't have any prior engagements.

"I had planned to be there anyway. It would be an honour to be your guest, Vincent," she said.

He then handed Cara a sealed envelope, requesting that she look at the contents later and let him know what she thought, before saying his thanks and taking his leave.

He wandered back through the casino to check up on the team, who even from a distance looked to be having a good time. The twins were playing at one of the blackjack tables and appeared to be holding their own while the girls were stood around one of the many roulette tables.

"Rien, ne va plus!" the croupier shouted as the little metal ball began to slow down and clip the pockets of the wheel.

Vincent wandered towards them. "How we doing ladies?" he asked them all, scanning the chips in front of them all. They were all surrounded by them except for Kerry, who looked to be on her last two black chips.

"Dad, it's fixed, I'm sure it is. I haven't hit anything all night," Kerry said, sounding very disappointed.

Vincent squeezed in next to her. "Okay Kerry, listen up. So, currently you are attacking the table with a scatter effect. This is costing you more than you are being rewarded with." He then took Kerry's black chips and asked the croupier to break them into 100s, giving her twenty chips. After looking at her previous numbers on the monitor, he noticed her pattern didn't include any middle teen numbers in the last twenty drops. He turned to her. "What's your favourite number?" he asked.

"Sixteen," she responded immediately.

Vincent then placed four chips straight on sixteen, with six further chips surrounding it on quarters and doubles, catching thirteen, fourteen, fifteen, seventeen, nineteen and twenty.

Saxby, Billie and Amanda decided to get in on some of the action and piled on top of Kerry's chips, making almost skyscraper heaps on those seven numbers.

"Rien, ne va plus!" the croupier shouted again. The table had now attracted a crowd.

It seemed to take an eternity for the metal ball to stop bouncing in and out of the pockets, before it eventually rested on black seventeen.

A cheer erupted from around the table. Though they hadn't hit sixteen, they had covered splits and corners at 17-1 and 8-1, giving Kerry about 3,200 back, with six-hundred still on the table. Vincent whispered in Kerry's ear to remake the bet with everything she had and let it ride. She looked at him with wide eyes and her mouth erupted into a smile. Vincent grinned back and left the table, but not before hearing another roar of triumph.

He found himself at the small private bar in the corner of the room. "The usual, Mr Natalie?" the barman asked.

"Thanks, Geoff," Vincent replied, turning his attention to

one of the TVs which was playing a rerun of the day's play at Gleneagles, showing the Europeans leading by two points.

Vincent had first started using roulette tables after poker games and had quickly worked out the most profitable way of winning. You had to pick a series of numbers and stick with them. For him, those numbers had always been sixteen, seventeen, eighteen, nineteen, twenty, twenty-one, with eighteen being the prime, giving him a 6:3 chance of winning on every spin. Once, his prime number had come in three times consecutively, winning him 100k each time. That was the first time he had met Cara.

Suddenly, Kerry and Saxby appeared at his side. "How did you know that number was going to come in?" Saxby asked suspiciously as she placed all her chips in perfectly symmetrical order on the bar in front of her.

"I didn't," he objected. "It's pure luck. But they're my numbers and, sooner rather than later, they always come in," he said before offering her a drink.

"Dad, do you have any idea how much I WON?!" Kerry said with a huge grin on her face.

"Twenty-eight thousand, with some change?" he said smiling. "Did you tip the croupier?"

Kerry's face fell. He took a black chip off her and went over to the table, handing it to Devina before apologising that they hadn't tipped her. She smiled understandingly.

As Vincent turned around, he saw Cara heading towards him, strolling hurriedly across the room with the envelope he had given her in her hand. He stood, waiting expectantly. "Vincent, you cannot do that," she whispered feverishly to him when she got close enough for him to hear. "It's not, well, it's not expected!"

"Don't be ridiculous," he said. "We are opening up another fifty casinos in the next three years and Jen and I want you on board." Vincent simply didn't understand why people always reacted this way. If someone was loyal to him, he tied them into the business. Before she had the chance to come back at him, he added, "Cara, if anything were to happen to me, Jen and Kerry will need you. All I am doing is making sure that will happen. Call me selfish, call it whatever you want, but a five percent share of the casino business means you're set up for life. What more could you want?" he said,

"It's not about the money, Vincent; you have my loyalty for free. Why would you want to give me this amount of money?" she said.

"That's exactly why. Because you don't expect it," he whispered back.

Head of Security Justin suddenly appeared behind Cara, Vincent raising his eyebrows at him to give him the opportunity to speak. "I'm sorry for interrupting, Mr Natalie, but there is a woman here asking a lot of questions... and I think they all relate to you."

"Cara, we will finish our conversation later. I'll stay here all night until you agree, remember," he said. She nodded. "Now then, can you find one of the private VIP areas and offer to chat with this woman. We've been being followed and tracked by some nosy journalist; from what I can remember her name's Claire Ashcroft, works for International News Corps. Find out what she knows. Use one of your comms and I'll take an earpiece and listen." Cara nodded again and turned to take this Claire Ashcroft into a private room. Vincent put the earpiece that Justin handed him in and went to sit by the bar. He pulled out his phone and sent a quick text to Antonietta:

'Antonietta, please pick up the feed from The Club. Nosy journalist Claire Ashcroft has shown up. Keep an eye on her. I will only get involved if I need to, VN.'

Vincent saw Saxby looking at him curiously and he

beckoned her over. "Keep an eye on Kerry and the team for me. I have a little situation to deal with." She smiled and said that was fine, then promptly disappeared.

Almost all casinos in the world were bugged by microphones, so that owners could listen in to conversations to catch scammers or cheats. In most cases, they're only used to settle disputes between players and dealers, but this case was for something far more serious and potentially dangerous: what does this woman know?

After only a few minutes of listening to the conversation, Vincent had heard enough and decided to intervene. He slid off his seat and headed towards the private room. He opened the door and found them both sat there in the middle of what appeared to be a heated discussion. Claire turned around, with an annoyed expression on her face, while Cara looked at him grimly.

"Claire Ashcroft, I presume," Vincent said, extending his hand out towards her.

She rose from the sofa and took his hand, shaking it briefly. "And you are...?" she said.

"The person you've been looking for," he replied, staring at her. He broke the eye contact after a number of seconds after Claire said nothing and turned to Cara. "Thank you for your time, Cara." He then pointed out the two MI6 officers who they could see standing outside the door. "Let those two kind gentlemen know that they are off the clock now; organise them some dinner if you would. They must have had a busy day following this journalist on and off planes."

Cara nodded and left the room and Vincent felt Claire's eyes snap on him, piercing into him suspiciously. There was an eerie silence. Vincent picked up the water jug from the table in front of them and filled up a glass for both himself and Claire. He allowed the silence to drift on for a further few minutes, as it sank in for Claire that she had been being followed for several days. She sat motionless.

"So. What would you like to know?" Vincent asked, making sure that his voice lacked any real emotion.

"Everything," Claire said.

"Why don't you fill me in on how you've found me and why you wanted to find me in the first place," Vincent asked reasonably. Claire appeared to hesitate for a moment, but it was clear that she was in no position to refuse his request.

"Well. I work for International News Corps in London. I was covering the recent abduction of the children and I stumbled on what I thought might be a world exclusive story... Although admittedly I never saw the rescue in action, I got to speak to several of the volunteers who were looking after the children and even managed to get some detailed stories from the rescued girls themselves. I had assumed the mission was completed by the SAS, but something didn't quite add up... I attempted to use my contacts in the military and government, who tend to give me a little wink or nod on who's responsible, but no one was giving me anything." She looked nervous and spoke haltingly, but Vincent nodded encouragingly and she opened her mouth to continue. "The most intriguing thing was the fact that the children spoke of some of the rescuers being women. I then knew for a fact that it couldn't be the SAS or the US Special Forces, because they don't employ females, so who actually carried out the rescue mission? The connection for me came when the paper asked me to follow up a story, referring to two camel herders who had been kidnapped by some 'demonic woman' in Chad. They told me, with some slight persuasion... that there had been a private plane, a group of 'hunters' who had led them to within a few kilometres of the camp where the children were rescued from. Well, neither of the camel herders had ever seen a plane before, so one took a picture on their phone. It was pretty poor quality, but the markings on the plane led me to a Malta registered company called The Club."

Vincent nodded. Jen had registered the plane to the casino purposefully so that there could never be a comeback on Vendicare. Claire hesitated again, but when Vincent stared at her, she quickly continued on with her story in the same, nervous tone.

"Well, then there was this diver rescue on Gozo. I checked the registration details on the helicopter which performed the rescue and it was registered to this place too. It all seemed like too much of a coincidence. Then I attempted to ring the girl who survived the rescue, but was met by a wall of silence. It was this that convinced me and the paper to follow this story all the way to Malta."

"So then what?" Vincent asked. He was intrigued. She was obviously bright and good at what she did. But he needed to somehow convince her that she didn't need to print this story. It could ruin everything if she did...

Claire took a deep breath. "Then... I landed in Malta and got the ferry to Gozo, arranging to stay in the same hotel as the one that the girl and her brother stayed in before the diving incident. I managed to talk to some divers in the beach bar about the rescue. They were able to give me rough directions as to where the helicopter had taken Molly. They told me that the local gossip was that this place that they took her was something to do with the movies. One of the guys told me that they thought the person who owned that place also owned The Club, where the plane and the helicopter were registered, so everything pieced together. Another guy told me it was owned by some millionaire on the island, but he thought that all the stories were just gossip and were exaggerated. Anyway, after talking with them, I decided to come here and see for myself."

Vincent remained silent for a few minutes and then smiled

for the first time. "Sounds like a BBC drama, or perhaps a very good book," he said.

She looked at him with a sharp frown. "So you're denying it all?"

Another uneasy silence ensued, in which Vincent took a sip of his drink and placed it slowly and deliberately back onto the leather coaster. He looked at her and she stared defiantly back. She certainly knows how to play hardball, he thought to himself. You can't argue with that. He leant back in his chair, before eventually saying, "It's all true. Well, nearly. Your version is a bit... mumsy."

He gave her the full, unedited version. He spoke of the children's graves at the rescue mission, the sexual savagery of the terrorist organisation. He talked of the bravery of his team, who risked their lives on every mission, just because everyone else in the world felt it was not important enough, not worth their time or money, because it wouldn't feed them back in votes. He explained that their company answered to no government or organisation, explaining the politics of their business, though he was careful not to mention VirtualTech, as it was clear she had not discovered the connection between the two organisations yet. He spoke of the death of his wife and his son, how they were brutally killed by terrorists whilst they were sailing, and how that had motivated him to start the business in the first place after the total lack of response from anyone in the world.

He eventually paused for breath, taking a sip of his drink. His voice felt hoarse. Claire stayed silent for a moment before asking quietly, "Why are you being so honest with me?"

"If I denied everything, I know you would keep digging. Eventually you would endanger your own life, but more importantly, you would endanger the lives of the people I love and my family. That is not happening."

"Is that a threat?" Claire asked, defiant again.

Vincent smiled again. "The only threat to you is yourself," he said simply. "In no uncertain terms, Miss Ashcroft, if you continue digging and attempting to write your story, or if you ever print a word of what we have discussed... every wannabe terrorist, hijacker, or criminal will seek you out, as you are one of very few people in this world who can identify us. And the others all have some serious security defending their lives, which I don't believe you do. If you print anything, your life will end, I can guarantee you that. I suppose it's up to you whether you think it will be worth it, but you'll have my family's blood on your hands too."

Claire looked well and truly terrified. He leaned over and saw her flinch before he whispered in her ear, "Don't be daft. Nothing's going to happen to you. It's not the bloody movies." Her body relaxed. "Get up, we're going for a walk, I've got something to show you."

She forced a small smile and stood up, following him past Justin and Cara who were looking across the casino floor. Billie and Amanda were sat at the bar, chatting to anyone who would listen while topping up their glasses with a Dom Perignon rosé champagne. Vincent sidled up to them and introduced Claire.

"Girls, this is Claire, a journalist from the UK. She wants to do a story on the rescue of the kids," Vincent said, watching the girls carefully for their reaction.

They both laughed. "No kidding boss, though I'm not sure I'm ready for the cover of Hello just yet," Billie said, puffing up her hair deftly before laughing again.

"Mmm, GI Billie does have a certain ring to it... it'd make a great story," Amanda said, joining in with Billie's giggling.

"No girls, seriously. Tell Claire honestly, and I mean honestly, what you do for a day job."

Amanda and Billie stopped laughing and looked at Vincent

to see if he was bluffing. He shrugged and nodded at them.

Billie, never knowing when to stop the joke, said sarcastically, "You mean... we AREN'T socialites spending all of your money in night clubs and casinos?" she said, sipping her champagne delicately.

"I'm serious," Vincent said in a tone that told her he wasn't joking anymore.

Amanda took over. "We kill nasty people and save nice people."

Vincent held his hands up to Claire, who looked at him nervously. He left the two girls to their drinking and pointed out Saxby and Kerry, standing with the twins at the roulette table.

"You know, Claire, somewhere in Syria or Iraq, right now, there are five hostages, including two British journalists, who did exactly the same job as you. They might be on YouTube any day now." He looked at her. "Do you honestly want their blood on your hands?"

"I understand what you're saying, Vincent. But I have always believed that freedom of the press should always come first. People have the right to know what's truly happening in the world." Vincent shook his head and attempted to keep his cool. This was a principle he had always, strongly, disagreed with.

As he looked at Claire, he realised that she had lost her confidence and her defiance. He realised she was beginning to come round. No one wants someone else's life on their hands, no matter what you believe regarding freedom of the press.

Vincent was about to say something else, realising that Claire was close to tipping over the edge and agreeing not to print the story, when he noticed Nikki running across the floor towards them. He stared at her in utter surprise. "Nikki!" When he saw how out of breath she was, the expression on her face, his heart dropped. "What is it? What's wrong?"

Nikki immediately looked to Claire. Vincent asked her to give them a moment in private. Claire looked at them both with a curious expression on her face, but stepped away nonetheless.

"Vincent. We have a problem. Well, two... but before I say anything, she's alive and her bios look good."

Vincent felt sheer panic take over. "Whose bios? Nikki, what's going on?"

"It's Jodie. We think Molly's ex-boyfriend has broken into her house. Her panic alarm went off. She's unconscious, but she's alive. The GS550 is up and waiting at Malta Airport so we can get to Manchester as soon as possible. I can fill you in more on the plane, but we've got to go. Now."

Vincent couldn't process it all, but felt Nikki's sense of urgency. "Grab the twins. Make sure Billie gets everyone home safe. Nobody mention it to Kerry. No one." He began to head towards the exit and the waiting helicopter as Nikki ran off to get the twins and instruct Billie to send everyone home, then saw Claire standing awkwardly a few feet away from him.

"You want a story, Claire?"

She nodded.

"Then come with us."

CHAPTER 33

MR SHINY BUTTONS

The boys from Hereford were just coming in to land in a school field only a few hundred yards from Church Street, where they had been urgently called out to deal with the situation. Gavi, the leader of the team, leant against the side of the helicopter and opened the door as they careered towards the ground. They had hoped for the opportunity to go in silently, but unfortunately with the noise and commotion caused by the helicopter and the local Bobbies, who had managed to wake up the whole bloody village, there wasn't a chance of that happening.

Some woman called Antonietta had sent them a link with the footage of what was taking place in one of these terraced houses with a live feed, which had allowed them to get up to speed on the situation. Gavi yawned. This type of hostage situation would have normally been handled by the local constabulary, probably overseen by the chief constable and dealt with by some police Armed Response Unit, but for some reason the PM himself had instructed that the SAS take control. So here they were.

Gavi was part of the four-man team, who had been on a surveillance operation at the airport, meaning they were already kitted up. Him and his friend Davey were regulars in their thirties and they immediately jumped from the helicopter, sprinting to 274 Church Street to evacuate the occupants of the neighbouring house to where the situation had erupted.

They were joined by O'Donnell, another seasoned operator, who had disappeared to the pub across the road and was surveying the property with some thermal imaging binoculars.

Gavi heard his voice come over the comms, "Team to leader, I have eyes on three. One seemingly immobile, one sat down, also appears unmoving, and the last looks to be our hostile. Pacing around the property with a possible weapon, over."

"Got that Donny, just drilling some holes to get a camera in there, over," Gavi responded.

Mac, the final member of their team, was younger than the rest of them and was bringing in, with the help of the local police, several Peli cases containing all their toys and tech. "That's what I'm talking about Maccy boy, pop 'em over here," Gavi said before returning to drilling the holes through the wall to fit the camera into place. They eventually managed to get some Borescopes in through the tiny holes and got some decent visuals on everyone in the room. "Yes lads, we're in business."

Suddenly, there was a knock at the door. Gavi looked around at his team, who all looked as perplexed as he did. "Who the HELL is knocking on the door? WE'RE IN THE MIDDLE OF SOMETHING, THANKS," Gavi yelled. There was another knock, louder and more persistent this time. Gavi cursed under his breath and hauled himself over to the door. He opened it, seeing an official dressed in an immaculately blue police inspector uniform, with huge, shiny buttons.

"Who's in charge here?" the man asked pompously, puffing out his chest and lifting up his chin.

Gavi rolled his eyes. "You can't come in here, mate," he said, dismissively.

"Why not?" the inspector asked.

"Because I bloody well said so. If you don't mind, we're very busy in here. Could you not go and wave your torches at some traffic or something?" Before the inspector could respond, Gavi slammed the door shut in his face.

"What was that all about?" Davey shouted over to Gavi.

"Oh some nobody twat, don't worry about it. How we doing over here?" he replied, moving back over to the group. There were several large Peli cases open with screens in the top cover, showing the live images being transmitted by the Borescopes. One screen was also streaming images from mobile devices belonging to the two non-hostiles.

"Just had a call in from the office Gav, they are patching someone through to you, it's a Steve. Says he knows you," Mac said.

Gavi grabbed the phone off him. "Steve, you involved in this little lovers' tiff?" he demanded down the phone.

"Yes, I suppose I am, but we are handing full operational control over to you as you're on the ground and we won't be there in time. We've got bios on the girl who is unconscious. Name's Jodie, she's alive but her heart rate is low. She may have lost quite a bit of blood, so if you could move soon, that would be much appreciated," Steve said quickly.

"Good man, Steve, that's what I like to hear, a bit of trust for the men on the ground. Not like this pleb inspector outside. Should be going in in about forty-five buddy, I'll keep you in the loop," Gavi said, hanging up the phone and chucking it to one side.

The hostile was pacing around the room; they had now managed to get an audio on him. "What's the dickhead shouting about?" Gavi asked.

"Says if anyone comes in he will kill them all and then himself," Davey said with a snigger.

"Tosser," Gavi said. There was another knock at the door. Gavi opened it. "Yes?"

The pompous inspector was standing outside. "I've rung the house phone several times and tried to talk him down. The man won't have any of it and appears to be getting more and more agitated with the lights and noise from outside," the inspector said, shaking his head in disapproval.

Gavi nodded and slammed the door again. "It's all getting a bit serious in there, lads; now how we doing?" Gavi said to the boys.

"Not long now boss, the C4 gel is in place. I'm just priming it. Pray it doesn't bring the roof down, will ya?" Davey said, grinning.

As the hostile had barricaded both the front and back doors, it would have been near impossible to get a clean entry. They would have to blow two holes in the supporting adjacent wall to give them any chance of an accurate shot at their target. There was another knock at the door. Gavi cursed loudly and opened it again, ready to curse this pompous guy's ass off. But it was someone different. "Who are you?" Gavi asked rudely.

The guy stammered, "I was told to come here... I'm from the electricity board." He looked scared to death of this 6'6" guy dressed in full black kit with a HK416 hanging over his shoulder, a knife strapped to his arm, a pistol attached to his leg and some grenades clipped to his Kevlar vest.

"Excellent. I need you to cut the power for the entire street in exactly fifteen minutes unless I tell you differently. You got that?!" Gavi demanded.

"Yeah, I got it, fifteen minutes exactly!" the guy said with a slight shake in his voice.

Gavi nodded approvingly. "Good man," he said, patting him on the shoulder. He was about the shut the door again when he saw the police inspector heading his way, an Armed Response

Unit officer in tow. Gavi sighed and glanced at his watch. Fourteen minutes to go. He supposed he had one or two minutes to spare arguing with this idiot. The man huffed up to the door.

"I want to know who has given you control over this operation," the man demanded, obviously attempting to show off in front of the ARU officer.

Gavi sighed and decided that actually, he really didn't have time for this. He pulled out a notebook from this top pocket and scribbled a number down on the paper before ripping it off and handing it to the inspector. "If you want to know, ring this number," he said. "And I need you to move everyone back. Get the medical team on standby. We are going in in less than ten minutes." He turned to the ARU officer. "Nothing personal mate. We've got our orders and you've got... well, him," he said before shutting the front door once more.

It didn't take long for Davey to announce, "Two minutes 'til the power's cut, boss."

"Alright boys, suit up and boot up, get ready to go. Now then, disable the target if you can. Lethal if not, but ONLY if you can't disable." The three of them raised their HK416s and the red dots flashed on the wall.

"Three...two...one...GO." The electrics went off at exactly the same moment as the C4 gel blew two holes in the living room wall. There was dust and debris flying around, but Gavi could see their target stumbling backwards, incapacitated momentarily by the implosion of the wall.

The familiar phutt sound of the HK416 in action surrounded Gavi and did its job perfectly. Two shoulder shots and a groin shot meant that the target was incapacitated, but not a fatality. He slumped on the floor, screaming in agony from the excruciating pain he would be feeling. It almost made Gavi wince. He and Mac entered and Mac kicked the shotgun over in the direction of the front door away from the target, then secured the hostile with plastic wrist cuffs, all before the debris had even begun to settle around them.

Davey had kicked open the front door and was helping a medic through. The girl on the floor had obviously lost a lot of blood, but she was squirming and seemed to be coming around. Gavi had freed the girl who had been strapped to the chair and attempted to evacuate her from the building, but she screamed and refused to leave, staring at the girl on the floor with tears on her eyes.

"Come on, Missy," Gavi said to her, rolling his eyes at how unreasonable people could be in these situations. "Let's get you to the ambulance. She's going to be just fine."

The girl slumped in his arms, appearing to have lost all her energy and turned to Gavi in a breathless, quiet voice. "Do you know, she'd never heard of fish and chips before...?" the girl said, sounding disorientated. Gavi almost dropped her at the oddness of her statement. He had been warned about how strange northerners were, but this?

Gavi pulled her gently from the room. A second medic had arrived and was tending to the man on the floor, who was bleeding pretty badly. It was unlikely he'd be using his manhood for quite a while, that's for sure, Gavi thought to himself with grim satisfaction. He took the girl over to the ambulance and the paramedics took over immediately. Suddenly, Mr Shiny Buttons appeared behind him.

"Excuse me," he said, sounding perturbed," but that number you gave me must have been wrong."

Gavi looked at him with fake astonishment. "Why? Who did it connect you to?"

The man flushed. "It was a helpline for erectile dysfunction."

Gavi pulled a confused expression, before saying in a concerned voice, "Oh I'm so sorry mate, I assumed that was what your problem was!"

Before he could reply, Gavi turned away from him and pulled out the satellite phone. "Aye, Steve, that alright for you? Everyone safe and sound now," he said.

"Cheers, that's fantastic. Hope to catch up with you soon," came Steve's hugely relieved reply.

"Just another day at the office, mate," Gavi said before turning off the sat phone and shrugging his shoulders.

CHAPTER 34

NOW THERE'S A STORY

Vincent's heart was in his throat and he could feel his anger rising. "I don't CARE if they have a 'no landing before 0500 hours policy', get us in the air and DO NOT take no for an answer!" he yelled at their poor pilot.

He turned his gaze to Nikki and, before he had a chance to ask, she said, "On it," and telephoned the duty officer at Hereford, asking him to make some calls and get whoever was necessary out of bed so that they could land as soon as the plane arrived in England.

"What about transport when we get there?" Vincent asked her

"Done. And don't ask anything else, just strap yourself in. I'm going up to the front as they need two pilots on the flight deck and I could only get one," she replied, snapping at him for second guessing her, then disappeared onto the flight deck.

Vincent did as he was told and sat down, strapping himself into his seat as he felt the engine warming up and rumbling beneath him. Scott and Lee had already strapped themselves in next to Claire Ashcroft, who appeared to be shaking, but he didn't care right now. All he could think about was Jodie, where she was, the situation she was in, praying that she was going to be alright.

Within moments, the GS550 was starting down the runway; a few seconds later it lifted off.

He tried to sit calmly, breathing deeply as the plane flew through the midnight sky towards Manchester.

He went to see Nikki after only a few minutes, unable to keep still, feeling useless. "How long?" he asked.

She sighed. "Ten minutes less than the last time you asked, Vincent," she said. "Just sit tight, stop stressing; we won't be able to get there any faster than we are going."

Vincent felt humiliated. He sat down next to her. "I'm sorry for how I'm acting, I'm just so terrified." She glanced down at him and gave him a squeeze on the shoulder, wordlessly. "Do you think I ought to ring Jean?" he whispered.

"I reckon you should ring her when we get there. With good news," she replied confidently.

As they were talking, the radio burst into life. "Alpha Oscar Sierra Three, this is Brize Norton control tower. Do you copy?"

Nikki grabbed the receiver. "Go ahead Brize Norton, we copy. Over," she said. Vincent prayed that they weren't ringing to say that they wouldn't be able to get clearance for landing at Manchester Airport.

"Good news, chaps. We have woken up Samlesbury airfield for you. Runway is a little short, but it's only five minutes from your final destination, I'm sending the co-ordinates to your navigation system now. Good luck. Over," came the voice. Vincent felt the relief ebb through his body, while Nikki breathed out next to him.

"Copy that, changing route, heading north-west now, over," Nikki replied.

Less than an hour later, they were touching down at Samlesbury. They all jumped hurriedly from the plane and sprinted over to the waiting, blacked-out Range Rover driven by an ARU officer. Within seconds they were travelling at ninety miles per hour along the bypass, en route to Ribchester. It took them only a matter of minutes and Vincent wasn't waiting for the Range Rover to make a full stop before he was out, heading straight towards the ambulance when he spotted Molly being led from the house by a member of the SAS. Someone attempted to stop him from going through the cordoned off area, but he just brushed them to one side. When Molly saw him, she broke away from the paramedics tending to her and ran to Vincent.

"Vincent, she's fine! She's fine! She's in the house!" Molly shouted over all the noise and pointed at the open front door of the middle terraced house that appeared to be missing a lot of its brickwork. Vincent gave Molly a brief hug and ran straight into the house.

When he saw Jodie, he felt relief flood through his body as he watched her motionlessly, standing in the doorway to the kitchen. She was evidently getting irritated with the medic who was attempting to patch up a cut on her head but was struggling due to the length of her hair, which had become matted with blood. He heard her muttering curses in Italian as the medic tried to calm her down. "Please miss, you must keep still while I clean this out... it looks like you may need stitches." She broke into louder cursing.

Vincent watched the proceedings and just smiled. Then the exhaustion hit him and his body slumped against the door frame. He wouldn't have to make a call to Jean with any bad news. He had been thinking about what on earth he would have said if anything had happened to Jodie the whole time since Nikki had first arrived at The Club, but it was all he could do now to tell himself over and over that Jodie was going to be okay.

The medic had secured the dressing on her head after the

huge palaver and had allowed Jodie to begin to move. It was then that she caught sight of Vincent in the mirror hanging on the wall. She turned in what seemed like slow motion. Vincent moved towards her, feeling the tears welling in his eyes, and threw himself down on the sofa next to her. She flung her arms around his neck and held him tight, sobbing into his shoulder, which set Vincent off too. The next thing anyone knew they were both crying as they held each other.

Eventually, Jodie calmed down and Vincent turned around to see Nikki and the twins standing in the doorway. Nikki looked on and Scott and Lee were chatting to the SAS team leader about how they had run the operation. Vincent asked the medic to check out Jodie's health and whether or not she was fit for travel.

"I'll have to run a few more tests, sir," he said. "The paramedics would feel far more comfortable taking her back to Preston Royal to stitch her up and give her an MRI scan."

"See what you can do," Vincent responded. "But if it's a possibility we can take her home with us, I'd much rather do that." Vincent knew that Jodie could easily have an MRI scan back on Gozo, but he did not want to compromise her health in any way. The medic grasped his torch and held Jodie's chin, moving the torch from side to side, checking for a positive retina response from Jodie.

Molly appeared in the doorway, having been checked over outside by the paramedics. She ran over to Jodie and threw her arms around her neck, sobbing desperately. "Jodie I'm so sorry, I can't believe the trouble I've caused, this is all my fault, what can I do to make it up to you..." she said as the tears fell down her cheeks.

Jodie wasn't having any of it. She grasped Molly tightly by the shoulders. "Molly, stop it now, look at me, I'm fine. We're both fine! Everything's okay," she said, holding on Molly as she sobbed, until eventually her tears became deep heaving breaths.

Vincent left the two girls on the sofa and made his way outside to where Claire Ashcroft was standing awkwardly. He was about to speak, but before he could, she interrupted. "Vincent... I have no intention of printing the story. I would never jeopardise what you're doing here, nor the safety of your family. I was wrong. There are more important things than the freedom of the press. The freedom for people to do as they please is one of them. I'm sorry for any upset I might have caused. I was just trying to do my job," she said, looking forlorn. "I've realised that there's more to being a journalist than putting innocent people in harm's way."

Vincent held out a hand, which she shook. He put his arm around her shoulder and steered her through the front door of Molly's house and pointed at the two girls on the sofa. "You've witnessed a pretty interesting story here, Claire. Stalking and its results. Why not see if your paper will do a piece that has a happy ending?" She looked up and nodded, smiling as she realised that he was right. "Just... don't mention us!"

She laughed. "No, of course not."

"I also have another proposition for you," Vincent said carefully.

"Oh, what's that?" she asked.

"Well, there are certain things that me and my team need out in the press and certain things that we don't. Maybe we can help each other out."

She seemed to think about it for a moment before she nodded carefully. "Now that's the kind of deal I like the sound of."

"Why don't we discuss it when I get back?" Vincent said, pleased.

"I would like that very much," Claire said, extending her

arm before she took her leave. “Thank you for everything, Vincent. You’ve taught me a lot.”

Vincent turned to his team. “Well! Now that’s all sorted, how about we go home? I’m exhausted!” he said to no one in particular, receiving a small cheer from the twins.

It was then that he noticed Nikki looking across at him. It seemed as though she was deep in thought.

“Nikki? What is it?” Vincent asked.

She spoke in a very small voice. “I said at The Club I had two things I needed to talk to you about.”

Vincent thought back to before the evening had taken off in a whirlwind and remembered that she was right. “God yeah, that’s right, I forgot, sorry.” She looked at him and he could see fearful anticipation in her eyes. He felt his heart stop. “What is it, Nik?”

She took a deep breath.

“We think Becci is still alive.”

Coming soon:

VENDICARE:
IS: WAR ON THE WORLD